W9-BMA-204

"People will talk."

"As I've said before, people always talk."

"Most won't understand. They'll question your judgment."

"I stand on my record, and I dare anyone to challenge it."

When he looked up at her, he couldn't hide the concern he was feeling. She reached over and tried to smooth his worry lines.

"You don't have to worry about me. I'm pretty good at taking care of myself." At least, she was now. Back on that lonely stretch of highway she hadn't been, but she'd sworn she'd never feel that helpless and vulnerable again. And she'd kept that promise to herself. It didn't mean she didn't still have nightmares about that incident from time to time, but at least when she woke up she could remind herself she wasn't that scared girl anymore.

Neither she nor Eric was the person they used to be.

Dear Reader,

From the time I was an elementary school student, there have been three types of settings and characters that have always fascinated me—those set in the American West, those involving Native American characters and those set in Asia. Maybe all of that was leading up to the creation of the heroine of this novel. Angie Lee is a lifelong resident of Wyoming and the daughter of a Shoshone father and a Korean mother who met during her father's military service. But Angie is so much more than her race and ethnicity. She's a good friend and a fundamentally kind and fair person who helps people make the right choices to better their lives, and who through her job as sheriff is a protector of those around her.

Eric Novak is also a protector, an army veteran who has returned home to the town he left behind so he can help his ailing and cantankerous father run the family ranch. Eric is also at the center of another type of story I love—those that showcase a character overcoming a difficult past to find happiness in the present. But he won't reach that happily-ever-after until he clears several hurdles, both new and old.

I hope you enjoy this latest visit to Jade Valley, Wyoming.

Trish Milburn

HEARTWARMING

His Wyoming Redemption

—

Trish Milburn

WORNSTAFF MEMORIAL LIBRARY

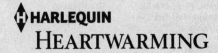

HARLEQUIN
HEARTWARMING

If you purchased this book without a cover you should be aware that this book is stolen property. It was reported as "unsold and destroyed" to the publisher, and neither the author nor the publisher has received any payment for this "stripped book."

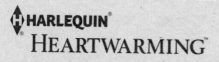

HARLEQUIN®
HEARTWARMING™

ISBN-13: 978-1-335-58489-2

His Wyoming Redemption

Copyright © 2023 by Trish Milburn

Recycling programs for this product may not exist in your area.

All rights reserved. No part of this book may be used or reproduced in any manner whatsoever without written permission except in the case of brief quotations embodied in critical articles and reviews.

This is a work of fiction. Names, characters, places and incidents are either the product of the author's imagination or are used fictitiously. Any resemblance to actual persons, living or dead, businesses, companies, events or locales is entirely coincidental.

For questions and comments about the quality of this book, please contact us at CustomerService@Harlequin.com.

Harlequin Enterprises ULC
22 Adelaide St. West, 41st Floor
Toronto, Ontario M5H 4E3, Canada
www.Harlequin.com

Printed in U.S.A.

Trish Milburn is the author of more than fifty romance novels and novellas, set everywhere from quaint small towns in the American West to the bustling city of Seoul, South Korea. When she's not writing or brainstorming new stories, she enjoys reading, listening to K-pop music, watching Korean dramas and chatting about all these things on Twitter. Hop on over to trishmilburn.com to learn more about her books, find links to her various social media and sign up for her author newsletter.

Books by Trish Milburn

Harlequin Heartwarming

Jade Valley, Wyoming

Reclaiming the Rancher's Son
The Rancher's Unexpected Twins

Harlequin Western Romance

Blue Falls, Texas

Her Perfect Cowboy
Having the Cowboy's Baby
Marrying the Cowboy
The Doctor's Cowboy
Her Cowboy Groom
The Heart of a Cowboy
Home on the Ranch
A Rancher to Love
The Cowboy Takes a Wife
In the Rancher's Arms

Visit the Author Profile page
at Harlequin.com for more titles.

CHAPTER ONE

SHERIFF ANGIE LEE finished typing the report about that morning's pickup-versus-cow accident north of town and hurriedly shut down her computer. She liked her job protecting the people of Jade Valley and the surrounding county, but even people who enjoyed their jobs needed a day off now and then. And as soon as she stepped out the front door of the sheriff's department office, she was going to have a rare two whole days off in a row.

She planned to pick up meals from both Alma's Diner and Trudy's Café so she didn't have to cook and didn't show favoritism to either of the women in Jade Valley's longest-running and most mysterious feud. Well stocked with delicious food, Angie could then devote part of her free time to reading the latest in the cozy mystery series set on a small Pacific Northwest island that had so many dead bodies per capita that the residents should be way more concerned than they were. She'd also devote a good amount of time to her home renovations. Car accidents, domestic disputes and anything else law enforcement related she was leaving to her deputies.

As she stepped out of her office, she noticed the department's secretary and dispatcher was on the phone. She waved to Sadie as she made for the exit.

"Not so fast," Sadie said right as Angie had her hand on the door, ready to push and make good her escape.

Angie knew what was coming. Well, not the specifics, but the result that she wasn't going home quite yet. She couldn't help the sigh, but she at least kept it quiet.

"What is it?" Angie asked as she turned to face Sadie Mitchell, who'd worked in this office longer than Angie had.

"Fight at The Bar, and Mike's not back from checking out that prowler report at Pippa Anderson's place."

"Okay, on my way. If Mike gets back soon, send him over there too. Must be something if Stevie can't handle it."

It only took her three minutes to drive to The Bar. After all, nothing in Jade Valley was very far from anything else. Angie supposed she was lucky that officers from her department weren't called to The Bar, the town's only drinking establishment, more often than they were. But usually all owner Stevie Baker had to do to get rowdy patrons to calm down or go home was pull out her golden baseball bat. If the bat hadn't ended matters this time around, it must be quite the brawl.

Angie heard the fight before she saw it. As she hurried inside, she noticed several men throwing punches, yelling insults and tripping over chairs and tables while a few other patrons watched from either along the far wall or their seats at the bar. Angie wasn't surprised to see Allen Novak in the middle of the fracas. She sighed. The man wasn't evil like some claimed, but he certainly made more than his share of poor life choices. And some of them, such as his current fighting and damaging of property, broke one or more laws. In the five years she'd been with the department, he'd been a visitor to a jail cell more than once. With his less-than-stellar health, she wasn't sure how he managed to take in enough oxygen to even participate in a fistfight.

With a glance at Stevie, who shrugged, Angie approached the melee.

"Hey!" she yelled as she grabbed one of the empty wooden snack bowls and slammed it down on the surface of a table.

Much to her annoyance, this attracted barely a glance. After eyeing the combatants and determining the best place to insert herself, she stepped toward one of the men she didn't recognize. Unfortunately, her step forward coincided with his elbow coming backward right into her eye. Pain shot straight from her eye to her brain, lighting up all her pain receptors like a fireworks warehouse hit by a meteor. She stumbled and tripped over a chair, nearly falling on her behind. Tears pooled and she bit her bottom lip as she covered her eye.

It took several moments before she was able to lift her gaze, but when she did the stranger was looking at her with a wide-eyed expression that telegraphed he knew he was in trouble. He still had a tight grip on Allen's collar and upper arm, and one of the other men involved had gathered up some common sense and was dragging his buddy away from Allen.

"I didn't mean to hit you," the man staring at her said. "I didn't even know you were there."

"Because you were otherwise occupied," Angie said as she grabbed her handcuffs and motioned for him to turn around.

She heard a faint curse under his breath as he shoved Allen down onto a chair. Remarkably, the older man stayed there. She braced herself against possible further attack, but to her surprise the unidentified man presented his back to her, hands at the ready for the cuffs. Perhaps he knew the drill from experience. At least it didn't appear she was going to have to chase anyone while it felt as if her eyeball might fall out of her head.

As she was cuffing and reading the man his rights, Allen grabbed a bottle of beer and took a long drink, fight evidently forgotten.

Mike arrived, scanned the bar and said, "Well, looks like I missed all the fun." Then he must have noticed the pain that had to be written on her face. "Are you okay?"

"Fine." She motioned for him to take care of the other combatants while she handled Allen and the man who'd hit her.

Mike helped her escort everyone toward the exit and a visit to the jail cells down the street.

"Still think you should turn this place into a yarn shop," Angie called out to Stevie as she guided the guy who couldn't be much older than her toward the door.

"Only if you take up knitting," Stevie replied. "Put some ice on that eye as soon as you can."

"Are you okay to drive?" Mike asked once they had everyone in the back of the department vehicles.

"Yeah." Granted, she drove with the injured eye closed half the time, but at least they didn't have to go far. And it wasn't as if Jade Valley had a tremendous traffic problem.

After a good many protests from everyone but the guy who had hit her, they had everyone inside and ready to be processed. When Allen tried to get up and leave, she pointed at him and used her stern voice to address him.

"If you take one step, I'm throwing you in a cell and throwing away the key this time." Of course, she'd never do any such thing. She followed the law to the letter no matter who she was addressing, but getting through the fog of inebriation sometimes called for shock statements. Thankfully, Allen settled himself and seemed to abandon any thought of bolting for freedom.

Before she could do anything else, she had to get some ice for her eye. Her eyeball was throbbing like a giant bass speaker at a rock concert.

"You should go to the hospital and get that checked. An eye isn't anything to play with," Mike said as he sat down at his desk to handle one of the other guys.

"After we're done with this," she said.

She headed toward the small kitchen, but Sadie was already coming toward her with an ice pack.

"Thanks." Angie winced as she pressed it against her eye. She paused long enough to take a slow, deep breath before turning back to the task at hand. She sank into the chair at the desk of one of her off-duty deputies and looked with her one uncovered eye at the man facing her. Focusing on the computer, she asked, "Name?"

"Eric Novak."

That drew her attention back to him.

"Yes, he's my dad. I was trying to pull him away from the others when I accidentally hit you." The way he said the words didn't make it sound as if he was trying to convince her to let him go, more a simple recitation of facts.

"I'll take your statement after I get all the pertinent information entered."

"If I can stand up, I'll get my ID for you."

She gave him a nod, a gentle one so the motion didn't make her eye start throbbing harder—if that was even possible.

He stood slowly, as if he knew any quick movements were not a good idea. Was that because he had experience being under arrest like his father? She wouldn't assume that without evidence, but it was a possibility. She'd know after she ran the usual checks. With his cuffed hands, he pulled his wallet out of his back pocket and let it drop onto the edge of the desk before he sank to the chair again.

When she pulled out his driver's license, she first noted it had been issued by the state of Texas. The second thing she noticed was that his photo was actually good. He was every bit as attractive in it as he was in person. Well, as much as she could tell with only one fully functioning eye. She'd looked at a lot of driver's licenses over the past few years, and most of the time the pictures didn't do the owners any favors. They either looked as if they'd just rolled out of bed or were new to the concept of flash photography.

After she input all the basic information awkwardly with one hand, she slowly lowered the ice pack and winced when the light hit her retina.

"I'm really sorry about your eye," Eric said.

Angie simply nodded once. "How long have you been back in Jade Valley?"

"Obviously too long," he muttered before exhaling a breath. "Since around noon."

She'd think that was some sort of record for time between entering the city limits and getting into trouble, but that wouldn't be true.

"And is this address on your license correct?" It was what she'd found in her search, but she wanted verbal confirmation too.

"Until a few days ago."

She considered the license photo and the man who sat next to her, the close-cropped way he wore his dark hair.

"Military?"

He nodded. "Was stationed at Fort Sam Houston in San Antonio until six months ago."

"And since then?"

"Working with an army buddy who has a construction company now."

"But you got homesick?"

"Not exactly." He sounded very much as if he wished he'd never stepped foot back in Jade Valley.

Angie didn't continue pursuing that line of questioning because whatever personal reasons had brought him back to his hometown didn't pertain to his assault on an officer, intentional or not. After she had all the information she needed, had typed in his version of events, then photographed him, and taken his prints, she escorted him to a cell then unlocked the handcuffs. Once she had him locked behind bars, she met his amber eyes.

"I will conduct my investigation as quickly as possible and will update you on the status once that is complete."

"Your deputy was right. You should get your eye checked."

His comment surprised her, and that didn't happen in her job very often. Things that shocked a lot of people—or what they claimed shocked them—did not have the same effect on her because she'd seen most of them before. Thankfully, she'd not had to deal with anything so heinous that she'd have to say otherwise, and she hoped that continued to be true.

She helped Mike book the rest of the bar combatants before she grabbed her keys. Two hours had gone by since she'd tried to leave the first time. And now, instead of going home, she was heading to the hospital because both Mike and Eric Novak were right. She needed to make sure there wasn't any serious damage that needed to be treated.

"Do you need a ride?" Mike asked.

"No, I'm fine. But thanks."

"I guess if you weren't taking off the next couple of days already, you would be now."

Of course all of her original plans might very well be toast. That made her grumpy enough to direct a look in Eric Novak's direction. But instead of gripping the bars or pacing the cell as the others were doing, he sat on his bunk with his forearms propped on his knees while staring at the floor. He appeared to be one part embarrassed, one part angry at his father and one part wishing he'd never left Texas. She got the strangest notion that though he was surrounded by people, she'd never seen anyone look so alone.

WHAT WAS THAT old saying? No good deed goes unpunished? Eric stared at the concrete floor, trying to ignore the grumbling of the guys in the other cells. At least his father wasn't one of them. Oh, he was in a cell, but he'd managed to pass out on the utilitarian bunk that matched Eric's. He could hear the snores that were similar to the ones he'd heard his entire life but now were louder and rattled more, thanks to the emphysema that resided in his dad's lungs.

Eric sighed then stretched out on his bunk. It wasn't the most comfortable bed in the world, but he'd slept a lot worse places—including lying on hot sand or ground frozen so hard it felt like solid rock. He stared at the ceiling, thinking about how he'd scraped up the vestiges of his feelings of familial duty to come back to Jade Valley. But when he'd seen the state of the ranch he'd left behind more than a decade before, he hadn't been able to hide his frustration with his father. So that they didn't have a full-blown fight on his first day back, he'd decided to go have a single cool-down drink while he decided if he would stick around to help his dad, whether his dad wanted it or not, or if he would retrace the miles he'd traveled to Wyoming.

He hadn't yet come to a decision when his dad had showed up and loudly demanded to know why Eric had stormed off. A guy sitting at a nearby table called out for him to be quiet because he and his buddies were trying to hear the TV. Before Eric could even get a word out, his dad had hurled a totally unwarranted insult at the other guy. It had been like watching a match tossed into a bone-dry forest. In the next moment, he'd been simultaneously trying to drag his dad out of the fray and defending himself from flying fists and any projectiles that were handy.

The approach of footsteps outside his cell had him lifting his head. The deputy, middle-aged and vaguely familiar, reached through the bars and placed a brown paper bag and a disposable cup on the floor of Eric's cell. He wondered if his dinner had come from the discount bin at the convenience store. Again, he'd eaten worse. And he'd been in situations overseas where he'd eaten less.

"You better hope the sheriff's eye isn't badly damaged," the deputy said.

"I hope she's fine too, but not for the reason

you're assuming." He had no beef with the sheriff, whose name was Angie Lee according to the nameplate he'd seen on what must be her office door. She wasn't Paul Genovese, the older, balding, pot-bellied man who'd held the position when Eric was a teenager hanging out with the wrong people and making wrong decisions. While Sheriff Genovese had legitimate reasons to watch Eric and his friends, he'd also been a complete jerk about it. Even when Eric hadn't been doing anything wrong, Genovese had harassed him. Had seemed to enjoy it.

Eric waited until the deputy moved on with his meal deliveries before he got up to retrieve his food. But when he returned to the bunk and opened the bag, the heavenly scent of a freshly grilled hamburger hit his nose and his stomach rumbled. It reminded him he hadn't eaten since he'd had a doughnut and coffee early that morning. And the fact that the hamburger was accompanied by a slice of chocolate cake made a night in jail not seem so bad.

The moment he bit into the juicy hamburger, memories of that taste zoomed to the front of his brain. His dinner was straight from the kitchen of Trudy's Café. It had been one of the two restaurants in town when he was growing up, and pretty much still was from what he could tell if you were only counting sit-down type places. The peanuts and chips at The Bar didn't count, and the little pizzeria he'd seen when he drove through town earlier didn't have a dining area. Alma's Diner, across from Trudy's, had been off-limits to him after his friend Tyler Langston had attempted to dine and dash. Eric and the third member of their trio, Wes Davis, hadn't been with him at the time, but Alma had banned all of them from her restaurant.

When Eric now thought about how Tyler had yelled at the woman that her cooking wasn't that good anyway, he cringed. What idiots they had been.

He'd say his identity was what had gotten him tossed in jail so quickly, but it had been obvious that Sheriff Lee hadn't known who he was. No, the fact that his elbow had ended up in her eye was the reason for his current lodgings.

"You going to eat that cake?"

It took Eric a moment to realize the guy in the cell next to his on the other side was pointing at the packaged slice of cake Eric had placed on the bunk.

"Yes." He didn't elaborate. He'd had a spectacularly bad day, so there was no way he was giving up the one bright spot.

The deputy gave Eric a hard stare on his way back to his desk from the coffeepot. Eric's reception by his hometown didn't improve his mood any, but he also couldn't blame people for how they looked at him. After all, he'd ended up exactly where most of them likely suspected him to. If not for one pivotal moment when he'd been eighteen, he might have been sitting in this cell even sooner. But he'd left to try to change his life, and he had. Based on his observations since he'd been back in Jade Valley, he was about the only thing that had changed.

Except for the sheriff. That was a huge difference. And though she'd escorted him to jail shortly after meeting him, he still considered Angie Lee a huge improvement over the man who'd occupied the position when Eric left town. Genovese was one of those cops who'd been in his position forever and had likely planned to stay there until he was good and ready to leave. And he'd gotten lazier and meaner with each passing year, but people kept voting for him. Eric honestly couldn't remember if it was because he didn't have any competition in the elections, or people were simply averse to change of any kind.

As he savored his hamburger, he thought about Sheriff Lee. Even in uniform, with her black hair pulled back in a ponytail, and one eye covered with an ice pack, it had been obvious she was pretty. If only he'd met her under different circumstances, he might have tried to strike up a conversation.

But that was the story of his life, wasn't it? There was a whole lot of coulda, woulda, shoulda. He'd left Jade Valley to stop making bad decisions, but now he wondered if coming back was the worst decision of all.

CHAPTER TWO

STEVIE WINCED THE moment she noticed Angie walk into The Bar the next morning.

"That is quite the shiner." Stevie pointed at Angie's eye then winced again. "I'd hate to be the guy who gave you that, no matter how hot he is. Or the fact he didn't do it on purpose."

"You saw it happen? Why didn't you tell me yesterday?"

Stevie shook her head. "I couldn't see the actual impact from my angle, but it's visible in the security footage. And I'm guessing that's what you're here to see."

Having put her days off on hold, Angie followed when Stevie motioned for her to come into her office. She watched the video of the fight from beginning to end along with a few minutes prior and afterward to get the full scope of the situation. Then she played it again, pausing just before she was hit in the eye, then watching it at a slower speed.

Stevie was right. Eric Novak hadn't hit her on purpose. In fact, he hadn't punched anyone. The extent of his contribution to the fight had been trying to drag his dad out of it and taking defensive stances when punches came his way.

"If Allen hadn't been so loud and rude, none of that would have happened," Stevie said as she flicked the computer screen lightly with her finger. "I don't ask for much, just for people to enjoy their beverages while not acting as if they've never been out in civilized society."

"Yeah, you don't ask much," Angie said with a little laugh and a gesture at their surroundings.

"Okay, I know it's a bar, but still."

Angie started to shake her head, but a throb of pain in her eye caused her to stop.

"You did go get that checked, right?"

"I did, and luckily there's no permanent damage. I'm just going to be extra pretty for a while."

Stevie snorted. "Yeah, not everyone can rock an eggplant-colored eye region like you can."

Angie would eye-roll if she didn't think

it would make her feel as if her eyeball was going to stab her brain with a spear. Instead, she stood.

"Get an estimate for the damage that was done," she said, pointing toward the seating area of the bar that had one less table and at least two fewer chairs postfight.

"Already on it."

Once back in her car, she placed to-go orders at both Alma's and Trudy's, ones she had intended to purchase the day before. She added a couple slices of Trudy's delicious pie—one apple, one blueberry—as a treat for having to work during her planned time off. With the pickup times set, she headed to the sheriff's department office.

When she arrived and approached Eric Novak's cell, he had the same reaction upon seeing her eye as Stevie had.

"Before you ask, it's fine," she said. "Just very colorful and sore."

"I'm sorry." His apology had the ring of truth.

She retrieved the keys to the cells and unlocked his.

"The security footage verified what you said yesterday, so you are free to go." She glanced toward where Allen was still asleep in his cell. "Your father, however, will be staying here at least until bail is set and made."

Eric looked at his dad and sighed. It was the same type of reaction she'd seen from parents whose children had misbehaved enough to have an encounter with law enforcement, as if he'd like to grab the older man by the ear and drag him home to be punished. In all honesty, Allen could use a good grounding. One would think running a ranch would keep the man too busy to get himself into trouble, but evidently not.

"Will you be staying in Jade Valley?" Angie asked him as she handed over his wallet and keys.

"I don't know. Can't say it's been a fun time since I got back."

There wasn't really anything she could say in response to that, so she didn't.

"We can let you know the next step when we hear, in case you need to come pick up your dad."

Eric shook his head. "He can get home on his own. He's a grown man, even if he doesn't act like it."

With that, Eric strode toward the exit without a glance back at his father.

Sadie *tsk*ed behind her, but Angie ignored the sound and what it meant. After all, Sadie's opinion of the Novak family mirrored that of what seemed like everyone else in town, that they were a nuisance and a thorn in the side of Jade Valley, the local ne'er-do-wells. She'd heard it on numerous occasions about Allen over the years, and no less than half a dozen times about Eric since his arrest. Angie wasn't one to be so simplistic in her conclusions about people, though. They were often more complex, for equally complex reasons, than most people liked to assume. Yes, some were just evil, but others ended up on a path paved with bad choices and seemingly unable to veer from that path. It didn't excuse when they broke the law, but she also always aimed to look at the facts of a case and not be swayed by public opinion or personal biases. She knew all too well from her own experience how someone's opinion could taint police work and end up hurting an innocent person. As long as she was sheriff, that wasn't going to be how she ran things.

IT WAS A good thing Eric had picked up a pizza on his way out of town because when he looked in his dad's refrigerator, he was greeted with a sorry state of affairs. He should have expected that, considering how run-down the house and other ranch buildings were. It all made him dread checking on the small herd of cattle. Were they even still alive? Or had his dad sold them off? And if he had, just how much debt was he in? The idea of spending a substantial chunk of his own savings to improve the condition of the ranch irritated him, especially after he'd just stopped by The Bar to apologize for his father's behavior and to pay for the damage he'd caused.

All those unanswered questions bombarding his brain, combined with the night in jail, gave him a headache. Still, it was probably nothing compared to the one the sheriff had. The thought of how painful it must have been when he hit her made him want to apologize again, even though it hadn't been intentional and apologies weren't going to take the injury away.

As he walked through the house eating

a slice of the pepperoni pizza, his thoughts
drifted away from the task at hand—mentally
cataloguing all the things that needed to be
repaired or spruced up. His thoughts instead
drifted back to Sheriff Lee. She wasn't like
any sheriff he'd ever encountered in his thirty
years. Being arrested by her within hours of
his return to Jade Valley hadn't been on his
to-do list, but it was enough to make him
wonder if there had been an alarm at the sheriff's department that blared, "A Novak has
returned to town. He must be up to something." He had to admit, however, that she
hadn't treated him unfairly, and she'd done
exactly what she'd said she would—investi-
gate quickly and release him if she found him
innocent of any intent to harm her, others or
property. That was a distinctly different experience than what he'd had with the previous
sheriff. Of course, he was a different person
now than he'd been then. Not that anyone in
Jade Valley knew that or would believe it.

He shook his head. He had to stop thinking
about the past. If he decided to stay in Jade
Valley, he would have to work to make people look at him differently. But as he considered how much work was ahead of him and

his dad's less-than-enthusiastic reaction to his return, he wondered again if he'd made a mistake coming back.

A sigh escaped him. The fact was he didn't really have a choice if he didn't want to be a rotten person who left his only parent to grow old and die alone. Despite his contentious relationship with his dad, he was still his dad. And the man wasn't in the best health. Granted, that was also at least partially caused by poor decisions, but there was no going back and undoing what had been done. And it wasn't as if Eric hadn't ever made his own poor decisions. The difference was he'd finally realized it and made a change. His dad hadn't.

Eric considered that maybe the state of the place was at least partially due to his dad's health and not any laziness or inept management skills. Or maybe it was all of those things. Somehow he needed to make this move home work. Or at least give it his best shot. If nothing else, he needed to make the ranch more inviting to any future potential buyers. Because once his dad was gone, Eric wouldn't have anything keeping him in this rural part of Wyoming.

As he ate a couple more slices of pizza, he mentally made a checklist of the most pressing tasks. He tried not to get overwhelmed by how lengthy the list was and focused instead on how getting things started in the house would definitely be easier with his dad temporarily elsewhere. He wished he believed that the time in a jail cell would change his dad, but he was a realist.

Before he did anything else, however, he needed to check on the herd. Having a small cattle operation had always made things difficult financially compared to the bigger ranches in the area, but there had been three of them to keep things going then. He dreaded seeing what had become of things in the years since he'd left town to join the army, and especially in the year since his mother's passing.

A pang of sadness tried to nudge away the annoyance and the threat of being overwhelmed by everything that needed his attention. He tried not to think about how long it had been since he'd seen his mother, and the fact that now she was gone. A wave of anger hit him, but he didn't have time to indulge it. After putting the other half of the pizza in the fridge, he left the house and made his way to the barn.

Even with a cursory glance, he could see repairs that needed to be done to the structure. Those tasks got added to his to-do list, which would no doubt grow even longer by day's end. He didn't want to think about that. He'd get through it all by focusing only on the next thing on the list.

Rusty, the horse that had been his when he was still living and working on the ranch, was long gone. He'd been sold while Eric was still in basic training, though he hadn't learned that fact until a year later. His father's horse from back then was no longer around either. In his place was a big gray named Oscar.

"Hey there," Eric said as he approached the stall and let Oscar sniff him.

Luckily, Oscar seemed to be friendly and well taken care of though probably hungry. Eric spent the next couple of hours feeding and watering Oscar, mucking out the stall, putting down fresh hay, examining the tack and taking a general inventory of the barn's contents and structural condition. He noticed some spots in the roof that should be repaired as soon as possible.

After saddling Oscar, who was good-natured about having a stranger ride him, Eric headed out with the hope that the cattle herd was in as good a shape as the horse.

He discovered the size of the herd was noticeably smaller than when he'd still lived at home, but he didn't know if that was because his dad sold off some to pay for bad habits or he'd simply winnowed down the number so the work was easier to handle on his own. There had never been enough money to hire help, and Eric doubted that had changed in recent years. While he noted ways to make improvements, he was thankful that the stock situation on the ranch wasn't as dire as it might have been. He'd imagined just about everything, including finding emaciated cattle. His list of things to tackle was still substantial and likely to grow, but at least the current state of the herd was decent as a starting point.

He reined Oscar to a stop at that thought. Was his brain already accepting that he'd stay? That he was going to commit to living and working with his dad again? To trying to somehow make the ranch profitable instead of a money pit?

He scanned the pasture, which was in need of a good rain. Still, it was a beautiful summer day with a slight breeze blowing down from the mountains to the west that never lost their caps of snow. Despite the reasons he'd left Jade Valley behind, there had been plenty of times during his military service when he'd longed to take a horseback ride like this under a wide blue Wyoming sky, far away from mechanized sound and people who wanted to shoot him. When he would have gladly traded seemingly unending sand or bleak conditions for this rural pasture.

Despite the state of things on the ranch, at least there was a roof to sleep under and easy access to food. He'd seen plenty of people who had neither. Those encounters had humbled him and made him extra ashamed of how he'd acted as a kid and teenager.

He remembered a young boy he'd briefly met during one of his patrols. He'd caught the boy stealing fruit from a wealthy man's orchard. The look of raw fear and desperation had hit Eric like a punch from Goliath. Instead of turning the boy in as he would have had to do if anyone else was around, he'd reached up and picked three apples and quickly given them to the obviously hungry, poor child. It was the first time in his life that he'd stolen something for a good cause. It was certainly a better reason than the dare that had precipitated his first lifting of a candy bar at the convenience store.

Not wanting to dwell on his dumb mistakes of the past or how he'd allowed others to convince him to make them, he urged Oscar forward. Before he returned to the house, he wanted to ride the fence line to see if any repairs would be needed and where. As he rode, he could get an approximate count on the number of cattle grazing his father's land too.

Thinking of his dad made him wonder if he'd caused a scene once he woke up in jail. He didn't envy Sheriff Lee if his dad was expressing his displeasure. But the surly deputy could get a continuous earful for all Eric cared.

As he reached the top of a rise, he noticed a truck outside the old Steagall place in the distance. As far as he knew, no one had lived there since he was probably seventeen, and it hadn't been in good shape then. To be honest, he was amazed it was still standing and that a strong winter wind hadn't toppled it.

He squinted to try to see better, but it was too far to be able to discern much detail.

Since he had more than enough tasks to occupy his thoughts, he turned away from whatever was happening on the neighboring property.

After he was satisfied that the fencing was intact, he headed back to the house. He searched for a notepad until he found one with the local bank's logo on it, one of those promotional giveaway types same as the cheap pen he grabbed that was adorned with the name and telephone number for A to Z Hardware. The pen was appropriate since the local hardware store was where he was going to be spending a substantial amount of money.

By the time Eric finished writing down everything he needed to buy, he wasn't sure it wouldn't be cheaper to just doze the house and build a new one. That was, of course, an exaggeration—but not by much. He was tired just thinking about all the work that awaited him. It was almost enough to make him want to reenlist.

ANGIE PULLED OFF her work gloves and wiped the sweat off her forehead. Since her bathroom sink was currently inoperable, she headed to the kitchen to wash her hands. She'd been stripping out all the ugly and outdated aspects from her bathroom since early that morning when she'd rolled over in bed and accidentally bumped her eye against her hand. The resulting jolt of pain had woken her faster than the tolling of cathedral bells right next to her ear.

Once the pain had receded, she'd decided to start her day with some of the *hotteok* she had brought home from her parents' house a couple of days before. She'd warmed up one of the sweet Korean pancakes and let her taste buds delight in the golden outside and gooey insides bursting with brown sugar, honey and nuts. Dessert for breakfast was totally allowed on one's days off.

Now, several hours later, she'd worked off the indulgence and then some. While she ate some of the barbecue she'd bought at Alma's, she made a mental note of all the things she needed to pick up in town. It was a risk, going into town on her day off. Being sheriff of a small community led to people bringing up their problems they felt law enforcement should address even when she was out of uniform. She routinely heard about everything from stolen ranch equipment to teenagers playing their music too loudly to Maisey Turner wanting "something to be done" about Sal Graybill's cat doing its business in her flower beds.

As she made her way into town several minutes later, she waved at everyone she passed because she knew them all. That was the way of things in a rural county and a small community that only had a handful of streets. Other than tourists passing through, they didn't get too many new faces in Jade Valley. But they had one now.

Well, she supposed Eric Novak's face wasn't exactly new to the area, but it was new to her. It was a handsome face, the kind she could easily picture staring out from a military uniform. She'd seen him earlier, out riding that big gray of his father's. No doubt he was surveying the state of things on the ranch. She didn't envy him. She had a lengthy list of improvement tasks for her place, but it wasn't a ranch and there were no animals requiring care and attention. She didn't even have a pet because she worked so much.

There were more waves and hellos as she entered A to Z Hardware.

"Hey, Sheriff," store owner Chris Easton said when he looked up from where he was ringing up Mary Weston. He winced and whistled when he saw her black eye before looking toward the back of the store as if something had drawn his attention.

"That looks painful," Mary said.

"Hazard of the job."

Angie grabbed a small cart, then headed down one of the aisles while suppressing a smile. It always struck her as humorous to see any of the Eastons and Westons together, as if the power of their last names might act as magnets in repelling them away from each other.

She made her way slowly up and down the aisles, making sure she didn't miss anything that she needed but had forgotten to put on her list. As she finished placing some boxes of teal blue tile in her cart, she consulted her list. Next up, the faucet for the bathroom sink. But as she rounded the end of the aisle into the one with plumbing fixtures, someone was already there. She shouldn't be surprised to run into Eric Novak again. It was a really small town after all. And yet she was. When he glanced up and saw her, the shift in expression on his face said he was surprised to see her as well. She watched as he saw her black eye, and she thought for a moment he might apologize again.

Her gaze shifted to the item he held, the exact faucet she had intended to buy. A quick look at the shelf verified what she'd expected, that it was the only one of that style.

"Looks like we had the same idea," she said.

It took him a moment to realize what she meant.

"You're doing some home improvement too?"

She nodded. "You could say that."

Angie didn't reveal they were neighbors because, considering the circumstances under which they'd met, he might feel as if he was being watched even at home. She'd investigated, found him innocent of any wrongdoing, and so now he should be able to go about his life.

"You should let her have that after what you did to her."

Angie nearly gasped at the unexpected rudeness of Chris's statement. She'd seen him approaching down the aisle behind Eric but had assumed he was coming to ask if he could help either of them with anything. She bit down on the retort that almost escaped her.

"No, actually I've changed my mind about what faucet I want," she said instead.

Eric looked down at the faucet in his hands then extended it toward her. "You can have this one. I can pick another."

She waved off his offer. "I've decided to do some things differently, so I'm good."

Which wasn't a lie. She had, in fact, chosen to go with a slightly different color of tile after doing some online mock-ups. Sure, she liked the style of faucet in Eric's hands, but not enough to let Chris's rudeness stand.

"Okay, if you're sure," Eric said.

She wanted to say that considering all he likely had to tackle at his dad's place, it was the least she could do to give up a simple faucet design. But she didn't want to sound as if she thought his family home was a dump. It wasn't, but the last time she'd been by there, it had been obvious it needed a good amount of TLC. A part of her wondered what had brought Allen Novak to the point where his son was having to clean up all of his various messes, but it wasn't really her business until those decisions broke the law.

Angie didn't confront Chris about what he'd said until Eric had left and she had everything in her cart she planned to purchase on this particular trip. When she reached the cash register, she made sure anyone else in the store was out of earshot before she looked at Chris.

"What you said to Mr. Novak wasn't necessary."

"You should have thrown the book at him as well as his father. Everyone knows that family is no good."

An infrequent anger started bubbling in her middle, but she didn't let it show.

"You should know by now that I don't use law enforcement for personal vendettas or biases, either mine or anyone else's." She didn't raise her voice, but it was firm and left no doubt how she felt about what he'd said. And to his credit, Chris appeared at least somewhat embarrassed. "This," she said, pointing to her eye, "was an accident. There is video proof of that. I hope people are not spreading that it was otherwise."

Chris didn't respond, but he didn't have to.

She'd gotten her point across without being rude or confrontational. She wasn't an unemotional person, but there were many situations in which letting emotions rule one's mouth didn't turn out well. That was true of police officers like her as well as normal, everyday people going about their business. It wasn't fair to judge someone based on things they couldn't control—the family they were born into, the color of their skin, their economic status to some extent. She wasn't perfect in that regard. She was human, after all. But since she'd been on the receiving end of the judgmental treatment, she did her best to stop herself in her tracks if she started to think in that type of way toward anyone. In addition to being the right way to approach her work, she felt it helped her have a positive relationship with most of the county's residents.

By the time Chris rang up her purchases and swiped her credit card, he had recovered enough to thank her for her patronage. Once again, she pressed her lips together to keep from smiling. As if she had a choice for her hardware needs unless she ordered them online or drove an hour and a half to the next nearest store that carried any sort of home improvement supplies.

"See you next time," she said before pushing the cart toward the exit.

She'd thankfully gotten a parking spot right in front of the store, so she was able to quickly transfer her purchases from cart to truck then return the shopping cart to the small corral next to the front of the store. Some extra sense had her shifting her attention down the sidewalk. There she saw Eric Novak approaching his pickup carrying two bags from Jade Valley's only grocery. She also noticed how people nearby, both outside and peering from shop windows, were staring at him as if he might suddenly attack them like some wild animal. She resisted the urge to go talk to him, to be extra friendly in order to combat the frostiness or outright hostility being directed at him by seemingly everyone else. But she had no legitimate reason for approaching him. And unless someone acted on that hostility that crossed over the legality line, it wasn't her job to protect him from unfriendly stares.

But then, just beyond him, she noticed some familiar friendly faces. She smiled and waved at Gavin Olsen and his son Max. The little boy waved back at her with the exuberant enthusiasm only a preschooler possessed, which caused her smile to widen. She headed toward the soon-to-be husband and stepson of her friend, Maya Pine, and met them right next to where Eric Novak was closing his passenger side door.

"Hi," Max said, this time looking at Eric. "I don't know you. I'm Max."

Both Eric and Gavin looked startled, but honestly Angie wasn't. In the past few months, Max had come out of his protective shell to become a completely different child. She'd even caved to his charms and given him a ride in her department vehicle and briefly allowed him to run the siren.

"Sorry," Gavin said to Eric. "My son is on a mission to make every stranger not a stranger anymore."

Angie knew that Gavin and Maya had sat Max down and had the "stranger danger" discussion with him, but she supposed he felt safe since his little hand was held by his father's.

"It's okay," Eric said, then lowered himself

into a crouch so that he was closer to Max's height. "I'm Eric. It's nice to meet you, Max."

And then Eric smiled and Angie felt the force of it like the sun emerging from a bank of dark clouds. Eric Novak was a handsome man even when scowling, but the smile transformed him into the type of man who made people of every sex and age trip over their own feet. She hadn't even imagined it after meeting him, so it took her completely off guard. It wasn't a feeling she was used to experiencing.

When Max thrust out his hand, Eric appeared every bit as startled as she'd been moments before. Eric hesitated at first, glanced up at Gavin as if the man might snatch his son away from the Big Bad Wolf. But Gavin was one of Jade Valley's newest residents, so he wasn't meeting Eric with any preconceived notions about him.

Eric, evidently sensing it was okay, took Max's hand and shook.

In the next moment, Max's attention was captured by Billy Burdock's rather rotund basset hound Sophie.

"Well, the newness has worn off," Eric said with a touch of lighthearted humor Angie had also never seen from him, which made sense considering their brief history of acquaintance.

"Sorry about that," Gavin said as Eric stood. "If it makes you feel any better, even I take a backseat to animals of all kinds. If he doesn't grow up to be a vet or a zoologist, I'll be surprised."

"I remember being all about animals at that age too."

Was she hearing a hint of loss in Eric's voice, or was it just nostalgia for simpler times when he didn't have so much on his plate?

Gavin was the one to extend his hand this time. "Gavin Olsen."

Eric accepted the handshake with only the slightest hesitation, likely the first friendly overture by an adult since he'd arrived back in his hometown.

"Eric Novak."

"Mr. Novak just moved back to town," Angie found herself saying, inexplicably wanting to help foster the potential positive relationship.

Eric looked at her, obvious but unspoken questions in his gaze. Why was she being friendly? Why was she introducing him to one of her friends?

"Welcome back," Gavin said. "I'm fairly new to Jade Valley, but I like it so far."

Eric made one of those noncommittal sounds accompanied by a nod. Angie imagined him thinking that Gavin was lucky he wasn't on the other end of the cautious or hateful stares from the locals. If he knew how the community had rallied behind Gavin when he was seeking to keep full custody of his son, Eric would probably feel even more of an outcast. Because even people she'd met who claimed not to care what others thought of them actually did care to some extent.

"If you'll excuse me, lots of work to do," Eric said.

To keep from watching him leave, Angie focused her attention on Gavin.

"So, how goes the wedding planning?"

Gavin's response was laughter.

"That good, huh?"

"It's actually going fine, but I'm pretty sure Maya is out now literally turning over stones to look for stories to cover so she can avoid her mother."

Maya was the editor of the fledgling *Jade*

Valley Journal, the online news site that replaced the newspaper that had been sold out from under her then shut down. And while Maya loved her mother dearly, Angie could very well imagine Maya's mom making a big deal out of the wedding, a much bigger one than her daughter wanted.

"Hopefully they can come to a compromise," she said.

"I hope so, or she might just drag me to Vegas to get married in a drive-through chapel."

"She won't do that because she would never hear the end of it."

"You're probably right about that. Well, I better rescue poor Sophie before my child smothers her with hugs."

As Gavin peeled Max away from Sophie the basset hound, Angie shifted her attention to where Eric Novak was turning the corner at the end of the block. Even after he disappeared from sight, she stood there staring at the spot where he'd been, questioning why she experienced moments of wanting to help him fit back into the community that he'd once left behind. Because she wasn't the type of woman whose opinion of a person changed with the appearance of a smile, no matter how transformative it was.

But she had to admit the smile certainly didn't hurt.

CHAPTER THREE

Maybe it was because he'd actually just had an unexpectedly friendly conversation, but when Eric stepped into Meecham's Ranch and Home Supply he'd swear he felt a chill. When he made eye contact with the vaguely familiar guy behind the counter, he received a quick but not overly friendly nod in greeting. Instead of letting it bother him, though, he went straight for the horse feed and the new horse blanket he needed for Oscar.

As he emerged from one aisle with a blanket and headed for the feed, he nearly ran into someone.

"Sorry." As he started to tack on an "Excuse me," his words halted.

Wes Davis, one of the friend trio he was part of back in middle and high school, stood staring at him with that crooked grin of his, one Eric suddenly realized he didn't like very much. Wes's presence in the store at the same time as him wasn't a good thing and probably explained the reception he'd received upon arrival.

"Well, look who's back in town," Wes said. "I'd heard but didn't believe it until I saw it with my own eyes."

"Wes," Eric replied, doing his best to keep any sort of identifiable emotion out of his voice.

"Heard your old man is in jail."

"That's what happens when you start a fight in a bar."

Wes chuckled. "You staying for good?"

"To be determined."

Wes took a moment to smile at a young woman passing by who did not return the smile and actually quickened her pace, which seemed to amuse Wes. As Eric had expected, Wes hadn't matured any. He was just an older version of the person he'd been in high school.

"You, me and Tyler should get together, catch up."

"I'm busy at the ranch." He experienced a moment of curiosity about how Wes and Tyler were making a living, but he was afraid he knew the answer to that already. And he wanted no part of it. He wasn't that person anymore, no matter what anyone else might believe.

"Help you all with anything?" The guy from the front counter stood a few feet away.

Eric knew what the guy's tone meant, that he wasn't there so much to ask what they needed as to make sure they weren't pocketing merchandise. If he did end up staying in Jade Valley, he was going to have to make people look at him differently. It wasn't going to be easy, and that was his fault. But he had to start somewhere.

Before some comment that definitely wouldn't help slipped from Wes's mouth, Eric asked, "Horse pellets where they've always been?"

The guy nodded, then Eric did the same to Wes before heading for the next aisle. He wasn't about to say "Good to see you" or "See you later" to Wes because it wasn't the former and he didn't want the latter. Even if no one was watching, he wouldn't have said or done anything differently with his departure.

He made quick work of the rest of his shopping and headed home. As he was getting close to the ranch, he slowed down when the driver of the vehicle in front of him flicked on their left turn signal and applied the brakes in front of the sad little house where the Steagall family used to live. To his knowledge, no one had lived there since Mrs. Steagall died and her husband went to live with his daughter in Cheyenne when Eric was a senior in high school. It had evidently been left to the ravages of the weather since then. Had someone actually bought the place and planned to live there?

As soon as he wondered that, the driver turned into the driveway and stopped. Before he drove past, he got a glimpse of the person.

Sheriff Angie Lee. Had she set up surveillance on the neighboring property to make sure he wasn't reverting back to old ways? That seemed extreme, even by small-town standards. And she'd been friendly enough back in town, both in the hardware store and when chatting with him and her friend.

He drove past while she was distracted by something on her phone screen. Was she not aware of who had been following behind her? As he looked in the rearview mirror, he saw her approach the mailbox then retrieve something. The realization that hit him made him bark out a laugh of disbelief.

His closest neighbor was the woman who'd tossed him in jail on his first day back in town.

AFTER GRABBING HER mail and responding to a text from her cousin Julie, Angie headed back to her car. A loud bang from behind her had her spinning on her heel, automatically reaching for the weapon that wasn't currently at her hip. She wouldn't have needed it anyway because the mailbox that currently sat on its side in the ditch was already dead.

"Guess I should have replaced that before now," she said to herself.

Her bathroom renovations she'd planned for the day would have to take a backseat to replacing the mailbox. Good thing she'd already purchased both a box and a post to mount it on.

A very different sound became audible in the wake of the mailbox's demise. Her heart leapt as she walked toward the opposite side of the road. There in the other ditch sat four little puppies huddled together, crying for a mother who was nowhere near.

Anger shot through her. She would never understand people who could just toss defenseless animals away like trash. But she reined in her anger so she hopefully wouldn't scare them any more than someone that much bigger than them naturally would.

"You poor babies," she said as she eased toward them. As one yipped and shied away, she did her best to soothe him. "It's okay, sweetie. I won't hurt you."

But the short-haired puppies with a mixture of fur colors were understandably skittish. She really needed some help to corral them, to make sure one didn't run onto the road and get hit while she was grabbing another. But she wasn't exactly awash in neighbors or passersby. She looked toward where Eric Novak had just arrived home. She'd been aware of him behind her as she'd driven away from town, but she had deliberately ignored him. From his perspective, it would likely seem suspicious that she kept crossing his path. Even in a community as small as Jade Valley, three times in one day was reason for suspicion even if it was coincidence.

The fact was, however, that protecting the puppies was more important than giving Eric distance. And one of her skills was easily remembering phone numbers. She pulled out her phone again and called him. After four rings she thought perhaps he wouldn't answer. Not answering a call from a number you didn't recognize was a valid response.

"Hello?"

"Hello, this is Angie Lee. You may or may not know, but I'm your neighbor. And right now I'd like to request some help."

There was a pause, probably during which Eric had to be asking himself why he couldn't seem to avoid her.

"What kind of help?" To his credit, there didn't seem to be hesitance in his actual words.

"Somebody dumped some puppies on the side of the road up here, and it would be easier to gather them up with two people."

"I'll be right there."

As she waited for him to arrive, she wondered if he'd joined the military because of some sort of protective instinct, if she'd just triggered that same instinct by telling him about the puppies.

When he arrived, he left his truck in the road with its hazard flashers on and approached her slowly. He peered into the ditch.

"There's a special ring of Hell for people who do this," he said.

"I don't disagree."

She half expected him to take charge like so many men tended to do, but instead he asked how she wanted to approach the situation. Working together, they were able to capture two puppies each in a fraction of the time it would have likely taken her.

"Good teamwork," she said.

"Guess I can add puppy rescue to my resume."

The comment was so unexpected that Angie smiled. "Thanks for your help."

"No problem." He chuckled a little when one of the puppies, evidently the bravest of the four, licked him on the chin.

"I think you've made a little friend."

"Looks like." He glanced back toward his ranch. "If you want to have the vet check them out, Dr. Parsons is coming out to give my dad's horse his vaccinations this afternoon, in about an hour."

"Excellent timing." Angie readjusted her hold on the wriggling puppies in her arms and then went still at the feel of wetness on her T-shirt. "Well, I'm going to need to change shirts before then. Someone just had her anxiety get the better of her."

She shifted the puppies to see the evidence on her stomach.

"Let's put them in the box I brought," he said.

As they carried the puppies to Eric's truck, he stopped and stared into the opposite ditch then back at her. "Did someone hit your mailbox?"

"No, it gave up the ghost and died all on its own."

After placing the puppies in a tattered cardboard box in the front of Eric's truck, Angie shifted her attention to him.

"Do you mind taking them with you? It'll be more convenient to have Doc only make one stop. Don't worry—I'll be there after I change and will pay for the puppies' examinations separately."

Eric seemed hesitant for a moment but then nodded before opening his driver-side truck door and slipping behind the steering wheel.

After changing and washing up both herself and her wet shirt, she headed down the road. As she pulled into the driveway, she saw that the property looked a bit worse off than when she'd last been there. It had even been quite a while since she'd driven past since town was in the other direction and no work calls had sent her in the opposite one.

The one thing that was different from her previous visit was the handsome man sitting on the edge of the front porch, the puppies next to him drinking from a water bowl. As she got out of her truck and walked toward him, an "Awww" bubbled up in her chest at the sight.

Angie sat on the other side of where the puppies were drinking then pulled a tan one onto her lap when it looked up at her. She laughed when the pup immediately tried to climb up her like she was a ladder, but then a pang of sadness hit her and she ran her hand softly over the puppy's head.

"Poor little thing. Not everyone in the world is as cruel as the person who did this to you."

"A lot are," Eric said.

"Again, I don't disagree, unfortunately." Still, she'd like to think the majority of people drew the line at tossing puppies into ditches.

"They seem to be in decent shape, considering. I doubt they've had any vaccinations, though, or flea treatments even though I've not seen any fleas. I don't think they'd been there that long. If they had, they would be in worse shape."

"I wish I'd seen who did it. I guarantee they would be having a very unpleasant day right now," she said.

"Enjoying the sheriff's department's fine accommodations?"

"Exactly." If she wasn't a by-the-book type of sheriff, she'd toss the offenders in jail only after tossing them in a ditch to see how they liked it. But there was no place in her policing for personal animosity or vendettas, no matter how attractive. She'd made that decision a long time ago, the moment she'd decided to take the law enforcement path—equality before the law.

She switched puppies, much to the first one's displeasure.

"You have to learn to share," she said, giving the first pup a gentle scratch between the ears.

Angie glanced up and saw Eric looking into the distance toward her house.

"So, you bought the Steagall place?"

"I did."

"To live there?" The disbelief in his voice was understandable.

"Yes. I'm certainly not going to use it as an expensive chicken coop."

"And I thought I had my work cut out for me."

Angie shrugged. "The price was right, and I enjoy doing renovations. I'm a bit of a home improvement fan. Love the shows on TV, and I've watched countless how-to videos online."

"Want to fix up this place for me?" he asked, followed by a brief laugh.

"Afraid I already have enough on my plate." A familiar red truck appeared down the road. A few moments later, Doc Parsons pulled into the driveway. "Ready to have your ear talked off?"

"I'd say you're more in danger there."

The tone of Eric's words wasn't self-pitying, rather matter-of-fact. And she couldn't blame him for feeling the way he did based on the way she'd seen people talk to and about him since his return to his hometown.

"Oh no, I'm not going to be alone here."

She turned out to be 100 percent right, which seemed to somewhat surprise Eric. To his credit, after a couple of minutes he held up his end of the conversation as Doc examined Oscar.

"Didn't figure you'd come back here," Doc said as he injected the horse with a flu vaccine. "Most people who leave don't come back."

"Can't say it was in my plans either."

Doc nodded as if he completely understood. "Sometimes life takes our plans and tosses them in the trash can."

Angie certainly knew that from experience. Probably most people did to some extent.

When Doc was done with everything he needed to do with Oscar, he took a moment to gentle the big gray by rubbing his hand along Oscar's shoulder and flank.

"Now, let me take a look at these little cuties," he said as he crossed to where Angie had put the box of puppies atop a workbench. "Hate to say I've been seeing more of this. People either can't afford vet care, or they just don't bother."

Anger welled up inside Angie again, but she held it in check. Not for the first time, she wished people as a whole were more empathetic toward each other and animals—both wild and domesticated.

The same puppy that had made Eric laugh

by licking his chin did the same with Doc Parsons.

"Well, aren't you frisky?" Doc looked over at Angie. "Overall, they seem to be in decent shape. I'd like for you to bring them to my office, though, and we can make sure they have everything they need."

"I'll bring them in tomorrow."

"Sounds good. Well, I'm off. You all hear of any young, energetic vets who are looking for a job, I could sure use some help."

With that, Doc headed to his truck.

"That wasn't anywhere near as painful as you indicated it would be," Eric said.

"I'm fairly certain that's the least I've ever heard him talk. I swear the man could manage to carry on a conversation with a cow."

"If cows start talking back, I'm definitely not staying here."

Angie pointed at him. "You and me both."

Even after she arrived back at her house with puppies in tow, along with the milk replacer Doc had given her, she kept thinking about how different he seemed when he smiled or laughed. She was glad he had relaxed enough to do both. The scene with Chris in the hardware store had been unfortunate, but at least now there had been four people today who hadn't treated Eric as if he suffered from some communicable disease.

She had finished bathing the puppies and was drying them off when someone knocked on her front door. Her heart leapt a little at the thought it might be Eric. Wait, what was that reaction about? Shaking her head, she made her way to the entrance.

"Well, if it isn't the bride-to-be."

"Oh, nice shiner," Maya Pine said.

In the midst of puppy rescues and dying mailboxes, she'd forgotten about her black eye.

"At least my eyeball didn't pop out."

"Eww." Maya smiled. "So, I hear you have puppies."

"You know, the speed at which news travels in this valley never ceases to amaze me. It shouldn't, and yet it does."

Maya gestured over her shoulder as she entered the house. "I just saw Doc Parsons. I was interviewing Isabelle Hardin about her scholarship to Stanford. Doc came by there to check out one of their horses that got injured."

A little bark came from behind the closed bathroom door.

"Puppies!" Maya clapped her hands together like a child about to be set free in a candy store.

"I thought you were a cat person. Blossom will scorn you if you come home smelling like dogs."

"Blossom knows I love her because I spoil her rotten. And when I don't, Max does."

"I saw Max and Gavin in town earlier. Max immediately tried to make friends with my new neighbor." Angie pointed in the direction of the Novak farm.

"That doesn't surprise me. And I heard Allen Novak's son was back in town and you'd already thrown him in jail."

"That was a temporary thing until I cleared up what happened at Stevie's." Angie eased the bathroom door open so she didn't accidentally hit one of the pups.

"Oh, they're darling." Maya lowered herself to the floor and sat with her legs crossed. The most adventurous pup edged toward the new arrival.

"Speaking of your new neighbor, you were actually at his place when Doc stopped by?"

Angie purposefully ignored the tinge of double-pronged curiosity in her friend's voice—

one part a journalist's natural state and one part friend hoping for a reason to tease her.

"Yeah, he helped me get the pups safely out of the ditch. I was afraid one of them would manage to get itself run over while I was trying to save it." She gave a rundown of the facts without any reference to how handsome Eric Novak was when he smiled or how her heart lifted when she heard him laugh. She told herself she just liked to see people happy and treated well, but she'd swear she heard a voice inside her head laughing as if it was calling her a liar.

She was surprised to find herself wanting to ask Maya about Eric, but she realized Maya wasn't the right person to ask. Like her, Maya didn't grow up in Jade Valley so didn't go to school with Eric. Their mutual friends Sunny and Dean likely had, but Angie had no valid reason to ask them about him. Plus, she figured given a little more time, she'd hear everything through the town grapevine anyway.

"I saw a picture of him in Sunny's yearbook once," Maya said. "Handsome, but she said he was a troublemaker. But I guess helping the woman who tossed him in jail to save puppies is a point in his favor."

"People change."

Maya leveled a way-too-perceptive look at Angie. "Oh?"

Angie knew that "Oh?" Maya had a way of getting people to open up and talk with just that one simple word. But Angie was good at keeping her expressions and responses neutral, a skill that came in handy on the job when showing emotion would just add fuel to heated situations. She also excelled at diverting conversations down different paths.

"Look at Sunny. She was a city-living world traveler until she decided to come back to Jade Valley. And Gavin used to be a hermit, and now he's fitted into the community rather well."

"True, but that's a bit different. Neither of them used to shoplift and vandalize."

Angie didn't make any excuses for Eric's past. One, she didn't condone criminal activity. But she also didn't know the extent of Eric's past. She didn't really know him at all. He might be nice to puppies and little boys, but that didn't mean he was leading a squeaky clean life now. Her gut told her that he had turned his life around—how he'd reacted when his father got in a fight was evidence of that—but she operated based on facts, not her gut instincts that could be completely wrong.

"Well, until I see current evidence of those crimes being committed by him, I will give him the benefit of the doubt."

Maya nodded. "Good policy as always. Everyone should strive for that kind of attitude."

It wasn't always easy. She was human, after all. Like everyone else on the planet, she made assumptions based on a person's appearance. The key was to be conscious of those assumptions and not act on them unless evidence backed them up.

"Are you planning to keep all of them?" Maya asked, indicating the puppies.

"Are you kidding? With my schedule? I'll find them good homes. Want them?"

"Actually, I probably will take one. Max would be beside himself if I brought home a puppy for him. But I need to talk to Gavin about it first."

"And Blossom."

Maya huffed out a laugh. "Blossom is the most chill cat ever. If she doesn't mind Max's enthusiastic hugs and petting, I think she can hold her own with a rambunctious puppy."

After Maya left, Angie knew she should tackle any of the many things on her to-do list as had been her plan for her days off. Instead, she found herself sitting in the middle of her living room floor playing with the pups. Her plans had continuously been turned upside down ever since Eric Novak's arrival in Jade Valley. But tomorrow was another day, hopefully one that was at least more normal than the past two.

SHE'D JINXED HERSELF. By thinking that surely the next day would be without quite so much upheaval, she'd tempted fate. Rain had moved in during the night, and it felt as if she'd only just fallen asleep when she was awakened by water dripping on her face.

"You've got to be kidding me." She thought of Eric's obvious disbelief that she'd taken on overhauling her little house to make it livable. But while she liked a challenge, a leaky roof was something she hadn't counted on. After shoving her bed out of the way, she put a plastic bucket under the drip. She'd have to keep the puppies away from it so they didn't knock it over.

Speaking of…

"Good morning, little monsters," she said in a teasing voice. "Surely you've heard rain before. No reason to whine and keep me awake last night."

The response was a collective plea for sustenance. Angie chuckled.

"You four sure are cute." Despite what she'd told Maya the day before about not having time for pets, she was already growing attached to the pups. She'd caught herself thinking about possible names for them, one set based on the Norse pantheon, another on the seasons, and yet others in Korean like her parents' dog Hodu.

After feeding the pups and shutting them in the bathroom, she went outside to check on the roof. She immediately saw the problem: a strip of the old metal roofing had come loose in the wind and now lay against the worn wooden fence at the edge of the yard.

She stood with her hands on her hips and sighed. So much for remodeling the bathroom and enjoying some reading on her days off. She reminded herself that this was all just part of the adventure that came with buying a home in need of a lot of work.

Resigning herself to another trip to town,

she got ready and loaded up the puppies. After dropping them off at the vet office, she headed to the hardware store yet again.

"You're going to roof your house yourself?" Chris asked, looking as if she'd said she was going to build a hang glider and sail off the summit of Grand Teton.

"Yes. It's not that big of a roof and doesn't have any complicated angles." Besides, she'd already quickly watched a few do-it-yourself roofing videos to know what she needed and felt confident she could do the job. It wasn't going to be the fun part of home renovation, but what the inside looked like wouldn't matter if it got soaked with rain.

When Chris realized he wasn't going to convince her to hire a roofer, he placed the order for materials.

"In the meantime, I need a tarp, ladder, two-by-fours and some screws."

"I sure hope you don't break your neck," Chris said as he started gathering the supplies. "We finally got a good sheriff, and I'd like to keep it that way."

She hadn't been the only one to suffer at the hands of her predecessor. There was no chance of the man reclaiming his former position, but elections were unpredictable with no guarantee the next person elected would approach the application of the law with the same impartiality she strove to use.

"I'll be careful."

With the pups' vet visit not scheduled to be finished until later that afternoon, she headed home with her new purchases and another sizable charge on her credit card bill.

IF HE WAS getting paid for all the work he was doing, Eric would be making some good money. So far, he'd been a plumber, electrician, carpenter and rancher. He needed to put on an accountant hat, but that could wait until he found a genie in a bottle and wished for an amazing proficiency with numbers.

Needing a break after wrestling the new bathroom faucet into place, he grabbed a soda from the fridge and went outside to enjoy the fresh breeze that was blowing in the wake of the previous night's rain. He glanced to his left and something blue in the distance caught his attention. When he looked more closely, he couldn't believe his eyes. Was the sheriff really standing on the roof of her house? Was she crazy?

Other people in his position would simply turn away, thinking it wasn't their problem. But that wasn't the person he wanted to be. And if she fell off the roof, no doubt many of the locals would think he had something to do with it. With a huff of frustration, he went inside to grab his truck keys then headed up the road to help the woman who evidently liked to do things the hard way.

When he pulled into her driveway, she stood from where she was attaching a blue tarp to her roof. He'd seen plenty of those during his time working construction. He'd been on a crew that spent two weeks in Oklahoma putting them on the roofs that had survived mostly intact after an outbreak of spring tornadoes.

"That doesn't look like the safest way to spend your day," he said when he was halfway between his truck and where she'd stationed her ladder.

"And yet necessary until my new roofing comes in. I woke up with water dripping on my face this morning."

Eric stopped in his tracks. "Wait, are you planning to roof your house by yourself?"

"Yes."

She really was crazy or an adrenaline junkie. Considering her profession, either was possible. Or both. Maybe with a generous dose of control freak thrown in. That would also support her career choice.

"You know you can hire someone to do that, even in a town as small as Jade Valley."

"I can also save a lot of money by doing it myself."

"Unless you end up in the hospital with a bunch of broken bones when you fall off the roof."

She snorted. "Why does every man I talk to today think I'm going to fall off the roof?"

"Because people fall off roofs all the time. It never ends well." He shook his head and walked toward the ladder.

"I can handle this," she called over the edge of the roof.

"It'll go faster with two people."

"So the man who says people fall off roofs on the regular is climbing up onto a roof that isn't his? That's a strange choice."

He reached the top of the ladder and stepped onto the roof. "I'd like to go home with you safely on the ground. I don't want to be accused of tossing you off the roof if you fall."

"I know some people haven't been particularly friendly toward you, but that seems a stretch."

"Maybe I just know their mindsets and why they have them better than you do. Remember, I grew up here."

"Sometimes people just need to be shown that their views should change."

He bent to line up a two-by-four atop the tarp. "You're very Pollyannaish for a sheriff. I know Jade Valley hasn't changed so much that there's zero crime."

"Not Pollyannaish. Just matter-of-fact."

He could tell from the look on her face and the conviction in her statement that she was being totally honest.

Together they made quick work of attaching the tarp. Once they were finished, she sat just below the ridge of the roof and looked out across the countryside.

"It's beautiful from up here."

Now that he was done with what he'd come to do, he should leave. Instead, he found himself sitting as well, stretching his legs out in front of him and leaning back on his hands.

"It is that."

"You've probably seen some interesting places during your military years."

"I have. Some pretty like this, some not fit for man or beast, others somewhere in between." He scanned the horizon, appreciating Jade Valley for its natural beauty if nothing else. "There were times I literally dreamed about this valley. Of course, it was probably because I'd baked my brain in my helmet."

"Or you were homesick."

He shook his head. "I didn't have any desire to come back here."

To her credit, she didn't press him to explain why. Or maybe she knew enough about his past to piece it together.

Because if she knew it all, there was no way she'd be sitting alone on her roof with him. No way she'd be so friendly toward him.

CHAPTER FOUR

"IT HAS TO be them," Dan Lintz said as he stood with his arms crossed, staring at the mess in aisle four of Meecham's Ranch and Home Supply. "It's no coincidence that I saw them here chatting like old times, and then a couple of days later someone breaks in and robs me blind."

Angie continued taking notes and photos on her tablet, refraining from correcting Dan that the crime had been burglary and not robbery since the theft had taken place while the store was closed and he had not been present. She didn't think he'd welcome being corrected when he looked like he was going to explode with anger.

"You should go arrest them now before they do this to someone else, before they can sell all my stuff."

"Dan," she said calmly without looking at

him. "We don't know they did this, either together or one on his own."

"You might not, but I know it in my bones. No good, neither one of them."

At that Angie did stop with her crime scene documentation and looked squarely at the man next to her. "Dan, do you not think I'm good at my job?"

Her question obviously surprised him because he stumbled over his answer. "Well, uh, of course. It's just that you're not from here and—"

"I didn't grow up here, true, but I have a pretty good sense about all of the people who call this valley home. I have had Wes as a guest of the jail before, so rest assured I am aware of his past."

"And that Novak boy too. Suspicious that this happened right after he returned to town."

"Just because they were in the store doesn't mean they did it. At some point, nearly everyone walks through your doors." In fact, she had been in the day before to buy a large puppy playpen. Until she could find homes for the pups, she didn't want them piddling all over her house and gnawing on every chewable object they could find.

"Seems like common sense to me. I mean, he couldn't make it a day after coming back before being arrested."

"He was cleared of any wrongdoing, and you know that because this town has an amazingly fast gossip network."

Based on the grumbling under his breath, she could tell she hadn't changed his mind about who he thought the culprits were. But that was his problem. There would be no arresting anyone based on assumptions. Could she see Wes doing something like this? Yes. Eric? She hoped not, but that feeling could very well be based on the fact that he'd helped her with the puppies and her roof. Not all thieves were pure evil. It was possible they could steal things and occasionally do something kind for someone else too. Most people weren't all bad or all good. They were more complex than that.

Eric Novak sure seemed to be. One minute she got an "I just want to be left alone" vibe from him, and then he turned around and helped her tarp her leaky roof unprompted. Part of the time he seemed to put forth the effort to be cordial, to fit back into a community he left behind. But he also obviously realized that a sizable portion of that community wasn't interested in welcoming him back, and perhaps thought it a better strategy to keep to himself. She'd seen both sides of him up on her roof. He'd helped her but he'd also made a quick departure after they were done. He'd claimed he'd assisted her so he wouldn't be blamed if she fell off the roof and injured or killed herself, but she wasn't so sure that was the only reason. Even though she did her job based on evidence, she couldn't totally turn off her instincts. And they were telling her that he'd helped out of genuine concern that had nothing to do with protecting himself. Maybe that was a product of his military experience, or maybe it had always been a part of him that for whatever reason no one ever saw.

Still, she would do her job. If her investigation led to Eric, then she would have to act accordingly.

"I've got all I need here," she finally said. "I'll leave you to clean up."

"Are you going to their houses now?"

"Dan, I don't tell you how to sell feed and tack, so I don't need you telling me how to do police work." It was a more curt response than she typically used, but Dan's attitude was grating on her nerves. "I assure you I will do everything necessary to find the perpetrator and see justice served. Now I suggest you call your insurance company, and I'll update you when I have more information." She headed for the exit but then paused. "One other thing, remember that spreading malicious and unfounded rumors about people can lead to being charged with slander. Just an FYI."

As she left the store, she spotted Maya getting out of her car.

"Be prepared," Angie said. "He's in a mood and has definite opinions that he's no doubt going to share with you despite the warning I just gave him."

"It's not the first time I've interviewed Dan. But since I have you here, let me get some information from you."

Despite them being friends, Angie stuck to her role of chief law enforcement officer dealing with the press as she gave the facts as she knew them.

"Any suspects yet?"

"No." The fact that she didn't elaborate had Maya looking up at her with obvious curiosity. Before her friend could probe further, Angie's radio crackled and Sadie, the dispatcher, informed her there had been a car accident a few miles out of town. "Duty calls."

"I'll call you later for details." Maya didn't specify if she was referring to the accident or more about the burglary, but it was probably both.

Angie waved as she headed to her department SUV. When she arrived at the scene of the accident, she was met with an unexpected cast of characters. Camille Becker had crashed her land barge of a car into the back of Carrie Mason's little truck. Some sales flyers that Carrie had no doubt been putting into mailboxes were caught on brush up at the edge of the tree line. And there, crouched next to where Camille sat on the embankment, was none other than Eric Novak. She'd seen him more since he'd returned to Jade Valley than she had some of her deputies.

As she was stepping out of her vehicle, the ambulance showed up. Lizzy and Elijah Owens, twins who worked as local paramedics, got out.

"We have to stop meeting like this," Elijah said when he saw her.

"That's not likely."

As Lizzy went to check on Camille, Angie and Elijah approached Carrie. "What happened?" Angie asked as Carrie waved off Elijah with an "I'm fine."

"I was out re-sorting some mail when she came down the hill and didn't even see me. I had to dive off the side of the road. The woman shouldn't even have a license anymore."

Carrie wasn't wrong. Despite having been born when FDR was president, Camille hadn't seen fit to slow down her driving. And it didn't help that her eyesight was getting worse by the day. Angie was going to have to call Camille's granddaughter in Coeur d'Alene, and she didn't envy Steph's conversation with her stubborn grandmother.

"Are you sure you're not injured?"

Carrie shook her head. "Nothing more than a couple of scratches. And having the bejeebers scared out of me."

"You should still let Lizzy or Elijah check you over anyway."

After getting more details of what had happened from Carrie, Angie strode over to where Camille was being checked for injuries. Angie would be surprised if she had any considering her car was built like a tank and probably weighed as much as one. She'd probably had it since it rolled off the assembly line in the 1970s.

When Eric noticed her, he gave a nod of acknowledgment. She crouched in front of Camille.

"Not having a good day, I see."

"What was she doing halfway out in the road like that?" Camille batted away Elijah's hand as he tried to take her pulse.

"Now, Camille, you know mail carriers can't pull all the way off the road to deliver mail." Angie examined the older woman's face. "I'm afraid maybe you didn't see her because your cataracts have gotten worse."

Angie fully expected Camille to snap back a reply. She'd seen it from so many older people who found it understandably difficult to accept that their bodies couldn't do what they once did. But before Camille could reply, she noticed Eric place his hand gently on the woman's arm, his much younger, tanned hand a stark contrast against Camille's lighter, papery skin peppered with a few bruises common on older people. That simple touch seemed to lower the temperature on Camille's upset. Instead, she sighed as if the state of her eyes was yet another heartbreak life had dealt her.

"I'm afraid I can't let you drive until you can see better." Angie said it as tenderly as she could, and for a moment she thought Camille might actually cry. She couldn't blame her.

"How am I going to get to my hair appointment?"

Angie pressed her lips together to keep from chuckling, but she almost failed when she saw Eric turn his face away in an effort to do the same.

"I'm sure Emily will reschedule it for sometime after you get examined at the hospital and have time to recover from the understandable shock of having an accident."

"I don't need to go to the hospital. I'm not made of money."

"You should go just to be on the safe side," Eric said. "Sometimes we don't think we're hurt when we are. I know from experience."

Angie didn't know why Camille seemed to listen to Eric when she didn't to anyone else, but she was thankful she did.

"And I'll have Theo check out your car at the same time," Angie added.

"Fine. I can't take the money with me anyway."

"You're going to be around for a long time still," Lizzy said in a teasing tone she'd no doubt used with a great many patients.

"How am I going to get home?"

"Don't worry about that," Angie said. "I'll see that you get home safely."

Camille ignored her and looked up at Eric. "Could you take me home?"

Eric appeared genuinely startled by the question. "Wouldn't you rather someone you know drive you?"

"I know you, have since you were little. You're Jessie Novak's boy."

The look that passed over Eric's face revealed that while he may have had a difficult relationship with his parents, he still missed his mother. Angie wondered if the state of their relationship or his military service had prevented him from coming to Jessie Novak's funeral.

Once Camille was on her way in the back of the ambulance, Theo Kent arrived with his tow truck. As he backed up to Camille's behemoth, which didn't look to have any damage other than a broken headlight, Carrie finished retrieving all the mail that had blown up into the trees. She stood at the back of her truck and sighed at the sizable dent in the tailgate.

"I just got this thing paid off last week."

"I'll get you a good deal on a new tailgate," Theo said.

Angie had no doubt of that. Theo had his finger on the pulse of the Wyoming salvage yard world.

When Theo pulled away with Camille's car in tow and Carrie was underway again, Angie finally turned to Eric.

"Well, aren't you just everywhere?" She hoped one of those places wasn't Meecham's the previous night.

"It does seem that way."

Sticking to business, she asked him to recount what had happened from his perspective.

"She didn't see the mail truck. Whether she wasn't paying attention or, as you said, she couldn't see it, I don't know."

"You were good with her."

He shrugged.

"Little kids, puppies and octogenarians—quite the range," Angie said.

"I guess."

She wanted to ask him so many questions, only a few of which had to do with the break-in at the ranch supply store. But it wasn't time for any of them. She had other investigative steps to take first unless she wanted to treat every single person who'd come into the store recently like a potential thief. And the other questions—well, they were all personal and none of her business.

"Do you need anything else from me?" he asked. "Before I play taxi driver, I have to pick up another faucet from the hardware store. Be glad you didn't buy the one you wanted originally. It's already broken. As I discovered when I was halfway done shaving this morning."

Angie had the oddest urge to know what his face felt like right after a shave. The unheralded thought surprised her so much that she turned half away from him and motioned that he could go. It wasn't until she was back at the sheriff's department, sitting in the parking lot, that she realized Eric Novak wasn't just an objectively attractive man. She was attracted *to* him.

Two things she knew for sure. One, she couldn't allow that realization to color her investigation of the Meecham's theft at all. And two, if she didn't want to be the hot topic of gossip, she couldn't let anyone else know.

ERIC STEPPED INTO the hardware store and greeted Chris Easton with a nod and a hello as if the man hadn't made his dislike of him obvious during his previous visit. But Eric was determined not to let other people's opinions bother him, at least not to let it show. Because the fact was that if he stayed, some interaction with the locals would be required and he'd rather it not always be negative. And even if he left again, until then he had to patronize the stores in town unless he wanted to drive a lot farther or wait for online orders to be delivered. And Jade Valley wasn't exactly a metropolitan area where those shipments arrived the same day, or the next.

He didn't, however, linger to engage in small talk about the weather or what type of pie was on offer that day at the two cafés in town. He made his way straight to the plumbing aisle and examined his choices. Chris was no doubt watching him, but at least he wasn't being obvious about it. After checking some online reviews from satisfied customers for a particular faucet, he grabbed it and headed for the cash register.

"Replacing a lot of faucets?" Chris asked.

"Same one." Eric didn't mention that the first one was defective. He hadn't even bothered bringing it back for a refund because he could already guess what Chris's reaction would be—that there had been nothing wrong with the faucet, that Eric had broken it out of negligence or ignorance. It wasn't worth the hassle. Simply buying another one was easier and might even plant a seed in Chris's mind that Eric wasn't the person he used to be.

That chance was likely blown to smithereens, however, when Eric stepped out of the store and encountered not only Wes Davis but also Tyler Langston.

"Wes, Tyler," he said simply, then started to walk toward his truck.

"Is that any way to treat old friends?" Tyler said.

Eric knew if he continued walking away from them, Tyler could choose to make a scene. Eric and Wes had done their share of the misbehaving and lawbreaking back during their high school days, but Tyler actually had a mean streak in him that Eric hadn't wanted to tempt back then. Same went for now. Even though Eric turned back to face them, he didn't approach. No doubt everyone on Main Street was watching, wondering what the three of them were cooking up. He'd swear he could almost hear "Up to no good" being murmured up and down the street.

"Wes says he invited you to hang out with us, and you declined." The way Tyler said *declined* had a suspicious edge to it, delivered deliberately slowly.

"As I told Wes, I have a mountain of work to do. Dad has let the ranch go a bit."

Understatement of the year.

"Well, aren't you being the good son all of a sudden." Tyler looked over at Wes. "Where was that guy the last few years?"

Eric didn't rise to Tyler's bait. In that moment he thought of Sheriff Lee and her policy of sticking to the facts.

"I was wearing a uniform and trying to do something decent with my life." If he had also been running from his life prior to putting on that uniform, that wasn't something he needed to share. They didn't need to know that one overheard conversation had made something click in his head, had made him realize that his path needed to diverge from that of his friends.

"Are you calling us worthless?" Wes asked.

"Did you hear those words come out of my mouth?" Eric kept his tone even and not argumentative.

"Maybe he thinks he's too good for us now that he's all worldly," Tyler said.

"Again, didn't say that."

"Then let's go have a drink. That is if Stevie lets you into her bar after your dad made a mess of it."

"It's the middle of the day, and I have work to do." Eric held up the box with the obvious photo of a faucet on it.

"You didn't used to be so hung up on working all the time. I guess the military brainwashed you."

"No. People grow up." At least some of them did. "See you guys around."

He actually hoped he didn't, but the likelihood of being able to totally avoid them in a town of five hundred people wasn't very high. As he turned back toward his truck, he made eye contact with the deputy who'd been with the sheriff when Eric was arrested. The man stood on the opposite side of the street, obviously watching the interaction between him, Wes and Tyler.

Just great.

Eric nodded once at the man before slipping into his truck. He was so annoyed, that he was driving out of the edge of town before he remembered that he needed to head over to the hospital instead. With a sigh, he turned right and doubled back. He sure was having a weird day.

When he arrived at the hospital, Camille was sitting outside on a bench.

"I guess you must be okay," he said as he approached her. That or she'd turned surly and stubborn again and had walked out of the ER.

"I told them I was okay. But they just wanted to get some money out of me."

"It's better to be safe than sorry." As he helped her to and into his truck, he found himself telling her the story of one of his army buddies who'd knocked his head pretty good during, of all things, a game of football.

"He said he was fine, but he didn't have any choice in going to get checked. And good thing he did because he had a bleed in his head."

That seemed to get through to her because she made a small—albeit probably somewhat reluctant—sound that said that maybe he was right.

After they left the hospital, Eric chauffeured Camille around to the various errands she was going to run following her now-postponed hair appointment. He noticed more than a few looks coming from other residents, some of them curious and others openly suspicious, as he helped her in and out of his truck. He could almost read their thoughts, that he was taking advantage of an old woman who didn't know she should stay away from him. He was honestly surprised that no one approached him on her behalf. But there was always the possibility that people who weren't confrontational would instead contact Camille when he wasn't around to issue their warnings.

"Come on, let's go," Camille said as she waved him out of the grocery store with her cart of purchases. "I've had enough of other people for the week."

The fact that she said it loud enough for everyone nearby to hear made him chuckle silently. Camille was evidently one of those people who had passed the age where she cared what other people thought about her.

When Camille told him that she still lived in the same place, he made his way out of town down the road he lived on. But a couple of miles before he got to his house, he made a turn onto a smaller road that headed off toward the mountains. Camille's husband had died well before Eric even got to high school. At her age and with her obvious vision problems, it wasn't the best idea for her to live way out by herself. But he suspected that would be a touchy subject too.

"That sheriff sure is a nice little gal. Way better than that dirtbag we had before."

Camille's comments were so out of the blue that Eric didn't know how to respond at first. He wasn't sure he'd call Angie Lee a "little gal," but she did seem nice.

"I don't know her well enough to comment on that first part, but I'll agree on the second."

Even if she had arrested him on his first day in town.

Paul Genovese had been one of those lazy cops who nevertheless loved throwing his authority and power around. Eric wouldn't say he hadn't deserved getting in trouble back then, but Genovese hadn't really followed the letter of the law either. He would conveniently forget to read Miranda rights, then say the person in his custody was lying when they claimed they hadn't been read them. And people just tended to go along with the authorities because those making the complaints were criminals. When Eric had heard that Genovese had been arrested himself, tried and found guilty of embezzlement and theft from his own department, the feeling of satisfaction had been profound. He remembered exactly where he was when he read the news—eating a fresh soft pretzel at a music festival in Munich.

"I cackled so much when I heard he was going to jail that I nearly gave myself a hernia," Camille said.

Eric smiled at that mental image then told her what he'd been doing when he found out.

"Bet you've seen some interesting places.

Never did much like traveling, though I'll admit I would like to go to Italy. I make an excellent lasagna, if I do say so myself. You have to come over sometime and I'll make it for you. Bring the pretty sheriff."

Yet again, Camille startled him with an unexpected string of sentences.

"The sheriff and I don't exactly hang out together." Unless you counted rescuing puppies and covering leaky roofs. But those had been necessities, nothing more.

"Maybe you should. She's single, you're single. You are single, aren't you?"

"I am, but I'm fairly certain Sheriff Lee doesn't date people she's jailed."

"You should ask her out and see."

Eric couldn't help it. He laughed at this little firecracker of a woman.

"I'll make you a deal. I will come over for lasagna after you recover from cataract surgery."

He saw her start to object, so he cut her off. "You want to live several more years, right? It's easier to do that if you don't crash into things because you can't see them clearly."

Camille *hmph*ed then reached for the door handle. Eric got out of the truck and hurried around to her side in case her luck for the day ran out and she broke a hip getting out. She latched on to his forearm and allowed him to help her to the front of her modest home.

"Been a long time since a handsome man walked me to the front door."

Eric released her. "Just think how much more handsome I'll be once you can see me properly."

"I don't know. Maybe you're better looking this way."

"Guess you'll have to find out."

"I expect you to keep your promise. I get these peepers fixed and you come for dinner and bring the sheriff."

"I believe I promised that *I* would come for dinner."

"Darn. I was hoping that would work." She sighed and looked to the west. "It would be nice to see the mountains clearly again. I just hope I don't die like Norma Agee did."

So that was the reason she hadn't gotten the surgery?

"I've never heard of anyone dying from cataract surgery."

"Norma wasn't supposed to die having her gall bladder removed either, but she did."

"That's a more serious surgery than cataract removal." He started to tell her that she'd even be awake for the surgery, but if she didn't already know that it might freak her out.

"I guess I have no choice if I want to get my car back."

He wanted to ask her why she still lived out here by herself. If he remembered correctly, she had a daughter. But maybe she was as stubborn about staying in her home as she was other things. She wouldn't be the only one. He had a strong feeling that his dad was going to be the same, no matter how sick he eventually got from the COPD that had already compromised his lungs.

Part of Eric just wanted to drive away and let someone else take responsibility for Camille, but he couldn't. Something had started to change in him that day when he'd decided to leave Jade Valley, the same something that had continued to change the more time he spent interacting with people from places far from this valley. He'd discovered an instinct to help people, one that he'd evidently ignored while making one poor decision after another, same as his father before him.

"Why are you being nice to me?" He realized he'd wanted to ask Angie Lee the same question, same with Gavin Olsen and his young son, but for some reason it was easier to ask this somewhat grumpy older woman.

"Even with these old eyes, I know a kindred spirit when I see one."

"Kindred spirit?" Was her mind perhaps not quite what it used to be either?

"Two people dealt a bad hand in life. My husband up and died, leaving me with a ranch to run myself until I sold all of it off but this little bit with the house. Then the Lord claimed my daughter much too young. So all the family I have left is a granddaughter who lives over in Idaho, and I'm stuck out here watching the world fade away."

If he'd gone through all that, he'd probably be surly too. Did she equate him losing his mother to them being so-called kindred spirits?

"Your bad hand got dealt the day you were born. Your poor mama had a chance when she was young, but she picked her husband poorly. And then kept making bad decisions by staying with him. Only good thing to come out of their marriage was you."

Eric couldn't have been more stunned if Camille had said that she was actually thirty-five years old.

"I think you are not remembering me correctly. I was not the best person before I left for the military."

"A certain amount of acting out when your home life leaves a lot to be desired isn't unusual. Add in that Langston boy's influence and you did make some bad decisions. But you changed your direction, didn't you?"

He hesitated for a moment, stunned by Camille's view of him. "Yes, ma'am."

She made a dismissive wave. "None of that 'ma'am' stuff, and don't you dare call me Mrs. Becker. It all makes me feel old."

Eric pressed his lips together to keep from laughing or pointing out the obvious.

"And I know I *am* old. I just don't want to be reminded. So it's Camille," she continued, stating her preference firmly.

"Okay, Camille."

"Now, you run along. I'm sure you have better things to do than gab with a crusty old lady on her front porch." She made a shooing motion toward his truck.

Eric suddenly didn't like the idea of leaving her by herself, even if she'd been living out here alone for years.

"Hang on a minute. Do you have a cell phone?"

"Of course I have a cell phone. Who doesn't these days?"

"Let me put my number in it, just in case you need anything while you're waiting for your car to be fixed."

"See, that's proof you're a hundred times better than your daddy. Sorry if that offends you." She didn't sound particularly sorry, but he didn't blame her. He wasn't sure he was worthy of that much praise, but he was grateful for it.

"I'm not offended," he said as he accepted her phone and input his name and number.

After he texted himself from her phone and then handed the phone back, Camille surprised him again by patting him on the arm.

"Go on. I got things to do."

As he drove away from Camille's, he glanced in his rearview mirror. A hazy memory of leaving his grandmother's house when he was young rose up from wherever it had been hibernating in his brain. He remembered very little about any of his grandparents.

They'd either passed before he was born or shortly before he started kindergarten. Now he wondered what it would have been like to grow up with grandparents. Would they have been a refuge for him? A place to run to when life at home wasn't great? If they had lived longer, would they have filled the space he'd instead filled with Wes, Tyler and a litany of bad decisions?

Since time travel wasn't actually a thing, he'd never know.

CHAPTER FIVE

ANGIE TURNED DOWN the volume on the radio strapped to her belt as she walked into Trudy's Café for an end-of-shift milkshake. She spotted Maya and Sunny sitting at one of the tables and headed toward them.

"Is this the wedding-planning command center?" Angie asked.

"Please tell her that eloping to Vegas is a very bad idea," Sunny said. "Not only would her mother disown her, I'm pretty sure you and I would be personae non gratae as well."

"Me? What did I do?" Angie motioned between her two friends and the written notes on the table. "I've got nothing to do with this beyond showing up at the wedding as a guest."

"Would you like to be the maid of honor?" Sunny asked. "Maybe you could handcuff her until she comes to her senses."

"Okay, you can stop now," Maya said with

an exaggerated sigh. "I'm not really going to elope. Gavin would never go for it. My parents love him, and he would never jeopardize that."

"So what is your mom doing that's driving you so bonkers?" Angie asked.

"She texts me constantly, suggesting things to change. And guests to add to the invitation list. I may have vented my frustration when she called me when I was in the middle of an interview and told her to just invite the entire reservation if she wanted to."

Angie snorted. "I'm sure that went over well."

"You have no idea."

Actually, she might. If she ever started dating someone, she imagined her mother would be totally up in her business too, to say nothing of a wedding.

"I have the sudden need to stay single my whole life," she said.

"Oh no, you're next," Maya said.

"Excuse me?"

"When was the last time you went out?"

"You mean with all my free time?"

"If you have time to watch home improvement videos and do home renovations, you have time to go on a date."

After Angie let the waitress know she wanted a banana milkshake, she leveled her gaze at Maya again.

"And just who am I supposed to go out with? And no, I'm not going out with Simon Harris again. He's obviously not a big believer in deodorant."

"Eww," Maya and Sunny said in unison.

"What about the new guy in town?" Maya asked. "Gavin said he was nice."

Angie saw the momentary look of concern cross Sunny's face before she adopted a neutral expression.

"You don't think that's a good idea?" Angie asked her.

Sunny shrugged. "It's been years since I saw Eric. He could have changed."

"Well, Camille Becker evidently likes him," Maya said. "I hear she had him toting her all over town today. And when T.J. Downey at the electric company made a negative remark about who she was hanging out with, she told him she didn't ask for his opinion and he wasn't one to talk since she knew for a fact that he'd been down at The Bar flirting with other women while his wife worked her nursing shifts at the hospital."

"Oh no, she didn't," Sunny said.

"I assure you that she did. I've heard about it from three people already."

"How is she so up on the local gossip?" Sunny asked.

Angie and Maya eyed each other with a knowing look.

"The 3C," Angie said as she accepted her milkshake then took a big sip.

The 3C was the local salon which, reportedly, had once been called the Clip, Curl and Color. That was too much of a mouthful, so everyone just called it the 3C. Eventually, one of the past owners officially changed the name.

"It's a cliché, but it's the best place to get the latest gossip," Maya said. "Better even than Trudy's and Alma's. I've lost count how many story leads I've gotten there."

"Is it the same with you and investigations?" Sunny asked Angie.

"I'll listen to what is said there but take it with a grain of salt. Gossip tends to be influenced by the opinions people already have of others."

"Like with Eric Novak," Sunny said, understanding the genesis for Angie's comment.

"Exactly."

"You're good at judging people based on what they do, not what they've done or who they are."

"That's what police officers should do," Maya said. "We're lucky to have you."

Angie appreciated the compliment even though neither of her friends knew why she held so firmly to her convictions about how to do her job. She'd never told anyone.

"Any progress on figuring out who broke into Meecham's?" Maya asked, switching from friend- or future-bride mode to journalist mode.

Angie shook her head. "Not yet."

"You were right. Dan is totally convinced he knows who did it. Speaking of judging people based on their pasts."

"To be fair, Wes is still a troublemaker," Sunny said.

Sunny wasn't wrong. Angie had hauled in Wes Davis and Tyler Langston for everything from drunk and disorderly to shoplifting. Not anything serious enough to get them any substantial time behind bars but enough for lawbreaking to be a pattern. It was entirely possible they were guilty of other crimes, even the break-in at Meecham's, but she didn't have any evidence to use as a reason to arrest them for anything more serious.

"He is that," Angie said, but even trouble-makers got the benefit of the doubt until there was evidence to indicate otherwise.

After a few more minutes of chatting, Angie paid for her consumed milkshake and headed for the vet's office to pick up the pups.

"I hate to see these little ones leave," said Stacey Burns, who worked the front desk at the clinic.

"Want one? Or four?"

Stacey shook her head. "If I bring home one more pet, my husband will divorce me."

Angie doubted that. Stacey and Jason had evidently been together since middle school and had three small children who were prob-ably at least part of the reason for the abun-dance of pets at their house.

"Besides," Stacey said. "I think you're going to fall in love with all of them and keep them for yourself."

Despite what Angie claimed about not hav-ing time to take care of pets, she was afraid Stacey was right. The evidence? The amount of money Angie spent at the store to buy them not only necessities but also an array of toys. Between puppy treats and a new roof and home renovation supplies, Angie was going to have to take on delivering pizzas for Little Italy in addition to being sheriff to pay for everything.

At least she didn't have rent or a mortgage. Because her property wasn't big enough to ranch and didn't have a ready-to-move-in house on it, she'd gotten it for an amazingly low price. Sure, she'd drained every cent of her savings, but her home was hers free and clear. And she could make it exactly what she wanted, even if it took years to complete.

When she arrived home, she noticed that Ginny, the mail carrier for her route, had put her mail under a rock on her front porch. That was nice of her, but so that she didn't have to make the effort again, Angie got the puppies settled in their pen and dragged the new mailbox and pole down to the road. As she was headed back up to the house to get the bag of quick-setting concrete, someone pulled into her driveway.

If Maya knew about how many times Angie and Eric had crossed paths since his arrival back in town, she would no doubt make something of it. Even Angie was beginning to wonder at the frequency. It was a small community and, yes, they were neighbors, but this was a bit much. And yet she didn't mind. Eric Novak was not a difficult man to look at—tall, fit but not overly muscular, tanned from being outdoors often, dark brown hair and striking amber eyes. Were it not for his past and his family, she suspected all single females in the county would have flocked to him as soon as word spread that he was back in Jade Valley again.

"That's certainly noticeable," Eric said as he stepped out of his truck and nodded toward the bright blue mailbox attached to the cobalt blue pole. "Blue your favorite color?"

"Perceptive."

"Want some help?"

While Angie was perfectly able to do things on her own, she wasn't so stubborn as to deliberately deny help when it was offered and could prove useful.

"Sure." She motioned for him to follow her. "I heard Camille had you driving her all over town today."

"I just count myself lucky I didn't end up at the hair salon."

"That would have been the talk of the town for sure."

"Pretty sure I already was."

Angie looked up from where she was pouring water in a bucket for the concrete.

"Does that bother you, the way people talk about you?" There was no use in trying to deny it was going on when it was so obvious. Even her deputies had offered their unsolicited two cents' worth on the topic.

"It's not awesome, but it's not unexpected either. And not without cause."

Eric lifted the bag of concrete mix onto his shoulder and together they walked back down to the side of the road.

Angie lifted her hand in a wave as Ronnie Pickett, who lived a few miles down the road, drove by pulling an empty horse trailer.

Eric set the bag on the gravel driveway and picked up the mailbox pole. After setting it in the hole in the ground, he motioned for her to hold the pole in place. She complied and watched as Eric ripped open the concrete mix and poured it in the space around the base of the pole, followed by some of the water.

"Since you know people are talking, you might want to be aware that there are suspicions you had something to do with the break-in at Meecham's."

"I wondered how long that would take," he said with a sigh. "I'm sure me being seen talking with Wes and Tyler in town today didn't help either."

"Did they say anything about the break-in?"

"No. They wanted to hang out together, and I told them I was too busy."

"Working on the ranch?"

He stood to his full height and faced her. "Yes. Regular running of the ranch. Fixing everything that's been neglected. Keeping my nose clean."

"So you don't want to hang out with your friends?"

"Former friends. Time and distance does a lot to give one a clearer view of things."

Angie swatted away a wasp while keeping the mailbox pole steady. "Such as?"

"That I was stupid when I was young, and that Wes and Tyler are not good guys to hang around. But I'm sure you know all of this. I doubt they became model citizens while I was away."

"No, I can't say that they have."

"So, do you suspect me?" he asked.

"I don't have any evidence saying I should. Gossip and assumptions not based on provable facts are not evidence."

"Well, at least I don't have to find someone to take care of the herd yet."

"If you hear anything that indicates your former friends are behind the break-in at Meecham's, please let me know. Or anything else. There are always unsolved disappearances of farm equipment, horse tack, checks out of mailboxes. I like being able to clear those and hopefully return property to the rightful owners."

Eric chuckled as he shifted from one foot to the other and looked out across his pasture on the opposite side of the road.

"Something amusing?"

"Yeah, the idea of me going from criminal to informant."

"Well, that sounds very TV police drama," she said. "More like misguided youth to concerned citizen."

"Semantics."

He was right. It was just semantics, but for some reason she found it didn't seem quite right for him to refer to himself as a criminal. Technically, he did have a juvenile record of shoplifting, a bit of vandalism, more minor things like speeding and playing music too loud. She didn't condone any of that, but sometimes kids acted out and then grew up to regret it. She'd seen plenty of that well before she went into law enforcement.

Eric's phone rang, and he pulled it out of his back pocket. A look of surprise preceded him saying, "Well, that was fast."

Not revealing who was on the other end of the call, he answered and carried on a short conversation before hanging up.

"I guess Camille really wants her car back," he said as he slipped the phone back into his pocket. "She scheduled her cataract surgery for next Tuesday."

"That's the day the surgeon from Casper is here each week."

"So she said."

Angie smiled. "She must really like you. I've never seen Camille change her mind about something so quickly before."

"Probably has more to do with wanting to be independent and mobile again."

"I'm not so sure. I think perhaps you've charmed her."

Eric actually snorted. "Charming is one thing I've never been accused of being."

Angie thought he could probably be charming if he tried and if other people gave him the opportunity.

"What happened to Camille's daughter? She mentioned she passed away."

"Brain tumor. She died a couple of years ago."

Eric nodded slightly in understanding. Angie suspected that the mention of cancer had brought back thoughts of his mother and her own short battle with the disease.

"If you could hold this for me, I'll go get the boards to prop it up," she said, tapping the mailbox.

After retrieving the necessary supplies, she grabbed a couple bottles of water from the fridge before heading back down to where Eric stood like a sentinel at the end of her driveway.

"Thanks," he said when she offered him the water.

As they worked to support the mailbox pole, a couple more vehicles went by. Both slowed down after passing but didn't stop.

"You're going to be the talk of town if you're not careful," Eric said.

"People always talk, whether you give them reason to or not. Whether it's vindictive, because they get a thrill out of it or they're just bored, it's going to happen. Neither you nor I have done anything wrong, so I choose to ignore things not worth my time and mental energy."

"I can't decide if you're remarkably well-adjusted or just naive."

"I assure you I'm not naive." Not anymore. Her predecessor had cured her of that.

"You okay?"

She was surprised by his question and the…was that a look of concern on his face? Now that she thought about it, perhaps there had been more heat in her answer than she'd intended.

"While most people seem to be satisfied with the job I do, there are those who question my age and gender—at least at first."

"Some of the toughest soldiers I served with were women. I knew one female MP who I wouldn't cross even if I did outweigh her by at least a hundred pounds. Nobody crossed her. No one with any sense anyway."

Angie smiled. "I like her already."

Their conversation trailed off and Eric took a couple of steps back.

"Got my own work to do now," he said. "Thanks again for the water, Sheriff."

"Thanks for your help. If you need any in return, let me know. And I'm not in uniform, so it's Angie."

She detected the slightest pause before he gave her another one of those single nods that obviously signaled he'd heard what she said but didn't feel it required a verbal response.

Angie didn't intend to watch Eric head down the road but her steps slowed halfway up her driveway. She glanced toward the entrance to his dad's property right as Eric was making the turn into the ranch. For someone who she noticed tried to keep at least some distance between himself and others, she found him easy to talk to. Most of the time she didn't mind being alone out here, actually found it restorative after having to deal with people all day long—many of them upset about one thing or another. But she had enjoyed spending time with Eric when he showed up to help her right when she could use it.

And if she was being honest, she wouldn't mind him showing up again. Might actually be looking forward to it.

OVER THE COURSE of the next few days, Eric kept his distance from Angie. No matter what she said, being seen with him could start rumors that would hinder her in her job. Then there was the realization as he'd driven away from helping her with her bright blue mailbox that he liked being around her, as in a physical attraction kind of like. He'd literally laughed out loud at the idea of him with the head cop in the whole county.

Others wouldn't laugh, though. Angie might have been dealing with the locals for the past few years, but he'd grown up here, spent his first eighteen years steeped in Jade Valley. Overall, it was a nice place filled with good people. But it was still a small town, and small towns around the world were hotbeds of gossip and residents being typecast into certain roles they couldn't escape with a rocket. He'd seen the same types of looks and attitudes on three continents and heard preconceived notions in half a dozen languages.

As it happened, it wasn't difficult to find

things to occupy his time and keep him firmly entrenched on the ranch. There was the business of actual ranching, repairing of equipment and the barn, general maintenance on the house and the area immediately around it. Then there was the cleaning and culling. His dad wasn't a hoarder, but he didn't exactly toss things when he didn't need them anymore either. The most difficult part was walking into the room his parents had shared and still seeing all his mom's things sitting around as if she'd done no more than go to the grocery store and would be back in a few minutes. The only clue that she wasn't coming back was the layer of dust on the single perfume bottle, the various ceramic knick-knacks, the pair of brown dress shoes she would wear when she left the ranch. Those shoes still being there made him wonder what his dad had buried her in.

Eric picked up the perfume bottle and wiped it off. He couldn't even remember what the perfume smelled like because his mother had worn it so infrequently. She'd likely saved it thinking she could make it last years. Only she hadn't known she had fewer years than she'd planned for. He set the bottle back down on the dresser harder than he'd intended, but thankfully it was made from a thick, sturdy glass.

He went to the kitchen and grabbed a trash bag, then retraced his steps to the bedroom and started shoving his mother's cheap, worn clothes into the bag. He didn't even consider that his dad might be keeping any of it for sentimental reasons. His parents hadn't had that kind of relationship.

Camille's words about how his mom had once had a chance came back to him. He wondered if she'd meant something specific, or if it was simply that his mom's life would have turned out better if she'd married anyone but his dad.

As he carried the filled bag into the living room and placed it next to the front door, he heard the distinctive beeping of a truck in Reverse. He stepped out onto his porch and saw a flatbed truck backing up Angie's driveway. Looked like her roofing supplies had arrived.

Telling himself it was none of his business, he returned to the bedroom and filled another bag with clothing and shoes. He set the box of paperback mystery novels next to the bags of clothing. Though none of it was worth much, he would still donate it to the local thrift shop that was operated together by all the local churches. There was always the need for cheap necessities and entertainment in areas like Jade Valley. People lived here for a variety of reasons—it was where they'd grown up, to be near family, the peace and quiet or the natural beauty and access to great hiking and fishing—but getting rich wasn't one of them. Many made a decent living, but others were barely able to pay their bills and had to cut financial corners where they could.

And all of his mom's things were doing no one any good where they were. Getting them out of the way now would make it easier to clean, fix up and possibly at some point sell the house. That might not be for many more years, but it would happen eventually. Because if he was being honest, his reception so far had shown him that his return wouldn't likely be permanent. He might be able to settle into the community okay over time, but he'd never be able to escape who he was or what he'd done when he'd been an idiot teenager. If only he could go back in time and shake some sense into himself.

After his mom's belongings had been removed from the closet, he started carrying the bags and boxes out to his truck. He noticed the delivery truck from the hardware store leaving up the road. Movement in Angie's yard caught his attention, and it only took him a couple of seconds to realize what he was seeing. Angie carried her ladder over to the spot where they had ascended to the roof before.

She really was going to roof the house herself. He wondered how many online videos she'd watched in order to learn how to do that. But roofing wasn't like putting down tile or painting walls. If you messed up, water would still find its way in with the next rain.

Not my problem.

He headed back toward the house. Halfway there he growled in frustration. Was he really going to let her crawl up on that roof alone when he could no doubt do the work in a fraction of the time because he had the hands-on experience? After letting out a long sigh, he hurried into the house to get his truck keys then headed off to be neighborly to his nearest neighbor again.

His very pretty neighbor.

ANGIE TUGGED HER ponytail through the back of her baseball cap then pulled on her work gloves. The day was the hottest one of the year so far, but it was also the only day she had off all week. And it was supposed to rain the next day. So today was roofing day, whether she liked it or not.

The friskiest of the pups, the one she'd started calling Loki because he was full of mischief, barked at her as if to say, "Let me out of this pen. I want to be free!"

"I brought you outside so I wouldn't give you a little puppy headache," she said. "But I'm not letting you and your brothers and sister run all over the hillside. Or, heaven forbid, into the road I saved you from."

As she put her foot on the bottom rung of the ladder, she heard the approach of a familiar vehicle. Instead of driving by, however, Eric turned into her driveway and parked next to her truck. Without hesitation, he got out and strode toward her.

"Hello," she said.

"Just so you know, I'm doing this for my own peace of mind—not because I don't think you're perfectly capable of doing it yourself." He took the piece of tin roofing from her hand and gestured for her to go up the ladder.

She didn't argue. This hot job would go much faster with help. She did, however, have to bite her lip when she turned away from him to keep from laughing. The annoyed look on his face was unintentionally amusing. He was trying so very hard to keep his distance from people, but what seemed like a natural desire to help others kept defeating his resolve.

After he handed several pieces of the roofing up to her, he carried up everything else they'd need and they set to work. Angie wasn't even surprised when they settled into an easy rhythm and made steady progress.

"I'm going to guess that in your construction job in Texas you did a fair amount of roofing," she said as she straightened her back when they were about a third of the way through and wiped the sweat off her forehead.

"I did." Eric didn't pause, and she couldn't help but laugh a little.

That did cause him to look up at her. "What?"

"You are zipping across this roof as if the hounds of Hell are after you."

"I wouldn't be surprised if they showed up. It's about that hot up here today."

"It does make a person have daydreams of banana splits or buckets of lemonade."

"Or vacations to the South Pole."

"Okay, that's a bit too cold even for someone used to Wyoming winters. I read a book about the Amundsen base, and the weather sounds miserable."

"I had some days in the field I would have gladly traded for that yeti weather."

"Where all did you serve?" she asked as they moved to the next sheet of roofing.

"Germany, Afghanistan, a few missions in places I can't talk about. Last place before my discharge was South Korea."

"Really? Did you like Korean food?"

"I did."

"Then you're in luck. In payment for your help today, I'm going to feed you some of the mountain of food my mother sent home with me. I think she's trying to make me turn into kimchi."

"So you're…"

"Half Korean, half Shoshone. Family meals are always interesting."

"Have you been to Korea?" he asked.

"No, though I'd love to go at some point. My mom's only been back twice since she moved here with Dad before I was born."

"I liked it, though every place I went was interesting in its own way."

"Because it was different from here."

"Yeah. Both the landscapes and the people."

"I've only been out of the country once, but that was just across the border in Alberta. Pretty, but not so different from here that it felt like an entirely different world."

The sun continued to bake down on them as they finished up one side of the roof.

"Time for a break. Not looking to have either of us keel over from heat stroke," Angie said, motioning for the ladder.

"I'm fine. This is actually nothing compared to roofing in Texas in the middle of the summer."

"While I'm sure that was like being on the surface of the sun, it's still break time." She took hold of his shoulders to turn him around, and she only barely kept herself from gasping at the extremely solid feel of those shoulders.

When was the last time a man had made her breathless? She literally couldn't recall.

Either he'd seen her reaction or had been

surprised by the physical contact because Eric quickly stepped out of her grasp and made for the ladder as if it had been his idea all along. Angie waited for a few wild beats of her heart before she followed, taking slow, deep breaths as she descended the ladder. She motioned toward the large tree and the shade beneath it without meeting his eyes. Needing some time to bring her body's unexpected reaction fully under control, she told him she'd go get them some water.

Before getting the water to drink, however, she went straight to the kitchen sink and splashed water on her overheated face. She couldn't even lie to herself that the heat was totally the result of the sun. She hadn't been unaware of Eric's physical attractiveness, but it had really reached out and made itself known the moment she'd felt those just-the-right-size, firm muscles beneath his T-shirt.

With a shake of her head, she filled two glasses with cool but not too-cold water, grabbed a bag of plain potato chips and headed back outside. She found Eric sitting with his legs crossed next to the puppy pen talking to the little furballs in the type of voice people used with babies of all species. So much for cooling down her reaction to him.

"I see they've wrapped you around their little paws too."

"Too? Does that mean you're keeping them?"

"They've been trying their best to make me answer yes to that question."

He accepted the water with a thank-you and leaned back against the tree trunk. Angie lowered herself to the ground—close enough that he could reach the chip bag she ripped open but not awkwardly close.

"Have you given them names?" he asked, a hint of a grin tugging at the edge of what she realized was a disturbingly attractive mouth.

"Maybe."

Eric laughed. "You're keeping them. Names mean you're attached."

Angie popped a salty chip in her mouth, allowing herself to crunch it loudly. With her other hand she reached into the pen and rubbed the cool nose of the one girl pup that she'd named Frigg.

"One will probably go to my friend Maya. You met her fiancé and his son, Gavin and

Max Olsen. Max has never met an animal he didn't fall immediately and completely in love with."

"Yeah, he nearly tackled a rather hefty basset hound that day."

"Ah, Sophie. All the kids love her." Angie scratched the head of little Loki and sighed. "Having pets, especially young pups, isn't really a good idea with how much I work. I hate the idea of leaving them alone that much. But they sure are cute."

They ate chips and drank their water in silence for a bit, both recovering not only from the heat but also the intensity of the sun.

"How are your renovations going?" she asked.

"Slowly. Every time I fix or upgrade one thing, I discover something else that needs doing."

"That's just par for the course with renovations."

"And you enjoy that?"

"I enjoy watching people do it and fixing up my own space the way I like it, but I'm not going to be going into that field of work."

"What made you want to be a cop? Seems like a dangerous job."

"Says the man who went soldiering all over the world."

"Okay, that's fair."

She took another drink of water before answering.

"You're not alone in thinking that," she said. "I've lost count of how many times my mother has told me how inappropriate my job is. I think she's actually embarrassed by it. She's never said it out loud, but I can tell."

"Why would she be? They have female police officers in Korea. I know. One ticketed me for speeding."

"I guess since I'm her only child, she wishes I'd get married and start giving her grandchildren instead." Angie sighed again.

"I can understand mothers wanting that to an extent, but you're your own person. You shouldn't be known simply as someone's wife or mother."

Angie looked up from where she was petting the shyest pup of the litter. "Why, Eric Novak, I think you are my new favorite person."

He chuckled. "That certainly didn't take much effort."

"You'll cement the spot permanently if you go and tell my mother that."

"Yeah, that's where I draw the line."

Angie turned toward the pups. "And here I thought he was brave."

"I'd rather face enemies in the field than upset mothers."

He grew quiet as that last sentence trailed off, and again she wondered if he was thinking of his mom.

"I'm sorry about your mother's passing. She seemed like a nice lady."

She glanced over at Eric in time to see the surprise on his face.

"You're different than most people," he said.

"How so?"

"I think they either pitied my mother or thought that her situation was her own fault. It was no secret that my parents didn't have the happiest of marriages."

She sensed he almost said something further but stopped himself.

"Too many people don't look beyond the surface. They are so wrapped up in their own lives that they don't spare enough time and deep thought for others. Some of it is understandable because just living day to day can be a challenge. But it's also too easy to try to feel better about our own life decisions by criticizing those of someone else. Cruelty is sometimes a defense mechanism. Not saying it's right, just that it's a thing."

"And sometimes cruelty is just cruelty."

Again, she had a feeling there was something specific that prompted his words, but they weren't close enough for her to ask those types of personal questions.

"Unfortunately, you are right about that."

But at least one of those people, the man she'd replaced, wasn't around anymore. He was behind bars, having gone from law enforcer to lawbreaker.

CHAPTER SIX

AFTER THEY FINISHED the roof, Eric was in need of a shower and clean clothes.

"It's best I just go home," he said, indicating his sweaty T-shirt. "I don't want to stink up your house."

"Go take a shower then come back. It'll take me a bit to clean up myself and get dinner ready."

"You don't have to feed me."

"And you didn't have to spend your day roofing my house. This is the least I can do."

As he surprised himself by agreeing to come back, part of his mind tried to convince him it was a mistake. But the fact was he liked her. She was nice, funny and beautiful even when she was dripping sweat standing on a roof. And the thought of having some Korean food with her held a lot more appeal than eating a sandwich at home alone.

When he walked into his dad's house, however, he second-guessed his decision. That voice in his head again told him it was a bad idea to allow himself to get closer to her. She was just being friendly, and he needed to remember that and only respond in kind. But it was surprisingly difficult when the sound of her laughter made his heart feel lighter. When her smiles and the accepting way she talked to him made him want to believe that other people's opinions could change, that he had a chance for a real life in Jade Valley.

He shook his head as he strode toward the bathroom. He needed to be realistic. She was just a neighbor who was thanking him for his unsolicited help.

Still, after showering he found himself actually taking too much time thinking about what shirt to wear. Good grief, this wasn't a date. He grabbed a blue T-shirt that had the Alamo on the front and quickly got dressed in that and clean jeans. Before he could talk himself out of going, he drove back to Angie's. He almost passed on by when he saw a sheriff's department vehicle parked next to her truck. But he didn't allow himself to because he hadn't done anything wrong.

As he approached the front door of the

little house, however, his steps slowed then stopped. He wasn't one for eavesdropping, but the conversation carried through the door and it only took a couple of seconds to realize the topic of conversation was him.

"I don't think it's a good idea for you to be out here with him alone."

"Mike, I've been up on the roof with him by myself all day. He didn't have to help me, but he did."

"Knowing his family, it's probably a con of some sort."

"What, he's going to abscond with my left-over roofing nails?"

"You're not being serious."

"And you're being like too many other people in town, judging a person on his past instead of his present behavior. I also know you've been watching him, tailing him around town. You're going to stop that."

"Have you asked him if he broke into Mee-cham's?"

"No. How about I ask you instead? Mike, do you use the fact you're a deputy to deflect attention away from yourself so you can steal stuff around the valley?"

"Of course not. Why would you ask that?"

"See, doesn't feel awesome when you're accused of something with no evidence, does it?" Her sigh was loud enough for Eric to hear it through the closed door. "Listen, I appreciate the concern, but it isn't necessary. You know I'm a decent judge of character. So unless something happens to change my opinion of him and I tell you to act differently, you will leave Eric Novak alone."

"Do you like him?"

Eric didn't like the deputy's tone, and he nearly stalked into the house uninvited so he could toss the man out on his head.

"That is none of your business."

Once again Angie proved that she was perfectly capable of taking care of herself. Eric found himself smiling and wishing he could see the expression on Mike's face.

He got his wish when the door suddenly opened and the man stepped out. Mike halted when he saw Eric and gave him an angry look. It hit Eric that Mike liked Angie, and either she didn't see it or she did and wasn't interested. He hadn't known her long, but he still couldn't imagine her with the big man. They didn't seem to have meshing personalities at all.

Without a word, Mike headed back to his vehicle and backed out of the driveway as if it was about to swallow him.

"I don't think he likes me very much," Eric said when Angie stepped out onto the porch.

"Well, he's just going to have to get over it."

"I do, however, think he likes you."

"He's going to have to get over that too. Not only am I not interested, I would never date one of my deputies."

He followed her inside and was surprised by how sparsely the house was furnished.

"It doesn't look like it now, but mark my word. When I'm done with this place, it's going to be awesome."

Somehow, he didn't doubt her. She seemed like the type of person who when she set her mind to do something did it to the best of her abilities.

"Come, sit." Angie motioned toward the small table that was accompanied by two chairs. He could tell by the style of the furniture that it had once been that utilitarian brown wood of decades of dining room furniture, but it had been redone in that kind of painting that was called distressed—white with hints of pale blue.

"Your handiwork?" he asked as he tapped the top of the table with his fingertips.

"It is. Refinishing old furniture is how I got started with the whole renovation thing. I had next to no money back then, so I furnished my little rental with old things I found at the thrift store or that people were throwing away. As you might remember, there's not a lot to do in Jade Valley at night. So I watched lots of online upcycling and furniture restoration videos."

"And that somehow led to 'I'm going to buy an old house and totally redo it on my own.'"

"Exactly. Makes perfect sense."

He liked to see this easy, humorous side of Angie. It seemed so different from the person she was in uniform. Not that she was mean or hateful while working as sheriff, just more serious. He supposed that came with the job. He hadn't exactly done stand-up comedy routines when he was out on patrols. Goofing off could have gotten him killed, and it was the same for her. He hated that realization despite not having known her long.

When she placed two generous bowls of *bibimbap* on the table as well as familiar side dishes of kimchi, spicy tofu and *gamja jorim*—

Korean braised potatoes—his mouth literally watered.

"I forgot to ask if you like spicy food."

"Love it."

"Oh, good. My family is all about the spicy. It's how my mom won my dad's heart, through her *tteokbokki*. That's rice-and-fish cakes in chili sauce."

"I know. I've had it."

"Dad was stationed near her family's restaurant and would come in and flirt with her. She had no interest at first, so she kept making his *tteokbokki* hotter and hotter. And he just kept coming back. She said when he still ate it when it was hot enough to make his eyeballs sweat, she caved. They got married three months later, much to her parents' displeasure."

"Wyoming must have been a culture shock for her."

"Yes. She said she felt as if she'd been dropped on another planet. A beautiful planet, but another planet nonetheless."

He took a big bite of his *bibimbap* and savored the flavors of the seasoned beef, vegetables and red pepper paste mixed with rice.

"This is delicious," he said, sounding reverent.

"I may be able to do home renovations on my own, but no matter how hard I try, my Korean food is never as good as what my mom makes. Now I do make a mean fry bread with honey."

"I'm good at grilling and sandwiches."

Angie laughed. "Said every man ever."

As they ate, Angie shared her plans for the house, growing more animated the longer she talked.

"Too bad I can't just hire you to fix up Dad's house. I look at it and all I can come up with is making sure things that need to be repaired get done and maybe paint some walls."

"You refer to it as your dad's house. Do you not consider it yours too?"

"Well, my name isn't on the deed."

"A technicality," she said.

"Considering I haven't bailed him out of jail, he may actually kick me out when he does get released."

"He has indeed had a few choice things to say about you."

"I can only imagine."

"I'm glad you didn't bail him out, though," she said.

Eric speared a piece of cabbage kimchi with his fork, glad she'd not expected him to eat with chopsticks. He'd never been able to get the hang of those, no matter how many times he tried.

"Why's that?"

"Maybe it'll make him think twice before doing something dumb again."

Eric nearly choked on his kimchi. "Yeah, good luck with that." He wiped his mouth and took a drink of his soda. "At least it's not winter now. If he kicks me out and I have to live in my truck, I won't freeze to death."

"Your dad wasn't glad to see you after you've been away so long?"

"No. At least he didn't act like it, and I doubt him ending up in jail because he followed me to The Bar has changed that opinion."

"He ended up in jail because he got in a fight and destroyed property, not because of you."

But his dad might not have been at The Bar if Eric's reaction to the state of the ranch hadn't been such obvious frustration and no small amount of anger. But then again, he might have been. Eric had no idea how often his dad might frequent The Bar. It appeared he'd been spending his time in some way other than keeping his home and livelihood in good condition. It wouldn't surprise him if his dad had been trying to add cirrhosis of the liver to his COPD diagnosis.

He didn't want to talk about his dad anymore.

"You never answered my earlier question about why you became a cop."

Angie didn't immediately respond, and even with their brief acquaintance he knew it wasn't like her. There was a faraway look to her expression, and it caused him to be both curious about her answer and wish he could take back the question.

"You don't have to tell me if you don't want to," he said instead.

"No, it's okay. I've just never told anyone the real reason."

Was she really going to tell him, a virtual stranger? But then he remembered one night in the middle of miles and miles of nothing in Afghanistan, some well inside him had finally broken and he'd told Tony about his growing-up years and what had made him flee Jade Valley in favor of military service as far away as he could get. Tony had then shared his own less-than-ideal childhood, and thus they'd become close friends. When his service was over two years after Tony's, Eric had taken his friend up on his offer to come to San Antonio and work construction with him.

Only a call from the hospital in Jade Valley when his dad had been a patient back in the winter, his lungs desperately trying to clear pneumonia, had caused Eric to start thinking about another life change. No matter the tension and difficulties he'd left behind, and the contentious relationship he had with his dad, the man was still his father and had no one else to take care of him as his health deteriorated.

"I thought I could do a better job than my predecessor," she said.

"A toad could have done a better job than him. Not that I'm calling you a toad."

She smiled, but only a little this time as if her memories were weighing down the edges of her mouth. "That's good to know."

"I know that Wes, Tyler and I deserved to be punished for the stupid things we did back then, but the sheriff always took too much glee in doling out that punishment."

"You mentioned people who liked to be cruel," Angie said. "He was one of them. He thought he could do whatever he wanted and get away with it."

"Until he didn't."

Angie nodded slowly. "Until he didn't."

She looked over at where the puppies, now well-fed, were curled up together sleeping.

"I know the exact spot where I was sitting when I made the decision to not only become a police officer, but that I was going to run against him at some point and win."

Eric's middle tightened, and the senses he'd developed during his time in uniform told him her decision hadn't come about as a result of anything happy. He resisted the urge to reach across the table and place his hand over hers. Every time he'd seen her she'd come across as strong, determined and self-assured, but he was seeing a glimpse of some younger version of her that wasn't—at least not as much so as she was now.

"I was coming back from a basketball game our school had played against Jade Valley, and I got pulled over between here and

Wind River, just shy of mile marker twelve. I could see it illuminated in my headlight when I pulled over. It was the sheriff who'd pulled me over for a headlight that had gone out. It had literally flickered out five minutes before, and I told him that and that I'd get it fixed the next day when the auto parts store was open. He accused me of lying to him, and he made me get out of the car."

Eric's fists tightened atop the table.

"The next thing I knew he had my face pressed against the hood of my car and was yelling at me that the law didn't look favorably on liars, and then he called me... Let's just say he used some rather racist language. Probably the only reason he didn't throw some Asian hate in there too was because he thought I was full Native."

"Did he hurt you?"

When Angie met his gaze, he saw the recognition of what he was asking and she shook her head.

"I was afraid he might, but he stopped at some manhandling and scaring me so bad that I ended up sitting on the side of the road crying all night. I pulled myself together enough to call my parents and to do the thing the sheriff had accused me of doing. I lied and told them I was staying at a friend's house that night. I was too afraid to drive on, afraid he'd pull me over for that single headlight again. And that he'd do worse to me the second time."

"You didn't tell your parents what happened?"

She shook her head and sighed. "I was embarrassed and afraid they'd blame me for being out there by myself."

"They wouldn't have done that, would they?"

"Now I know they wouldn't have. At the time, I let it get into my head that what had happened was my fault. I didn't want to get yelled at or punished on top of what I'd already gone through."

"You never told them." It wasn't a question, and it explained part of why her mother couldn't understand her career decision.

"Even if they had believed me, I knew how things would likely go with other people. 'She must have done something wrong.' Or 'What was she doing out by herself that late?' Or 'She was asking for it.' People who look like me don't get the benefit of the doubt in those types of situations."

"How were you able to beat him in an election?" That question was nothing against her or what she brought to the position, more a comment on how entrenched people in positions of power often were. The longer they stayed in those positions, the harder it was to dislodge them.

"It turned out there were way more people who'd had negative interactions with him than I anticipated. And I refused to lower myself to the name-calling tactics he used against me. I stuck to the facts and my vision for better policing for the county. People responded in a positive way. There were some who didn't think a woman, or especially a nonwhite woman, should be in the position, but thankfully they were a small minority—much more so than I would have ever imagined. Sometimes I still can't believe it. It's why I have faith that people can change their minds, even if it takes a while."

He admired her positive attitude and wished he shared it. Even though there had been a few people who'd been nice to him since his return, he wasn't under any illusion that their attitude was shared by the majority of local residents. Would those attitudes change over time if he showed himself to be a changed man? Or would his name always come up whenever some crime was committed?

"So he's behind bars for embezzlement now?"

"Among other things like abuse of power. When I won the election, it was as if the floodgates opened. People kept coming in to report things he'd done, things they couldn't do anything about when he was in charge. People who didn't have the clout and power and money to avoid becoming his target. I wasn't alone in listening to their stories, though. I cleaned house once I became sheriff, so the people of Jade Valley didn't just get a new sheriff. They got an entirely new sheriff's department, with the exception of Sadie the dispatcher and one of my deputies who had only been on the job a month when I started. Even in that short amount of time, Jace had seen enough that he was able to testify at the trial."

"I'm sorry about what that man did to you."

"I'm just glad something good came out

of it and that he can't do that to anyone else again. Even when he gets out, he'll never hold a law enforcement position again. If for no other reason than I hear his health hasn't fared well in prison."

Eric considered whether to ask the question uppermost in his mind, partly because he didn't know what he wanted the answer to be. But the curiosity was too much to ignore.

"If you've never told anyone about what happened, why tell me?"

"I don't know. Just felt easier somehow. Not sure why I never told my friends in all the years since. Maybe the natural time to say something just passed by and it would seem weird to suddenly go, 'Hey, remember the guy I replaced? Yeah, he physically assaulted me.' I couldn't even make myself admit it when I handed over evidence for his prosecution. I think some part of my brain thought there was enough already to convict him, and I didn't want all the people who'd just elected me to always look at me as a victim. I didn't reveal it during the campaign because I wanted to get votes based on my promises for change, not on pity."

"He should pay for what he did."

"He is, whether everyone else knows it or not. *He* knows it."

And maybe that was the most important thing.

ANGIE THOUGHT SHE might make it through her shift without having to get out in the rain too much. After all, she'd begun the day at a meeting about the upcoming Fourth of July festivities, then went to the board of education office for a meeting about improving school safety. Following that, she'd had a series of phone calls with everyone from an FBI agent who was looking for a missing young woman who'd supposedly been tracked to the adjacent county. And one of the older residents wanted to know why the pothole on her street hadn't been fixed yet. After directing her to the county road department and texting Keith over there to expect the call, she leaned back in her seat and rubbed her eyes.

Sadie appeared in the doorway and surreptitiously pointed toward the front of the office and quietly said, "Dan Lintz is here, and he doesn't look happy."

Angie was beginning to wonder if Dan ever looked happy. If he had any competition for feed and tack, she suspected he might have to shave a bit off his surly edges to stay in business.

Instead of inviting him into her office where she might not be able to get rid of him in a timely fashion, Angie stood and followed Sadie out to the main area of the building.

"What can I do for you, Dan?"

"You can do your job."

Though Mike hadn't talked to Angie as much after their heated conversation at her house, she caught sight of him pushing back from his desk, ready to come to her aid if necessary. Angie made a small hand motion at her side to tell him she was okay.

"I assure you I do my job every time I put on this uniform. If you are upset that I haven't yet found the culprits who broke into the store, these things can take time." It would have helped if the security camera in the store hadn't been a fake, but she didn't verbalize that thought.

Dan pointed in the general direction of the middle of downtown, anger pulling at all his facial muscles. "Wes Davis just smirked at me. I know it's him, and he knows I know it's him."

"Even if you're right, I can't get a search warrant based on gut feelings."

He started to object, but she interrupted him by saying, "Tell me this. If you went into the hardware store this afternoon and Chris saw you, and then tonight someone broke in and stole a bunch of expensive tools, how would you feel if I showed up at your house looking for those tools simply because you'd been a customer in the store?"

"I'm not a criminal."

"Just because someone has been found guilty of one crime doesn't mean they are automatically guilty of others."

With a sound of disgust, Dan spun on his heel and stalked out the door.

"We're going to have to watch him," Mike said. "Got a gut feeling he's going to do something stupid."

"I'm afraid you might be right," Angie said.

"Must be tiring, being that grumpy all the time," Sadie said.

The phone rang, and Sadie quickly answered. By the sound of her side of the conversation, Angie knew this wasn't going to be good.

"That was Amy Croft. She said the bridge

over the creek out by her place just washed out."

"Call Keith," Angie said as she grabbed her rain slicker and boots. She looked at Mike. "Come around to the opposite side so we can block both sides of the road."

Sadie was already dialing the road department as Angie and Mike hurried out the door into the heavy rain. Angie turned on her blinkers and siren as she raced through and out of town. Uppermost in her mind was making sure someone didn't accidentally drive off into the swollen creek.

When she arrived, she caught sight of a vehicle on the other side of the raging water. She stopped well short of the drop-off, not knowing how much the creek had eroded the ground beneath the pavement. As her windshield wipers made a swipe, she recognized the truck on the opposite side. As she got out to inspect the damage, she called Eric's number.

"Are you okay over there?" she asked when he answered.

"Yes, but I have Camille with me. Her surgery is this afternoon, but I don't want to drive away and risk someone not seeing the bridge is out."

"Mike is on his way to that side, but it's the long way around and it'll take him a bit. You might want to call and see if they can push Camille's surgery until later this afternoon, maybe switch her with someone else."

She heard Camille fussing in the background and Eric's slight laughter.

"I think you're earning karma points," Angie said.

"I could use them."

"Just stay there until Mike arrives. You know how to get to town the other way?"

Eric snorted. "Who grew up here?"

"Point taken."

Her radio crackled as soon as she hung up the phone in order to focus on directing a couple of vehicles to turn around.

"Water is over Greenacre Road," Mike said. "Not safe to cross."

Angie glanced across the creek. Eric and Camille weren't going anywhere but back to her house.

"Okay. Stay there. We'll get some road barricades out there as soon as we can."

Angie made a flurry of calls, both on her

phone and her department radio. The situation required all hands on deck. Sadie said calls were coming in from all over the county about rising water. When she finally had a moment, she called Eric to update him on the situation.

"I don't know how long you're going to be cut off," she said.

"Don't worry about us. We'll be fine." He started to say something else but stopped himself.

"What?"

"Could I ask you to check on Dad's horse?"

"You helped me put on a roof. I think I can manage to feed and water a horse and muck out a stall."

"Thanks."

She got busy with calls and turning motorists around again, and soon an hour had passed. Still, Eric's truck sat on the other side of the increasingly angry creek. He'd backed up a bit, no doubt to make sure he was a safe distance from the eroding bank. If the rain kept up much longer, the creek was going to overflow.

Angie radioed Sadie to get her Reggie Brewster's phone number. A few seconds later she called the rancher who lived between her current position and Camille's. After a quick conversation, Reggie agreed to move his backhoe to block the road on the other side. He also offered to send one of his sons with a tractor to block Greenacre Road.

Long after the roads were blocked to prevent any tragedies and Eric had driven Camille to her house Angie finally made her way toward home for a few hours of sleep before she got up and went back to work. Just as she was about to turn into her driveway, she remembered her promise to Eric. Continuing down the road to his family's ranch, she placed her hand against her growling stomach. It had gotten louder and louder as the day wore on and she didn't have time to eat.

"Are you as hungry as I am?" she asked the horse when she walked into the barn.

His only answer was a snort, which despite her fatigue made her laugh.

A bang from deeper in the barn made her hand go immediately to her weapon.

"Who's there? Show yourself."

No one stepped out, and she didn't hear anything else other than wind and rain. Still, she eased forward and checked the dark corners at the back of the barn but found no one and nothing threatening. She used her flashlight to check the area behind the barn and the exterior of the house. Even though she found no evidence anyone was close by, she didn't want to linger too long. Her arm and neck hairs were standing on end. She hurried through all the necessary tasks, gave the horse an affectionate pat, then checked the area near the front of the barn again before closing the door behind her and jogging toward her truck.

Even when she was safely inside her own house, the on-edge feeling didn't pass. Instincts honed through her years of police work told her she hadn't been alone on the Novak ranch. Whether it was a person or a wild animal watching her, she had no idea. That either was out in the current weather added to her sense of unease.

As she warmed up a can of chicken-and-rice soup, tended to the puppies' needs, and as she prepared for bed, she paid attention to the sounds around her house. Gradually, however, exhaustion won out over caution.

When she woke, the rain had thankfully passed and the sun was just beginning to peek over the horizon. She made a pot of coffee that would hopefully infuse her with enough energy to launch her into another long day of work. She threw a couple of slices of bread into her toaster oven then quickly cleaned up after, fed and gave water to the pups. Their little yips and tail wags helped to lift her mood after an exhausting day the day before and a night of not particularly restful sleep. She'd awoken feeling as if she'd run a marathon while she slept, a result of near-constant dreaming.

She let the pups out of their pen to allow them to run around more. Three of the four—Frigg, Odin, and Balder—immediately attempted crawling into her lap, making her laugh. Loki, true to his name, ran off and came back with one of her house slippers as if he'd slain a monster.

"You're a little rascal, aren't you?" An adorable little rascal, but one all the same.

After a quick breakfast, she freshened up and put on a clean uniform. As soon as she stepped outside, she could hear the rushing of the creek in the distance. Before she tackled her professional duties, however, she needed to check on Allen's horse.

The creepy feeling of the night before was gone in the bright light of a new day, so much so that part of her wondered if she'd spooked herself for no reason. No, she trusted her instincts. Something hadn't been right. With that in mind, after tending to the horse, she walked around the barn and the house to see if she saw anything amiss. The only thing notable was fresh lumber where Eric had made some repairs to the side of the barn as well as a corral behind it.

Her instincts still telling her she'd been right the night before, she scanned as far as she could see in every direction. She didn't really expect to detect anything suspicious, but she needed to check anyway. Once she'd done everything she could, she got into her truck and headed toward town. She'd tell Eric about her concern later, but there was no need to worry him when he couldn't get back to his house. She did, however, text him that she'd taken care of his dad's horse again.

As she drove toward Jade Valley, she noticed that the road to Camille's was now blocked off with a concrete barricade. Beyond it in the distance, she saw a county road crew assessing the damage and probably figuring out when the creek was likely to go down enough that they could start work.

Angie wondered how Eric was doing as Camille's guest. She couldn't help smiling at the idea that he'd signed up for way more than he'd bargained for when he stopped to help Camille the day of her accident.

CHAPTER SEVEN

GROWING UP ON a ranch followed by years in the army followed by working construction each day had engraved the habit of getting up early deep in Eric. But evidently Camille was part chicken because when he woke up in her guest bedroom, he heard her already moving around in the kitchen. He quickly went to the bathroom and washed his face with cold water, using a bit of it to smooth his sleep-mussed hair.

When he went back into the bedroom and grabbed his phone, he was actually surprised by how late he'd slept. He'd slept like he'd been on patrol for a solid week. He wasn't even sure he'd moved from the position he'd been in when he fell asleep. It was strange to have slept better in someone else's bed than in the one he'd grown up using.

"Well, look who decided to get up," Camille said when he joined her in the kitchen. "You snore, by the way."

Eric laughed at her bluntness. "You do too."

Camille huffed. "I do not."

"I assure you that you do. I heard it loud and clear before I fell asleep."

"I ought to take your breakfast out and feed it to Reggie's cows."

Eric peeked around her and saw she was making pancakes and sausage. "Looks delicious."

"Of course it is. Just because I'm old doesn't mean I've lost my touch. Now pour us some coffee." She motioned toward the coffee maker that seemed right out of an episode of a 1970s' sitcom. It was definitely more than a decade older than he was. But as long as it made decent coffee and didn't burn the house down, that was all that mattered.

His phone buzzed with a text as he was placing the two filled coffee cups on the table. It was a message from Angie to let him know she'd gone by the ranch again to take care of Oscar. A second message followed that said, Enjoy your vacation. And she had the audacity to follow that with a laughing emoji.

Eric laughed despite himself. When he'd

first met her, he never would have imagined her having the sense of humor she did. Granted, she'd just busted up a fight and gotten his elbow in her eye for her efforts, so there hadn't been much to be amused by. Thank goodness the eye hadn't been seriously damaged, but he still felt a stab of guilt when he saw the bruising that was gradually fading.

Camille placed a plate of three fluffy pancakes with butter melting atop them and two sausage patties in front of him. His mouth watered at the sight. He couldn't remember the last time he'd had a home-cooked breakfast like what sat before him.

"The pretty sheriff texting you? With you smiling like that, I sure doubt it's your dad."

He thought about ignoring the question, but only for a moment. Trapped as he was at Camille's, he decided the truth was the best way to try to deflate her ill-fated match-matching balloon.

"Yes, the sheriff was letting me know she took care of Dad's horse again this morning."

"I doubt very much the welfare of a horse is what makes you look all lit up from the inside."

"Now I know you're exaggerating," he said

as they took their seats. "Besides, I thought you couldn't see well."

Camille swatted him on the upper arm. "I see well enough to see something that obvious."

Thank goodness the subject of Angie fell away as Camille dug into her own breakfast. Eric nearly laughed again, this time at the sight of his breakfast companion. Seeing such a small woman tackle a big plate of food with enthusiasm tickled his funny bone.

"So, I've got a way for you to pay for your room and board," Camille said suddenly, right as Eric had taken a bite of maple-syrup-covered pancake.

"My taxi service isn't enough?"

"Well, I don't think your taxi is going anywhere right now, do you?"

Eric nearly choked on his pancakes when she whipped a lengthy to-do list out of the pocket of the apron she still wore. It looked as if she'd been adding to that list since her husband died.

In actuality, it was good to have things to do because he didn't think he could mirror whatever Camille normally did with her days. By lunchtime, he'd knocked out several of the items on the list. Some of them—such as changing light bulbs and trimming a tree branch that Camille said rubbed against her bedroom window didn't take long at all but were things she couldn't do. A woman her age didn't need to be standing on chairs or ladders and certainly didn't need to be wielding an ax or saw. All of those scenarios had a high likelihood of resulting in a trip to the hospital or her lying out here injured and alone.

"Why don't you move into town or in with your granddaughter?" he asked when he took a break to get a drink of water.

Camille looked up from where she was working on paying bills by writing checks.

"This is home and it's paid for," she said simply. "And my granddaughter offered to let me come live with her, but she has a busy life. And she'd no doubt want to tell me how to do things differently than I want to. As long as I'm able, I'm staying put. Though I wouldn't mind having visitors now and then."

"Subtle."

"Subtlety is vastly overrated."

After a quick lunch of a tuna salad sandwich and cheese puffs—a pairing Eric was sure he'd never eaten before in his life—he got back to work, this time washing windows that appeared to have been through several seasons since their last cleaning.

"You missed a spot," Camille said, then giggled as she passed by.

He pretended as if he was going to spray the window cleaner at her.

And that's how they spent their day—joking with each other as they completed a variety of tasks big and small. Many of them Camille could have done on her own if she were younger and had better eyesight. Others he thought she still could have undertaken, but the fact that she hadn't made him wonder if she was lonelier than she would admit to and just didn't bother.

"So, do I get your famous lasagna for all this work you have me doing?" he asked as he finished using her broom to knock down cobwebs in corners.

"No. That's only if you bring Angie with you."

"You don't give up, do you?"

"You should have figured that out by now."

He shook his head while smiling again. "So what's next?"

Camille motioned for him to follow her

into her bedroom, which was painted a pale pink. If he had to guess, that color had happened after her husband's passing. He could remember Camille's husband and he hadn't been a mean man to his recollection, but he also hadn't seemed like the type of man who'd like sleeping in a pink room. Of course, Camille could have been just as much of a force of nature back then as well and told her husband that was just the way it was going to be, and if he didn't like it he was welcome to sleep on the couch.

Eric chuckled at the image.

"What are you snickering about now?"

"Nothing."

Camille gave a little snort as if to say, "Yeah, right." She then crossed the room to a closet and opened it. The contents appeared to be as much of a time capsule as his mother's closet. Men's shirts and pants hung from wire hangers. A collection of work boots, cowboy boots and a single pair of black dress shoes sat on the floor, a coating of dust on them.

"I need to get rid of this stuff," she said in a way that made him think perhaps she had tried in the past and hadn't quite managed it.

For all her swinging between grumpy and

unexpectedly funny, Camille no doubt still mourned her husband and her daughter. Time might ease the severity of the grief, but it never truly went away. When alone with those memories, they seemed even bigger and more present. More alive and demanding of attention.

"I even got boxes to do it, but I ended up just shoving them under the bed," she said, pointing behind her. "And then it got to where it was too hard to get down there to pull them out. But I ought to make it as easy on my granddaughter as possible when I pass, even if that's one less closet of old stuff to dispose of."

Eric didn't like hearing her talk about dying, wanted to tell her to not talk about it. But at her age, the truth was the vast majority of her life was behind her. At most, she likely only had another decade left. He hadn't really known her long, but he hated the idea of her suddenly not being there. It was strange to feel that way when he didn't even know how long he'd be in Jade Valley. The longer he stayed, the more connections he felt forming, surprising him when they did. But the negatives of staying weren't going away.

Wes and Tyler were not going to suddenly disappear, and with each passing day he dreaded his dad coming home more and more. Because the longer the man had to sit in jail, the more he was going to stew. Eric had paid Stevie for the damages because those affected someone else, but he refused to pay his dad's bail. The truth was they'd probably take care of him better at the jail than his dad took care of himself. At the very least, perhaps he wouldn't be able to smoke, giving his beleaguered lungs a break.

"You can keep any of it you like, anything your dad might be able to use. The rest can go to the thrift store."

"We must be on the same wavelength," he said, saying the words out loud even though he hadn't consciously meant to.

"How so?"

"I've been clearing out my mom's things."

"Maybe it was just time for both of us."

To Eric's surprise, Camille took his right hand in one of hers and patted it with the other. The pang he felt in his chest was unexpected as well. The gesture was so like a memory of his mother when he'd been young that a lump formed in his throat.

A knock at the front door interrupted the moment. Eric cleared his throat, trying to dislodge the lump.

"I'll get that," he said, and tried to pull away.

"No, I'll leave you to this," Camille said with a gesture toward the closet. Maybe she wanted to seize the opportunity to not have to see her husband's things go into boxes as if he'd never existed. "Probably one of the neighbors stuck out here like us."

Eric took a moment to take a deep breath after Camille left the room. Throughout his life he'd had a sometimes frustrating relationship with his mom, never understanding why she stayed with his dad, always wondering why she just went along with whatever her husband said and didn't stand up for herself more. By doing so, his father's reputation had rubbed off on her. He tried to remember if his mom had any true friends and was hit by a wave of sadness when he realized the answer was no. Had she at one point? Had his mother asked to borrow money one too many times? Had her friends gradually faded away because they didn't want to hear about or be near his parents' variety of troubles, afraid they were contagious?

Shaking off memories and a past that couldn't be changed, he lowered himself to his knees and pulled the dusty boxes out from underneath the bed. When he stood back up, he heard voices heading his way. Then there in the doorway stood Angie, looking as if she'd had a very busy day at work. Next to her was Camille, wearing the most mischievous grin he was certain he'd ever seen.

"I'll leave you to supervise," she said to Angie. "I was about to make some lasagna."

"I can help you," Angie said.

"No, no, I don't let anyone help with my lasagna." Camille nudged Angie farther into the room. "Have a seat and chat about young people things."

"I see what you're doing, old woman!" Eric called out to Camille, who responded with a self-satisfied cackle.

"What's that all about?" Angie asked.

He shook his head. "Never mind."

Angie smiled. Despite how part of her hair had come loose from her ponytail and there were smears of dirt here and there that showed she hadn't spent all day behind her desk or the wheel of her patrol vehicle, she looked beautiful in that moment—so much so that he had to turn away or risk her seeing his thoughts.

"I'm guessing you had a busy day," he said instead.

"I did. If I were a betting person, I'd lay down a substantial sum that you have as well."

"After today, I think I'm qualified to open a housekeeping service."

Angie laughed. "Now I'm picturing you in a frilly white apron and cap."

That comment got his attention. "Did you just picture me in a French maid's uniform?"

"Uh, no."

Was that a flush of embarrassment in her cheeks? The overwhelming urge to tease her came over him.

"Good, because I'm not sure my hairy legs would go with that whole look."

"So what are the boxes for?" She obviously wanted to change the subject, so he took pity and allowed her to.

He pointed at the open closet then spoke in a quieter voice. "I think she wanted someone else to remove her husband's things so she didn't have to face so many memories."

Angie nodded in understanding then

stepped forward to help him assemble the boxes using a packing tape dispenser that Camille had evidently placed on the nightstand earlier in the day with this project in mind.

"It must be hard to part with the clothing a person wore, like you're losing them all over again."

"It feels like you're erasing them." He hadn't even really acknowledged that truth to himself until that moment. When he looked up and saw understanding in Angie's eyes, it caused warmth in the part of his chest that held his heart.

"You've been clearing out your mother's things?"

She was certainly perceptive, which probably helped immensely in her police work.

"Yeah." He stared down at an empty box, imagined his mother's dresses and blouses folded neatly inside it. "Only it feels like the first time I'm saying goodbye to her."

"Because you weren't able to attend her funeral?"

"Because I didn't even know she'd died until a month after her funeral."

"What?" Angie asked, shock evident in her question.

"Yeah, dear old Dad didn't bother to contact me to let me know. He claimed he didn't know how to, that Mom was the one who had my number and my APO address."

"I'm so sorry, Eric. That was so wrong of him."

Not wanting to look at an empty box anymore, he turned and pulled some pants off a couple of hangers.

"I was very angry with him for a long time. I refused to talk to him. For a while I was so angry that I told myself I'd never see or talk to him again."

"But something changed?"

He told her about the call from the hospital, how the doctor had told him about how very sick his dad had been. Eric still hadn't made the trip to see his dad, but over the months that followed he'd gradually come to the realization that no matter what his dad had done Eric didn't want to be the type of person who abandoned his ailing father in his old age. He refused to travel down the same path as his dad or even his younger self.

As they talked, Angie moved around to the end of the bed and accepted the items he removed from the closet. She folded them and

placed them in the boxes, filling one after another until four were totally full and all that
remained in the closet were a couple of cowboy hats and an old Winchester rifle.

"I just had the funniest image in my head
of Camille toting this around," he said as he
pointed toward the gun.

"Don't even say that," Angie said as she
closed the final box. "With her eyesight she'd
probably shoot one of Reggie's cows."

"So the fact that you're here tells me Greenacre is passable now."

She nodded. "Not sure yet how long before
they get a new bridge over the creek. Going
to be a lot longer drive for you for a while."

"You could have just called or texted to let
me know. I'm sure you've had a long day and
didn't have to drive out here."

"I was already in the area for a domestic
call."

"Everything okay?" He knew that domes-
tics were often the most dangerous situations
to walk into.

"Yeah, got everyone calmed down and then
had a long, serious talk. Felt better walking
away from there than I often do with those
types of calls."

"You must get mentally exhausted dealing with other people's problems."

"Sometimes yes, but I like to help people make the right choices, to talk their way out of disagreements before things get physically violent. I've often used the phrase when talking to people that we should help each other, not hurt each other."

Her words brought to mind that boy in the orchard again, and he found himself telling Angie about him.

"That's what I think the world needs more of," she said. "I bet that boy will remember you well into his later years. That one small act helped someone a world away."

While they were in Camille's room, they swept, dusted and Angie decided that the curtains needed to be washed.

"I guess if I get kicked off the ranch and the whole sheriff thing doesn't work out for you, we can start a cleaning business. Cop and Criminal Cleaning."

"Yeah, that name is going to need some work. And I thought I told you to stop calling yourself a criminal. Maybe we could go with Cop and Cowboy Cleaning and Home Renovation."

As they proceeded to take down every set

of curtains in the house, they started tossing out increasingly ridiculous names for their fictional business. By the time Angie shoved the first set of curtains into the washing machine, Eric was about to choke on both the silly names and the dust they'd stirred up. All the while Camille was working in the kitchen, humming along to the radio. Feeling lighter than he had in a long time, he grabbed Camille and started dancing her around the edge of the table where he'd already shared two meals with the older woman. Camille tried to protest and push him away, but he didn't let her.

"After all the cleaning I've done today, you owe me a dance."

Despite her protests, in the next moment she was smiling and laughing like a young girl who'd just been pulled onto the dance floor by the cutest boy in school. When Angie returned to the room, she turned up the radio and started clapping along to the beat. After one more spin around the table, Camille backed away from Eric and pushed him toward Angie.

"You two dance. I've got work to do."

Eric hesitated for a moment, unsure if

Angie was up for dancing. But then his feet were moving forward because the need to dance with her demanded they do so. An uncharacteristic nervousness fluttered through him as he approached her, especially when she realized what he was doing and her dark eyes widened a bit. He extended his hand.

"You heard the lady."

He thought she might laugh at him, maybe even swat away his hand as if he was merely teasing her. Instead, she placed her hand in his and allowed him to place his other hand at the lower part of her back as they spun into the rhythm of the song. As he examined the pattern of yellow and fading purple around her eye, he winced.

"I'm sorry," he said, though he'd apologized for it multiple times before.

"I know."

When the song ended, he didn't want to let her go. He liked the feel of his large hand against her lower back, of his other one holding her hand in his. She was a fascinating combination of strong and delicate.

"If you two can bear to stop flirting for a few minutes, I think you both need showers before we eat," Camille said suddenly, breaking into the momentary bubble Eric felt had formed around him and Angie.

"I can shower when I get home," Angie said.

"Same," Eric added, though he didn't like the idea of leaving Camille alone, especially when the shortest way back to her was still inaccessible.

"Nope, you'll both feel better and be able to enjoy my delicious lasagna more if you're clean." Camille pushed Eric toward the bathroom as if he wasn't twice her size. "You first. How are you supposed to woo a beautiful young woman if you stink?"

Eric didn't get embarrassed easily, but a sudden whoosh of heat traveled up his neck to his face. Despite being afraid of what mischief Camille would get into while he was showering, he headed to the bathroom nonetheless. He'd have the opportunity to apologize to Angie later.

But as he stepped under the stream of hot water, he couldn't help wondering how Angie would react if he did attempt to woo her. Despite all her insistence that he not call himself a criminal, would she really be able to set aside his past and see him for the man he was now?

"YOU SHOULD BE nicer to someone who has helped you all day," Angie said as she leaned back against the kitchen counter next to the sink.

"I am being nice. I don't make this lasagna for just anyone. It's a lot of work, and I'm old."

Angie laughed. "Funny how you're old when it suits you and you're not when it doesn't."

"It comes in handy from time to time." Camille tapped an upper cabinet. "Plates are in here."

Gathering that setting the table was her assigned task, Angie pulled out three plates and put them on the table, followed by silverware and napkins. She pondered whether to ignore the obvious matchmaking or ask why Camille was pushing it. Had Eric said something about being interested in her? Those moments dancing made her believe it was possible. And each time they encountered each other, it was easier to interact. She'd told him about the assault she'd endured and how it had pointed her in a new life direction, and he'd shared how missing his mother's funeral hadn't been his fault.

Part of her wanted to keep Allen in jail longer just for doing that to his son. But being a jerk wasn't illegal in and of itself.

The shower was still running, so Angie decided to plow ahead with her main question.

"Why are you trying to push me and Eric together?"

"You're both single, both good kids. Being alone is the pits. I don't recommend it."

Angie made a promise to herself to come see Camille when she could, maybe take her out on occasion.

It sounded as if the attempted matchmaking was 100 percent Camille's idea, and Angie was surprised to be a bit disappointed by that fact.

"Do you like him?" Camille asked.

"He's a nice man."

"And handsome too. My vision might be compromised, but I can see that much."

Denying it would be an obvious lie. "I agree."

"Nice and handsome. And you are nice and pretty. Seems like a no-brainer to me, especially after listening to the two of you laughing together as you worked."

When Camille put it like that, it did make sense. Angie did like spending time with Eric, more than she would have ever expected after their first meeting. And when he'd placed his hand at the base of her back, warmth had spread through her all the way to the tips of her extremities. She hadn't been interested in anyone in a long time. Work, family and renovations had taken up all her time. But it had hit her in those moments dancing around the kitchen that she had looked forward to seeing him as she'd driven toward Camille's. How would he respond if she asked him out on an actual date?

She was still pondering that question when he walked into the room freshly showered and with his hair still damp. Her heart gave an extra hard thump against her ribs at the sight of him.

Wow, she did like him. How had Camille seen what Angie—someone trained to see even beyond the obvious—hadn't fully realized?

Flustered by her realization and not willing to have that fact seen, she made her way quickly to the bathroom for a quick shower to satisfy Camille's dining companion requirement. As the water splashed over her body, she wasn't sure if the heat flooding her was from the shower, the idea that she was interested in Eric in a romantic way or the knowledge that only moments ago he had stood in this same spot every bit as naked as she was now.

After she finished in the shower, she quickly dried off then put her uniform back on. Spotting some streaks of dirt on it from when she'd helped a couple of hikers push their stuck compact car out from the softened side of the road, she grabbed the washcloth she'd used and scrubbed the spots. After rinsing the washcloth and hanging it up, she did her best to dry her hair with a towel since Camille didn't seem to have a hair dryer. After finger-combing her hair and pulling it back into a ponytail, she took a couple extra minutes to try to fix her thoughts on anything other than the realization that she was attracted to Eric and probably had been since the day he'd helped her rescue the puppies.

After a slow, deep, heart-rate-slowing breath, she opened the door and was immediately greeted with the heavenly scent of baked garlic bread. Her stomach rumbled in response, reminding her she'd only had a corn dog on the go for lunch.

That's it, focus on the food.

"It smells awesome in here," she said as she reentered the kitchen.

"Then let's eat," Camille said as she motioned toward the chair nearest Angie.

Eric, wearing oven mitts, placed the lasagna on a woven trivet in the middle of the table. Camille followed behind him with a basket of bread.

"I think I could eat that entire basket of bread by myself," Angie said.

"I might have to arm-wrestle you for part of it," Eric said.

"I'd at least give you a run for your money," she said, though she wondered if being that close to him again would cause her to lose her competitive focus.

When Angie took her first bite of the lasagna, she closed her eyes and savored the explosion of flavors on her tongue. Camille might be getting up in years, but her abilities in the kitchen were still top-notch.

"This is delicious. It tastes like special-occasion food."

"It is a special occasion," Camille said. "I told Eric that I'd make it if he brought you here so we could all eat together. You came on your own, but I figured that was close enough since he's been stubborn about it."

Across from Angie, Eric covered his face with his hands for a moment before meeting her gaze.

"I'm sorry," he said. "She's incorrigible."

Angie smiled. "It's okay. If you had asked me, we could have been eating this sooner."

She took a bite of lasagna, surprised at herself because she wasn't normally a flirt. The words had just tumbled out as easily as anything she'd ever said. If anyone was more surprised by them than she was, it was Eric Novak. Though he didn't reply in words, she could almost hear them tumbling over each other in his head. She thought maybe he realized those thoughts were reflected in his expression because he lowered his eyes, focusing on his meal. She pressed her lips together to keep from laughing when he shoved an extra-large bite into his mouth.

She—and thankfully Camille—let him off the hook for the rest of the meal. Angie shared with them the details of her day helping to assess the damage caused by the flooding, aiding people who had been trapped either in their homes or away from them and setting up a detour around an area where an electric crew was repairing some downed lines.

"Never a dull moment," she said as she wiped leftover sauce off her plate with the end of a piece of bread.

After the meal was over, she insisted on washing the dishes while Camille went to put her feet up.

"I think she enjoyed tonight," Eric said when he stepped up beside her to rinse and dry the dishes. "But sorry about earlier."

"There's no reason to apologize." She considered saying something further to indicate her interest, but if he hadn't gathered that from her earlier teasing he either was a bit dense or wasn't interested. In case it was the latter, she chose to forgo being more direct. She wasn't one to force her feelings, even new and positive ones, on an unwilling recipient.

"If you want to go ahead and leave, I can handle this," he said.

"No, we can do it together. And we still need to hang the curtains."

By the time they had the curtains back in their proper places it was later than she'd intended to stay when she had arrived. Luckily, she'd been able to stop by her house earlier while passing by for work. She'd attended to the puppies, played with them for a bit, letting them run and stretch their little legs before she had to put them back in their pen.

Among the most surprising things that had happened to her lately occurred when Camille pulled her down to her shorter height to give Angie a hug.

"You like this one," Camille whispered in her ear. "Don't let him get away."

Before Angie could respond that Eric wasn't a fish, Camille had moved on to Eric. When he bent over from his even taller height to hug Camille, Angie's chest grew full with emotion. Eric looked uncomfortable at first, as if he wasn't sure exactly how this hugging thing worked. Angie blinked several times against unexpected tears as she considered that he hadn't had much experience giving or receiving hugs. She certainly couldn't imagine Allen doling them out to his son. And Eric had been robbed of an opportunity to seek even one more from his mother. Angie had to resist the urge to hug him too, to try to make up for all the affection he had not received in his life.

"Thank you, for everything," Camille said to Eric as he pulled away from her.

Eric cleared his throat, and he looked like a man standing next to his tiny grandma. "Call me when they reschedule your surgery."

Camille nodded, and Angie couldn't believe what she was seeing. The older woman's eyes were shiny. How long had it been since Camille had received any physical affection? Was she lonelier than anyone had guessed? And was her crotchety exterior hiding a vulnerability she didn't want anyone to see?

Once Angie and Eric were outside and walking toward where their vehicles were parked side by side, Eric slowed down and looked back at Camille's house.

"She'll be okay," Angie said. "I think you made her year with everything you've done for her in the past twenty-four hours. I wouldn't be surprised if she files adoption papers."

That made Eric laugh a little. He shifted his gaze to Angie, and she experienced the same flutter of awareness she'd felt when he'd been spinning her around the kitchen earlier.

"Be careful driving back," he said. "You've had a long day and are probably tired."

"I could say the same to you." Then she remembered her experience at his ranch the previous night. "By the way, I didn't want to worry you before, but last night I'm pretty sure someone was on your land. I had a strong feeling I was being watched when I went to take care of Oscar."

Eric's expression changed to one of concern and then guilt.

"I'm sorry."

She waved off his apology. "I didn't tell you to make you feel sorry. I was glad to help out. I just wanted you to be aware and careful."

He looked out into the night in the direction of his family's small spread. Even in the dim light outside, she saw his jaw tighten.

"Has something else happened like this before?"

He shook his head. "Not that I know of."

"But you have a suspicion about who it was?"

He looked back at her. "Could have been anyone. Wouldn't be the first time prowlers have come around ranches that are out away from town. I heard you mention one at some-one else's place when I was sitting in the jail cell."

"Pippa Anderson. She has an organic farm north of town."

Whoever had stolen items from Pippa could very well be the same person she'd sensed the previous night, might even be the same person who broke into Meecham's. Though she had no evidence, her thoughts went to Wes and Tyler. And she had a feeling that's where Eric's had gone as well. A chill ran the length of her spine. She was trained to take care of herself, but something about Tyler in particular gave her an intense sense of unease.

"Just be careful," she said.

"You too."

When she arrived home more than half an hour later, she searched the darkness beyond the reach of her headlights before turning them off. Once she reached her porch, she stood there and watched Eric pull into his driveway. She didn't realize she was holding her breath until she saw the lights come on in his house.

Standing there in the dark, she admitted fully what she'd started to realize earlier. She really liked Eric, and she hoped the feeling might be reciprocated. And this time she hoped he stayed in Jade Valley.

CHAPTER EIGHT

CAMILLE GRUMBLED AS Eric drove her away from the hospital, wanting to go home instead of to his house.

"You're not going to win this argument, so you might as well stop fussing." He needed to be able to help her administer the post-surgery eye drops and take care of her while also tending to his work around the ranch. Oscar needed regular attention, and he still had a lot of work to do in the house before his dad came back. According to Angie, Allen's mood had not improved any, so he no doubt would let Eric hear an earful when he returned home. Eric wanted to be able to escape it by working outdoors. Thus, the interior repairs and refurbishing needed to be complete before then.

"Then at least stop by Trudy's and get me some pie."

"Pie I can do."

Of course, when he stepped into Trudy's Café five minutes later, every set of eyes in the place turned toward him. He chose to pretend he didn't notice and made straight for the front counter. Trudy herself was standing there wearing a T-shirt from the previous year's Jade Valley Autumn Extravaganza, which had simply been known as the Fall Festival when he'd been a kid. According to Angie, when Sunny Breckinridge took over, they changed the name and the event that had been dying even when he was a teenager now drew thousands to Jade Valley for three days of events. If he was still in Jade Valley come October, he supposed he'd get to witness it for himself.

Maybe he'd even get up the nerve to ask Angie to go to it with him.

He shook off the thought as Trudy looked up at him and actually smiled. Of course, she always had been nicer than Alma across the street. Granted, she hadn't been the victim of his friends' dine-and-dash efforts either.

"What can I get for you?"

"A chocolate meringue pie," he said, pointing toward the display case atop the counter.

"That's some sweet tooth," she said as she retrieved the pie.

"While your pie is great, it's not all for me."

"Oh?" The twinkle in Trudy's eyes nearly made him laugh. It was obvious she thought she might be on the verge of some juicy romantic gossip. What was it with the older women in this town wanting everyone to pair up? Not that the idea of pairing with Angie didn't appeal to him, but he just couldn't imagine how that would work. If only he didn't have the past he did, and his dad wasn't a current guest of her jail. In a town this size, where gossip replaced the nonexistent forms of entertainment, he just couldn't see how the locals would allow their sheriff to date a criminal. Former criminal, he corrected himself.

"Camille just had her cataract surgery and wants some self-pity pie because I won't let her go home and stay by herself."

"That does sound like her," Trudy said on the heels of a chuckle. Then she held up an index finger. "Wait here for a moment."

She disappeared into the kitchen, reappearing shortly after with a takeout bag. She pushed it and the pie toward him.

"Tell her I'm glad she got the surgery and look forward to seeing her when she's able to be out and about again."

Eric started to open his wallet.

"No, my treat," Trudy said.

He shook his head. "No, ma'am. I can pay."

Almost as bad as everyone seeing him as someone who stole from others was the assumption that he couldn't pay.

"I have no doubt you can, but this is my gift. It's a good thing to take care of others." The look she gave him was praising him for taking care of Camille while also allowing for no argument about payment for the pie and whatever was in that bag. Not wanting to draw any more attention than he already had, he put his wallet away.

"Thank you, ma'am. I'll give Camille your well-wishes."

"Oh, that smells like Trudy's fried chicken," Camille said as soon as he slipped back into his driver's seat. "You must be trying to butter me up."

"If anyone is buttering you up, it's Trudy."

Camille laughed. "She better."

"What's that supposed to mean?"

Camille grinned and motioned between

Trudy's Café and Alma's Diner. "I'm probably the only person in this entire valley who knows what their feud is about."

Eric's mouth dropped open for a moment as he stared at Camille, sitting there in her dark postsurgery sunglasses. "You're kidding. What is it?"

The long-ago genesis of the feud between the two women, which had led to them opening up restaurants literally across the street from each other, had been cause for speculation for as long as he could remember.

"Oh no. You're not getting that out of me. I promised to keep that to myself, and it's good for a free meal from them every now and then."

"You're blackmailing them for fried chicken and pie?"

"Blackmail is such an ugly word. More like I get occasional gifts of gratitude."

Eric snorted as he started the truck. "Remind me to never get on your bad side or let you be privy to my secrets."

"Like the fact you're falling for Angie? But I guess that isn't really a secret. It's as plain as day."

Camille teased him relentlessly as he drove toward home.

"You should really let people do things at their own pace," he said.

The way Camille snorted told him exactly what she thought of that idea. "And some people need to stop dillydallying around and get to it. Some of us don't have forever to wait around to see love bloom."

"You need to decide if you're going to live forever or you're about to expire," he said. "Seems like your outlook changes to fit your needs."

"When you get to be my age, you have to be able to use all those years for something."

He glanced over at her. "And getting your way is it?"

Camille's big grin caused a laugh to bubble up from deep within him.

His laughter died when he pulled into the ranch and saw who was sitting on his front porch as if they were the owners of the rocking chairs there. His hands tightened on the steering wheel. Why were Wes and Tyler waiting for him? It couldn't be for any good reason. Why couldn't they have moved away from Jade Valley and stayed away?

"Wait here for a minute," he said to Camille when he parked.

"Who is that?"

"Don't worry about it. They'll be leaving soon." At least he hoped he could get rid of them without any sort of altercation.

He approached the porch, putting himself between his truck and his former friends.

"What are you two doing here?" He thought of what Angie had told him about sensing someone out here the night she'd come to feed and take care of Oscar.

"You sure aren't as friendly as you used to be," Wes said. "No wonder people in town talk about you all the time, wondering when you'll leave."

Eric didn't know if what Wes was saying was true or he was simply trying to rile him up, or if it was a combination of the two, but it annoyed him all the same. For a moment he imagined tossing the two of them off Novak land on their heads. Instead, he simply crossed his arms and stared at them.

Tyler nodded toward Eric's truck. "Have to admit, nice little long con you've got going there. I think Wes and I need to be in on that."

Eric's veins iced over, and he felt sick to his

stomach at the idea that his helping Camille had put her on Tyler's radar.

"There is no con here."

"Sure," Tyler said, then glanced over at Wes. Both of them laughed in a way that chilled Eric even more.

"You're going to want to get back in your truck and leave," Eric said. "And stay far away from Camille."

Tyler's laughter faded away, and he narrowed his eyes at Eric while making no move to vacate the rocking chair.

"I don't like your attitude since you came back," he said, menace in his voice. "*You're* going to want to cut us in."

There was no mistaking the threat, but Eric was no longer the hanger-on in Tyler's shadow. He'd grown up, was a trained soldier, had been through more than Tyler would ever be able to handle, let alone Wes. The sooner Tyler knew he was no longer in control of Eric, the better.

"I'm not your underling anymore. I made a decision to change my life, something you could have also done but you chose to keep living the same way, leeching off others because you're too lazy to do any actual work."

Maybe it wasn't a great idea to antagonize them with Camille nearby, but he needed to let them know in no uncertain terms that he wanted nothing to do with them or their way of life anymore.

"And if you ever set foot near Camille or her property, you'll answer to me. It would serve you well to remember how I've been trained." Let them hear his menace now.

"Maybe we should focus on the sheriff instead," Tyler said, his suggestive tone sending white-hot rage through Eric.

Only the sound of an approaching vehicle up the driveway kept Eric from telling Tyler exactly what he'd do to him if he got within an arm's length of Angie. His heart sank when he glanced over his shoulder to see Angie approaching in her department-issue vehicle.

"Well, well, well," Tyler said. "Looks like she came to me."

Eric's hands tightened into fists, but he couldn't exactly attack Tyler right in front of a uniformed officer of the law if he didn't want to take up residence next to his dad in the jail.

"Everything okay here?" Angie asked as she approached.

"Wes and Tyler were just leaving," Eric said, his words firm and inviting no dissent.

"Were we?" Tyler asked. "But we haven't had time to catch up."

Eric leveled his gaze directly at Tyler and did the one thing Tyler probably didn't expect—revealed the threats he'd just made.

"I have no interest in conning Camille or hurting Angie, unlike you two."

He saw the exact moment that Tyler's annoyance with him turned to hatred. There was no going back now. Eric turned to Angie and recounted the entire conversation he'd had with Tyler and Wes since his arrival back at the ranch.

"You can't prove we said any of that," Wes said. "Who would believe you anyway?"

Wes really was stupid.

"I believe him," Angie said, slowly moving forward at an angle that forced the two men on the porch to look in her direction, away from Eric and, more importantly, Camille.

"One man's word against two," Tyler said.

Eric hated that it was the truth, even if Angie did believe him.

"Eric has made his feelings clear, so it's time for you to leave," Angie said. "Unless you want to be charged with trespassing, which is something I'm seeing with my own eyes and you can't dispute."

Eric stood ready to spring into action if Wes or Tyler so much as made a single wrong move. But they stood and slowly descended the front steps. Tyler fixed his stare on Eric, and there was no mistaking that this wasn't over. He would have to watch his back from now on and make sure that neither Camille nor Angie paid a terrible price for befriending him.

When it appeared as if Tyler might walk right past where Camille was still sitting, Eric stepped into his path to divert him.

"You'll regret this," Tyler said so that only Eric could hear him.

"It's between me and you, no one else."

Tyler sneered in a way that told Eric he didn't play by the same rules. Eric felt even more nauseated, but he didn't let it show. Any sign of weakness around Tyler was a bad idea.

Tyler's truck tires spit gravel as he drove away, one last move to let Eric know he'd ticked him off. Eric didn't move from where he stood until the truck went over the hill beyond Angie's house. Only then did he utter the curse he'd been barely keeping in while Tyler and Wes had been in front of him.

"That retreat is only temporary," he said.

"Yep. But if anything happens to Camille or me, or even you, there will be a record of the threats."

"I would prefer nothing happen to any of us." He sighed then kicked a piece of gravel, sending it flying across the driveway. "I shouldn't have come back here."

"Don't say that."

The way she said those three words had him looking toward her. It had sounded like... somewhat like a plea. He thought back to the night at Camille's house, how he and Angie had briefly danced together, how a couple of things she'd said to him had seemed like flirting and interest. But after they'd parted ways at the end of the evening, he'd convinced himself that it had been a product of wishful thinking on his part. He liked her, liked her a lot, but getting close to him had now put her in more danger than even what she faced on a daily basis while on the job.

"People like them will steal more from you than physical items if you let them," she said.

He suspected she was thinking of the man who'd scared and humiliated her and who was thankfully behind bars now. She hadn't let what he'd done ruin her life or cause her to make decisions she didn't want to make. Could he be as strong and determined as her?

Setting aside his own life for the moment, he went to retrieve Camille.

"I figured out who they were," Camille said once they had her safely in the house. "I'm glad I'd already called Angie."

"You know I'm able to take care of myself," he said. "Wait, you'd already called her?"

"Yes. Told her to come have dinner with us."

"Nice of you to invite people over to *my* house."

"The more the merrier," she replied, undeterred.

"Yes, that's how I've always thought of you, the center of party merriment."

She swatted him on the arm. "Get me something to drink. I got parched out there waiting to see if you were going to punch those two in their stupid mouths."

"Camille, don't encourage violent behavior," Angie said as she came into the room with a glass of water. She'd been inside the house less than two minutes, and she'd already found the glasses in the cabinet.

Camille huffed as if she thought some people deserved to be on the receiving end of such behavior. Eric refused to take sides. His view of civilian life mirrored what he'd held while enlisted—not resorting to fighting unless absolutely necessary but not holding back when it was. He just hoped that Tyler and Wes stayed away from him, Camille and Angie, but he suspected that hope was in vain because Tyler was one to hold a grudge and was vindictive.

As Angie helped him set the table and pull the food out of the bag, Eric was struck by how at home she seemed. It would be way too easy to imagine eating dinner with her like this regularly. But the altercation with Wes and Tyler made him want to push her away. Of course, it might be too late for that. She was already being targeted by them because of her association with him. Would it be better to keep her close so that he could protect her? Not that he didn't think she was capable, but it never hurt to have another set of eyes scanning the perimeter.

After they finished dinner, Eric escorted a tired Camille to his room, administered her medication and waited until she was tucked into bed before he shut off the light and turned to leave.

"Don't let them scare you off," she said. "You deserve to be happy. Don't let them ruin that."

Camille could be rough around the edges and contrary, but his affection for her was growing every day. He would do whatever was necessary to protect her.

When he closed the bedroom door and rejoined Angie in the kitchen, she was already done with the dishes.

"You didn't have to do that," he said.

"Totally worth it for a free meal. I would have probably eaten cup ramen if I'd gone straight home."

"Well, then you owe Trudy, not me."

As if it was her kitchen, Angie crossed to the fridge and pulled out two sodas. "Let's go outside so we don't bother Camille." Angie bypassed the porch and headed toward the barn, but instead of going inside she sank onto the old wooden bench to the left of the door. Then she patted the seat next to her, indicating he should sit there.

Despite the fact he couldn't see very far in the faint light filtering out from the house, he still scanned their surroundings. He didn't think Tyler and Wes would come back tonight, choosing to bide their time, but he couldn't be certain.

"Relax," Angie said, then patted the bench again.

His heart rate kicking into a higher gear for an entirely different reason, he sat beside her.

"I need you to promise me something," she said.

"What's that?"

"That you won't try to settle things with Wes and Tyler when I'm not around. If they truly attempt to do something, then I'll be able to arrest them then.

"Not if they've hurt you so badly that you're not able to. I don't think Wes would hurt you on his own, but he's a follower. I know from experience that Tyler has a way of making people do things against their own best interests. I'm not excusing what I did in the past. They were my own stupid mistakes. But Tyler was definitely the leader of our trio." Eric leaned his head back against the side of the barn. "I'm embarrassed when I look back at my past self."

"Can I ask a personal question?"

"You can ask." Didn't mean he had to answer, though he probably would. He'd already shared more with her than he would have ever expected.

"What made you decide to break away? To leave and join the army?"

He hadn't expected that question, and he'd never shared his reasoning with anyone because it really highlighted just how many bad decisions he'd made during his teen years.

"Despite getting in trouble more than I should, I actually did okay in school. Not great, but okay. This might be surprising, but my favorite class was always history. Our class took a trip up to Cody to the Buffalo Bill Museum. Wes and Tyler skipped and thought I was going to as well. I told them my mom found out and made me go to school, but I just wanted to go on the trip. And I loved everything about that trip except…" He was surprised by how much remembering the next bit hurt, even all these years later, but it made sense considering it had changed the course of his life. "I always liked Mrs. Kirkland because she was the only teacher who didn't treat me like a lost cause, but on that trip I overheard her talking to one of the aides. She told her I was a decent kid but she'd be surprised if five years after graduation I wasn't in prison or dead."

Angie actually gasped at his revelation.

"Yeah, that was basically my reaction. I ran all the way back to the bus and sat scrunched down in one of the back seats until it was time to leave."

"What a terrible thing to say about a student."

"I never admitted it to anyone, but I was…" How did he even explain how he felt?

"Crushed."

He turned his head toward Angie, marveling again at how perceptive she was about people.

"Yes, that's exactly it."

"But you used it as a positive turning point instead of staying on the same path and perhaps proving her right. That's something you should be proud of."

Eric shifted his gaze up to the vast, starlit sky stretching out in all directions.

"I am." Until that moment, however, he wasn't fully aware of how proud he was to make that change. "Of course now that I'm here, it doesn't seem to matter to some and too much to others."

"At least to some extent, you can't control how other people feel about you. Even if you do everything right, getting some people to change their views is like swimming against rapids."

Something about the tone of her voice caused him to look at her again. He found her staring at him, and the look in her eyes made his body temperature rise by what felt like several degrees. He wanted to ask her how she felt about him, but he needed to be pushing her away instead of moving closer. Or did he? What Camille had said about him not letting Wes and Tyler steal his happiness echoed in his head.

"No pressure if I'm reading this moment wrong," Angie said, her voice softer than usual, "but if you want to kiss me I won't handcuff you."

Eric chuckled at her unexpected comment despite the fact his heart was going crazy.

"Is that your way of telling me you want me to kiss you?"

"Yes."

Extra points for forthrightness. He wanted very much to oblige her, but he still wasn't sure it was such a good idea. But he didn't think he could hold back from really going for what he wanted anymore. So he lifted his hand, cupped her cheek and looked into her eyes.

"This is probably a mistake," he said.

"If it is, we're both adults and can deal with it." She turned slightly toward him. "But I don't believe it's a mistake."

Her words shattered his last sliver of resolve to keep his distance. He'd deal with repercussions later. Right now, he wanted to kiss this woman. He brought his mouth to hers slowly so she still had time to change her mind. But she didn't, instead meeting his kiss with an enthusiasm that fueled his own desire. His hand slipped from her jaw to the back of her head as he deepened the kiss.

ANGIE FELT AS if she was floating through open space, and were she to lose her grip on

Eric's arm she would drift off into the black.
She'd been kissed before, but no kiss had ever
made her feel as if every cell in her body was
on a serious sugar high.

Eric was the first to pull away, and the way
he audibly caught his breath made her smile.
It was the most powerful moment she'd ever
felt, surprisingly even more so than when
she'd won her election or when her predecessor had been sentenced to prison time. This
was a positive, joyful feeling of power.

"Wow," Eric said, his forehead pressed
against hers, their breaths mingling.

Angie laughed softly. "Yeah. I second that
wow."

She recalled the conversation with Maya
and Sunny about the possibility of her dating and how that simply hadn't been too close
on her radar at that point. What had just happened between her and Eric wasn't technically dating, but she'd enjoyed it immensely
and wouldn't mind it happening again.

Eric eased away from her, leaning back
against the barn again. One look at him told
her the heaviness of the worries weighing
on his mind, and she was pretty sure she
wouldn't need a background in law enforcement and investigations to figure out what

those were. The situation with his dad, the work that still needed to be done around the ranch, taking care of Camille, trying to fit back into a community that thought of him as the person he used to be and not who he was now. As if all of that wasn't enough, Wes and Tyler were making threats and trying to drag him back into that old life. She wouldn't blame him if he left Jade Valley again, never to return, but for her own selfish reasons she hoped he stayed.

She could help make it easier for him to stay.

"What do you think about me bringing the puppies over here so that they can play with Camille while you and I are both working?"

Understandably, Eric looked confused by the turn in the conversation. What he didn't know was that there was more to her question than what she'd asked. He was already concerned about the threat made against her and her associating with him, so she doubted he'd allow her to help with fixing up the ranch house if she came right out and offered. Sometimes help had to be a little sneaky.

"You're welcome to bring them over. You took care of Oscar, after all."

She settled in next to him and looked up at the sky. It was the new moon part of the lunar cycle, so tons of stars were visible.

"When you were overseas, did you ever think about how when you looked up at the stars they were the same ones everyone in the world, no matter where they were, saw at night?"

"I did. I even remember the first time I had that thought, lying on the ground in the middle of Afghanistan. Where we were, there was no man-made light visible in any direction. I've never seen such an amazing night sky."

"Mom says when she moved to Wyoming, it almost felt as if it was an entirely different sky. You couldn't see this much in Seoul."

"That's true. I enjoyed the city, though. So much activity and culture and fast pace, very different than here. I could see where Wyoming would take some getting used to for your mom. Seoul has great history museums too."

"Have you ever considered working in the history field?"

Eric shook his head. "No. I don't want to make it into a job."

"Because it would rob it of being fun?"

"Yeah."

"I get that. I love doing my renovations, watching the videos, upcycling things, but it's how I relax from my job. If I made it a career, I'd have to find some other way to relax." Though sitting out under the stars with Eric was a nice option. Or even helping him with his own renovations. Working side by side at Camille's had proven they could have a good time and worked well together.

"Actually, I've been surprised by how much I've liked being back doing ranch work, especially since I resented it when I was younger. I did everything I could to get out of doing it."

"Maybe it wasn't the ranch you were trying to get away from."

He was quiet for a moment then sighed. "You're probably right."

Angie wanted to give him something positive to hang on to, to focus on, so she reached over and entwined her fingers with his. Eric stared down at their joined hands, lifted them slightly.

"Are you sure about this?"

"Yes." She ignored the flutter of nervousness that made its presence known. "I like you. I like spending time with you."

"People will talk."

"As I've said before, people always talk."

"Most won't understand. They'll question your judgment."

"I stand on my record, and I dare anyone to challenge it."

When he looked up at her, he couldn't hide the concern he was feeling. She reached over and tried to smooth his worry lines.

"You don't have to worry about me. I'm pretty good at taking care of myself." At least she was now. Back on that lonely stretch of highway she hadn't been, but she'd sworn she'd never feel that helpless and vulnerable again. And she'd kept that promise to herself. It didn't mean she didn't still have nightmares about that night from time to time, but at least when she woke up she could remind herself she wasn't that scared girl anymore.

Neither she nor Eric was the person they used to be. They'd grown up, matured, made positive changes whereas people like Wes and Tyler and even Allen were just older versions of who they'd always been.

"Easier said than done." Eric squeezed her hand, ran his thumb across the back of it. "I don't want my issues to bleed over onto other people, especially not you and Camille."

"That's not something you can control either."

"Won't keep me from trying." He took a deep breath, then stood without releasing her. "You should go home and get some rest."

She knew he was right, but the truth was she didn't want to leave. Not because she was afraid of going home alone, but rather the part of her that had fully admitted she liked him was afraid if she left he'd find a way to keep them apart because of his desire to protect her.

"Only if you promise me one thing."

"Another kiss?" he said, a mischievous grin tugging at the edge of his mouth. The mouth that she had really enjoyed kissing.

"Okay, two things."

His grin spread right before he pulled her close and kissed her again, threatening to scramble her ability to think coherently. Eric Novak was an excellent kisser.

"So what was the second thing?" he asked.

"Don't push me away. If you decide you're not interested, that's one thing and I'll respect that. But don't be a noble idiot and push me away out of some misguided sense of chivalry."

After a couple of long seconds, he nodded. "Okay. I can't promise I won't try to protect you, but I won't let Wes and Tyler ruin this."

Part of her wanted to know what his definition of "this" was, but there was plenty of time for them to figure that out together.

Several minutes later when she took the puppies out to do their business, she looked out across the distance to the single light shining from Eric's house. Whatever she had to do—within the bounds of the law—to free him from the final bindings of his past, she planned to do it. For his sake…and for hers.

CHAPTER NINE

ERIC SPENT MORE time away from the house than he'd intended, but then he'd narrowly avoided having both Oscar and one of that year's calves get bitten by a rattlesnake. He'd heard the rattle just in time to rein Oscar away from danger and use a crack of his bullwhip near the edge of the herd to get them to move away as well. Then he'd dispatched the snake to the reptile hereafter. He'd spent at least half an hour riding around the area to see if there were any other snakes. He couldn't guarantee there weren't but he didn't see any. With as small as the herd was, they couldn't afford to lose one animal. A snake bite likely wouldn't kill one of the full-grown cattle, but that wasn't the case for the calves. Plus, he just hated the idea of one of them being struck and suffering as a result.

After searching the area, he rode through and around the herd slowly, seeing if he could detect any sign that the snake had already bitten any of them. He didn't see anything and hoped that there was nothing that just wasn't visible yet. Tomorrow he'd check again, but for now he needed to get back to the house to make sure Camille was okay and to help her with her next dose of eye drops.

His heart gave an extra hard thump when he came within view of the house and saw Angie's personal vehicle parked out front. He'd been up that morning drinking coffee and eating a cream cheese pastry when he'd seen her pull out of her driveway and head toward town. She should have gone home earlier the night before and rested, but part of him—a large part—was glad she hadn't. It had taken him a long time to fall asleep. He'd lain in his dad's bed with his and Angie's kisses replaying on loop in his head. When he'd awoken this morning, he'd questioned whether it had really happened. But the memory had been too vivid for a dream, and he'd swear he could still taste her lips on his.

That first kiss had been, without question, the best thing that had ever happened to him. And he wanted another every time he thought about it.

His concerns about them being close hadn't gone away, but he'd allowed himself to like her too much to retreat now. But there was a constant battle going on within him— one side recognizing that she was a capable woman trained to deal with people like Wes and Tyler, but the other side finding it impossible to set aside his protector instincts that had only been honed during his time in uniform.

He reined in his unusual giddiness and desire to run inside to see Angie, forcing himself to take his time tending to Oscar's needs. When he finally did step through his front door, he stopped and tried to process what he was seeing. Angie was stripping the old wallpaper off the kitchen walls, and Camille was sitting at the table with what appeared to be the ranch's financial records spread out in front of her while the puppies played around her feet. Right as he noticed them, the pups saw him and came racing his way, their little paws sliding on the floor.

He crouched down and petted them all in turn, smiling at their enthusiasm.

"They seem happy to see you," Angie said

as she wiped a few flyaway hairs away from her face.

He wanted to ask if she was happy to see him too, might have had the courage to do so if Camille wasn't sitting there staring at them with a knowing grin.

"You know, I like being able to see better now," Camille said, her voice full of mischief.

"I bet you were a terror when you were younger," Eric said as he stood, one of the pups cradled against his chest.

"No, that came with age," she said. "Just decided I didn't care what people thought anymore and I was going to do whatever I wanted—within some boundaries, of course."

"Of course," he said, suppressing a laugh. He shifted his gaze to the rest of the kitchen. "Why does it feel as if I've lost control of the situation here?"

"We're just helping," Angie said.

"I heard you complaining about the books," Camille said. "Lucky for you, I'm excellent at keeping financial records. I kept all our ranch's books because Henry was just dreadful at it. We would have gone bankrupt if I let him do it. And your dad's bookkeeping isn't much better."

"I'm not surprised. It's part of why I dreaded even looking at it."

"And I heard you say you hated the wall-paper," Angie said.

Even his mother had hated it, but there had never been enough money to replace it.

"Don't you have your own renovations to complete?"

"I do, but they can wait. I don't mind doing them gradually, but don't you want to complete as much as you can before your dad comes back home?"

"Yes, but that's not your job. It's mine."

"Oh, let your girlfriend help you if she wants to," Camille said as she flipped a page in the notebook his dad kept the finances recorded in rather than using a computer program.

"She's not m—" He stopped himself and glanced at Angie. What exactly was their relationship now? They'd shared some kisses the night before, held hands for a few minutes. Did that equate to being boyfriend and girlfriend? He'd kissed the occasional woman who he wouldn't describe that way, but Angie was different. To be honest, he liked the idea of her being his girlfriend. But despite her evident interest in him, he didn't know what she thought about labels or that level of commitment.

"I thought if we got all the wallpaper off tonight, we could pick out a paint color you like tomorrow on my lunch break."

"It doesn't really matter," he said. "Anything is better than this wallpaper."

"Men sure are dumb sometimes." Camille turned toward him and sighed. "She's asking you on a date."

Eric looked at Angie, who smiled and shrugged as if to say Camille had hit it on the head.

"Oh."

"Oh," Camille echoed in a tone that said she couldn't believe how incredibly dense he was. "This is why women should be running the country. Like buy a clue."

Angie snorted at Camille's comment, and Eric followed. The sound surprised the pup in his arms.

"Sorry," he said to the pup that proceeded to lick him on the chin as if to say she forgave him.

"Looks like you have some competition from little Frigg," Camille said to Angie.

"Frigg?" he asked.

"Queen of the Aesir Norse gods, Odin's wife."

Eric looked down at the little bundle in his arms. "That's a lot to live up to for such a little girl."

"She's the only girl, therefore the queen."

"So, Norse gods. Why those instead of Korean or Shoshone mythology?"

"I've always been drawn to the Norse pantheon for some reason. Loved all the stories of Asgard, Valkyries, Valhalla."

"Plus, that boy who plays Thor is cute," Camille said, causing Eric and Angie to laugh.

"The mythology has been around a lot longer than those movies," Angie said.

"So have I."

The rest of the evening went much the same with Angie and Eric working side by side in yet another kitchen while Camille cleaned up the finances, tossing out occasional remarks about the unholy mess the books were in and random thoughts that caused them all to laugh. Before meeting these two women and having them somehow work their way into his life, he didn't remember ever laughing so much. It felt foreign but also like a piece of himself he hadn't realized was missing.

Before Angie prepared to head back to her house, they had removed all the wallpaper and the ancient glue. The walls were ready for whatever color paint he decided on the next day.

"Are you sure about lunch?" he asked after he helped her load the puppies in their travel carrier.

"Positive," she said as she turned toward him in the open doorway of her truck. "I want to and it'll be good for people to get used to seeing you doing the same normal, everyday activities they do around town. The more they see you shopping, eating out, paying bills or attending community events, the more their memories of past you will hopefully fade."

He wasn't so sure, though the idea of that sounded nice.

Angie lifted to her toes and planted a quick kiss on his lips. "I'll see you tomorrow."

As he watched her taillights grow smaller in the surrounding night, he was already counting down the hours.

As Angie and Eric exited the hardware store the next day with two gallons of pale yellow paint, they were still laughing about the story she'd shared about doing a traffic stop the previous summer and discovering the male tourist she'd stopped was wearing nothing but a thong.

"I would have cited him for that alone," Eric said.

"Nope, it was his right, but speeding wasn't," she said. "So I gave him a ticket for going fifteen over the limit and sent him on his way."

"To traumatize some other unsuspecting soul."

After leaving the paint in Eric's truck, they started toward Trudy's for lunch. She noticed the openly curious looks they were receiving, and judging by how he stopped laughing or even talking, Eric had noticed them too. She resisted the urge to take his hand because they'd not discussed being public with their new relationship, or even to what point that relationship extended. When she spotted Dean Wheeler, Sunny's husband, up ahead, she called out his name. Since he had gone to school with Eric, a positive public interaction between the two of them could be beneficial to Eric.

"Hey," Dean said to her, then gave a nod to Eric. "Been a long time."

"It has."

Okay, it was awkward, but at least Dean had been the one to initiate a cordial greeting.

"You heading to lunch?" Dean asked.

"We are," Angie said.

"I'm meeting Sunny. She's a bit stressed out."

"Because of Maya's wedding?"

He shook his head. "Something about whoever was supposed to build the stages for the Fourth of July festival falling through."

"I'm going to need blood pressure medicine before this is over," Sunny said as she stepped out from between two parked cars.

Dean immediately took her hand and gave it an affectionate squeeze. "You'll figure something out."

An idea popped into Angie's head, and she looked over at Eric. "You could build stages, couldn't you?"

He looked startled by the question but only took a moment to nod. "Yeah."

"Eric worked construction in Texas before coming back to Jade Valley."

Sunny's eyes lit up. "Really? If you can save me here, I'm totally buying your lunch." Sunny released Dean's hand and stepped forward to take Eric's arm. As she started leading an unsuspecting Eric down the sidewalk toward Trudy's Café, Dean just shook his head and laughed.

"I think we've been abandoned," Angie said, happy to see her friends pulling Eric into their midst.

"You know, I haven't been to Alma's in a while." Sunny suddenly steered Eric to the right so they could cross the street to Alma's Diner. As they moved out of Angie's line of sight to Trudy's, she saw what had prompted Sunny's change in destination. Wes and Tyler stood at the entrance to Trudy's, and the look on Tyler's face as he watched Eric cross the street sent a chill down her back. She didn't move, staring at the two until they noticed her. Tyler smirked as he gave her a two-fingered salute that contained not an ounce of actual respect. Contrary to how she normally viewed crimes and potential criminals, she found herself hoping that Wes and Tyler were the ones who'd broken into Meecham's and that she could prove it.

She stood there until they went inside the café, then took a moment to set her mind on the right path. She'd never let personal feelings interfere with how she did her job and she couldn't let that change now that she had someone she really liked. She doubted Eric would want her to shift at all from her principles because of him.

As she turned to cross the street, she was glad to see that Dean was the only one who'd noticed her lagging behind.

They got the usual stares as they entered Alma's, but Angie noticed that they were somewhat quicker to fade than they'd been the first time she and Eric had met in the hardware store. People shouldn't need a perceived seal of approval from others to give someone the benefit of the doubt, but that was just how the human brain worked most of the time. That Sunny and Dean were providing that seal of approval by sitting down and having a meal at the same table as Eric, laughing with him, working out a plan by which he would help Sunny and the festival committee, filled Angie with happiness. She liked Eric a lot, and she wanted others to like him too, to give him a chance. There was little doubt that when Allen returned home, things were going to be rocky for Eric. She didn't want him having to fight on multiple fronts just to be able to live a normal, happy life.

"Seriously, you are a lifesaver," Sunny said as she and Dean stood, preparing to go back to their ranch and make sure the twins weren't overwhelming their grandfather.

"That's a bit of an overstatement," Eric said. "But I'm glad to help."

Dean extended his hand. "Thanks for relieving a big stressor for Sunny."

Eric only hesitated for the slightest moment before accepting the handshake.

After Dean and Sunny left, Angie met Eric's gaze and smiled.

"That went well," she said.

"Did you orchestrate that?"

She shook her head. "I did not. Sometimes things just work out how they're supposed to."

After Eric bought a giant brownie to take to Camille, they left Alma's and walked toward his truck.

"Want a ride back to work?" There was a hesitance in his voice, as if after everything she might not want to be seen in the same vehicle as him. She considered saying yes, but the distance was so short that it would be a bit silly.

"Thanks, but I need to walk off at least part of that lunch."

He nodded as if he'd expected her response, and she couldn't let him go like that. She wouldn't go full PDA and kiss him on Main Street, but she did reach over and gave his hand what she hoped was a reassuring squeeze.

"I'll come by after work and help with the painting."

"That isn't necessary. I'll probably be done with it by then."

"How about I just come by because I want to see you then?"

When he started to scan their surroundings, she squeezed his hand again. "Look at me."

He did and she saw a soft affection in his eyes that she'd not seen before. It caused her heart to melt.

"If you weren't in uniform, I think I would kiss you right now."

A thrill at the idea, a feeling she'd never experienced, raced through her body. But he was right. She needed to maintain a level of professionalism while in uniform.

"Then if we're ever standing here again

and I'm not in uniform, I'm going to expect that kiss."

A grin tugged at his mouth. "Remember you said that."

As she walked back toward the sheriff's department a few minutes later, she couldn't stop smiling. That was until she answered a call from her mother and got an earful of upset Korean.

"Neo mich-yeoss eo?"

Angie knew immediately what this was about and wondered who had seen her with Eric and set a speed record for calling to report it to her mother.

"No, Mom. I'm not crazy. So nice to hear from you."

"Don't be smart-mouthed with me. You insisted on having that job, but now you're trying to lose it."

"Mom, calm down."

"Why should I calm down when you're consorting with criminals?"

"I don't know who told you I was doing that, and I don't care. But the fact that someone made mistakes in the past doesn't mean their entire life should be forfeit. People change."

"Bring him here. Your father and I need to

speak to this 'changed' man before we can even think of giving our approval for you to see him."

Angie rolled her eyes. It didn't matter that she was thirty years old and sheriff for a county that was bigger than some states, her mother still clung to the idea that she should have the final say in her love life.

"Goodbye, Mom. I have work to do."

It wasn't a lie. In addition to catching up on paperwork, she talked to everyone she could think of who might have information about what Wes and Tyler had been up to lately or who might have been anywhere near Meecham's the night it was burglarized. By the end of her shift, she was so frustrated that she spent a few minutes down at the riverside park forcefully throwing pebbles into the river, trying to think of another angle to solve the case. No matter who the culprit was, she needed to find out.

In addition to someone reporting back to her mother about Eric, several people had mentioned to Maya that Dan Lintz was questioning Angie's ability to do her job properly. It wasn't the first time someone had leveled that accusation. There were always going to be people who had problems with how the police did their jobs—some perfectly valid complaints, but others less so. She just hoped Eric didn't hear about it because she knew how he'd react.

When she felt she was able to leave enough of her frustrating afternoon behind that it wasn't detectable, she headed home. After a change of clothes, she made the short drive to Eric's. She found Camille on the front porch holding little Loki in her lap as she rocked and the other pups chased each other up and down the length of the porch. Beside Camille was a pile of clothing with a small sewing basket on top of it.

"Looks like you've gone from bookkeeper to seamstress."

Camille motioned toward the interior of the house. "Had to have something to do while he was stinking up the place."

Angie caught the scent of fresh paint coming through the open windows. She also detected the smell of smoke.

"He's grilling out back," Camille said.

Angie scooped up Frigg and Balder, nuzzling their noses and letting them gift her with puppy kisses. "You all are growing so fast."

"That's what love and good food do."

Angie got the distinct impression that Camille wasn't just talking about the pups. After a few pats and belly rubs, she put the pups down to let them play again and went into the house.

Eric had indeed finished painting the kitchen, and not just the walls. He'd also gotten some glossy white paint at some point and applied it to the previously dull brown cabinets. The kitchen looked like an entirely different room than when she'd left the night before. She had trouble seeing Allen in it, but it definitely had a cheerier and more welcoming vibe than before.

"How's it look?" Eric asked as he stepped in through the back door.

"Great. You might have a knack for home improvement after all."

He walked farther into the room and leaned against the counter opposite her. "I think Mom would have liked it. Yellow was her favorite color."

She hadn't known that when she'd suggested the color earlier, but now she wondered if there was some sort of echo of his mother left behind who'd somehow whispered that idea to her.

"I wish I could have done this for her before," he said.

Angie didn't say any of the things people would normally say in such a situation—statements like "I'm sure she knew you loved her" or "She's probably looking down at you and smiling." Those types of comments were what people said when they didn't know how else to respond, well-meaning but no less throwaway lines. Instead, she simply moved next to him and took his hand in hers, letting him navigate the moment how he needed to. Everyone had regrets about the past, things that made them wish they could go back in time so they could make different choices, but that wasn't possible and everyone had to learn to deal with the past and then leave it there.

It had taken her a while to leave her own such moment where it belonged, on that long-ago roadside. She hoped that the new, positive aspects of Eric's life would eventually outweigh the bad.

"ARE YOU SURE about this?" Eric asked as Camille opened the door on her newly returned car.

"Absolutely. An old woman can only take

so much lovey-dovey stuff before she needs a reprieve."

Eric snorted. "Says the woman who has taken every opportunity to push me and Angie together."

"And now that my mission is complete, I shall leave you two to carry on without me."

While most of the past week with Angie had been spent doing further updates to his dad's house, there had been time for more kisses too, a couple of walks hand in hand under the stars and lots of laughter. He'd gotten so used to having dinner with her and Camille each night that it was going to be strange to not have Camille around. Though that did create more privacy for him and Angie.

"If you need anything, call me," he said as Camille got settled in the driver's seat and clicked her seat belt.

"Remember you said that when I have you come over and do things."

He laughed at her sass as she headed off toward home. Now that the new bridge had been built over the creek, it would be easier to pop in to check on her from time to time. When he went back into the house, he'd swear it echoed with emptiness. No chatter from Camille. No hyper puppies since they were having a playdate with Gavin Olsen's little boy. And no Angie since she'd had to transport a prisoner to Casper.

Standing in the middle of the living room, the combination of quiet and the renovations made it feel as if he'd stepped into an entirely different house. It no longer had the dismal feeling of someone who had given up on life entirely. Angie had helped him breathe life into it—the way she'd done for him as well. He couldn't remember ever feeling so light and...happy. He'd enjoyed a lot about his years in the military. Being able to get away, starting his life over, seeing parts of the world he likely never would have been able to otherwise, making friends who weren't a bad influence—all of those things were invaluable. But he'd also seen abject poverty, lives without hope, devastation. And he hadn't been totally in control of his own life.

He still wasn't sure what he wanted to do long term beyond helping his dad, but each day staying in Jade Valley was more attractive. Old, toxic friendships were being replaced by tentative, healthier ones. Much to his surprise, he was involved in a community event. And he dared to say he had a girlfriend. There hadn't been any "Will you be my girlfriend?" voiced out loud, but he and Angie weren't seeing anyone else and they spent a lot of their free time together. With each smile, each laugh, each kiss, each moment of helping him in some way, Angie filled more of his heart. So much so that it actually scared him. He'd never been truly happy like he was now, and he couldn't shake the ominous feeling that it wouldn't last.

Any further work in the house could be done gradually, so he headed out with Oscar to move the herd to a new pasture. The job would be easier with both his dad and him working, but he managed. By the time he did that and some hot, muddy work on the irrigation system, he wanted nothing more than a shower and a huge glass of lemonade. After downing the second, he headed for the first in anticipation of Angie's return sometime that evening.

But as he walked into the living room rubbing a towel over his wet hair, it wasn't Angie he saw coming in the front door.

"So this is why you left your dad rotting in

jail," Allen said as he looked around. "What have you done to my house?"

Eric tensed, trying to keep himself from flying off the handle.

"The house needed some work. I did that work." In his mind, he added a sarcastic "You're welcome" but didn't voice it out loud.

"You didn't have my permission to do any of this. You better not have used my money."

"What money?" He probably shouldn't have asked that out loud either, but being attacked for doing good deeds caused anger to flare. "I saw the ranch financial records. Those are cleaned up now too, by the way. I'm surprised you hadn't sold off the entire herd."

"How am I supposed to make a living if I do that? It's not like anyone in town will hire me."

"And whose fault is that?"

"You came back all high and mighty, didn't you? I don't recall you being the local golden boy."

"I admit I made mistakes, but I deliberately changed who I am. It's never too late to do that."

His dad made a sound of disgust as he

stalked straight for the kitchen and grabbed a bottle of beer from the fridge. "If you think you can sell this ranch out from under me so you can have the money, you can forget it."

Eric stared at his father. "Is that really what you think of me?"

"What else am I supposed to think when you don't come back for years, and when you do you immediately leave me in jail and frou-frou up the place without my permission?"

"I wouldn't call a faucet that doesn't leak, clean windows and some fresh paint frou-frou. It's basic home maintenance."

"That sheriff tell you to do this? I hear you two have been spending a lot of time together."

"Be careful what you say next." Eric had expected to take heat from his dad, but he refused to let the man do the same to Angie.

His dad snorted, then took a long drink before stalking back into the living room, dropping into his recliner and turning on the TV.

Their conversation wasn't over, but Eric needed a few minutes to calm down. He headed into the kitchen and set about making a simple dinner of cheeseburgers and frozen French fries. He tried to tune out the talking heads on the news and resisted grabbing the remote and tossing it in the nearest stock tank full of water. Or, better yet, the river even though that would require a drive. Maybe he could just run over it with his truck in the driveway.

"Dinner's ready," he said when he scooped the fries out of the hot oil.

"Bring it in here."

"If you want any, you can come get it yourself. Maybe actually eat at the table."

"So you can berate me?"

"Dad, can you stop being so angry for five seconds?" Eric surprised himself by not raising his voice. In fact, the quieter, exhausted sound of his words seemed to catch his dad off guard as well.

Allen filled his plate with his burger, fries and a generous pool of ketchup. By the time he sat at the opposite end of the table, he was out of breath. Despite their tense relationship, Eric didn't like the sound of his dad's lungs and the fact that it was irreversible.

He debated initiating more conversation, wondering if just sitting quietly was preferable for both of them. Might as well start with one of the sources of Allen's irritation.

"How did your court appearance go?"

"It's not till next week."

Then how had his dad walked out of that jail cell?

"Wes did what my own son wouldn't."

That ominous feeling came back even stronger. "He paid your bail? Why?"

"Maybe he felt bad because you'd left me in there."

"Wes doesn't do anything without expecting something in return." The same was even truer for Tyler, who Eric's gut instinct was telling him was behind the bail payment.

"He didn't ask for anything."

"Just wait."

"Well, he won't be alone." Allen jabbed a fry into the sea of ketchup.

Eric dropped his burger back onto his plate. "I'm not here to take anything away from you. I spent my own money to fix this place up so it didn't look so dismal. I replaced the faucet before the leak rotted a hole in the floor. I took care of Oscar and the herd and everything else you either couldn't or wouldn't do."

"What do you want, a medal?"

Eric leaned back and ran his hand over his face. "No. I don't want anything except maybe not to be attacked for trying to help my father whose lungs sound as if it's all they can do to inflate."

"Did I ask for your help?"

"No, but I came anyway." They fell into silence again, and Eric just stared at his food while feeling like he was a kid again. Any appetite he'd had deserted him. He hadn't aimed to bring up heavy topics, but a question that was eating him up from the inside came out. "Why do you hate me so much?"

"What?" His dad looked up at him with a confused, annoyed look on his face. "What kind of dumb question is that?"

"Is it a dumb question?"

"Yes. Geez." Allen shook his head as if he couldn't believe Eric was his son.

"See, I don't think it is. When have you ever done anything to make me think otherwise?"

"I fed you, put a roof over your head."

Eric couldn't help the snort of disbelief. "Barely."

"You weren't exactly a model of hard work either."

Eric took a deep breath and looked briefly out the window before returning his gaze to his father.

"You're right. I made all the wrong decisions until I made the one to leave here and change my life."

"Running away."

"Yes, I was. And to be honest, I never had plans to come back here."

"Did the outside world not work out how you wanted and you came crawling back? Are you not too good for life here now?"

"I came back because you're my only parent and I'm your only kid. Who else will take care of you?"

"If you came back out of pity, then you can leave the way you came."

"I came back because family is supposed to take care of each other." Not that his father had gotten that particular memo. "My advice to you—figure out why you're so angry at the world all the time. Otherwise it's going to eat you up before the COPD does."

With that, Eric shoved his chair back and headed out of the room, leaving his largely untouched dinner on the table.

"Where are you going?"

"Out." Anywhere his father wasn't.

By the time he reached the end of the driveway, his anger had reached the point where he wanted to drive out into a middle of a pasture and yell as loudly as he could. He'd told his dad he'd come back to help him, but the bitter man didn't want it. Was it worth it to stay where he wasn't wanted? But he couldn't leave his dad to wheeze his way through the rest of his life alone. He wouldn't be that kind of person.

He turned onto the road, not knowing where he was going. All he knew was that he needed time to cool down. Staying within yelling distance of his dad would have done more harm than good. If his return to Jade Valley hadn't gotten off to a bad start at The Bar, he'd go have a drink. Maybe he'd just drive aimlessly instead, find that secluded field in which to scream at the sky.

But as he approached Angie's house, he saw that she was home. The sudden need to see her overpowered every other thought, prompting him to turn quickly into her driveway. He'd barely turned off the engine when he opened his door and strode toward the house, a strange new desperation driving him. Angie stepped out onto the porch as he climbed the front steps. Without a word, he pulled her into his arms and held her close.

He wished he could stay there forever.

CHAPTER TEN

ANGIE DIDN'T KNOW what exactly had happened, and she didn't ask. But she had a feeling it had to do with the fact that Allen had been bailed out by one Wes Davis, information he'd obviously learned before she had.

"Your hair smells nice," Eric said.

Angie laughed a little. "I should hope so since I just took a shower."

"How was your day?" he asked as he continued to hold her close.

"Long but thankfully pretty uneventful. I would ask about yours, but I think I'm getting the gist that it wasn't awesome."

"Dad came home."

"And I'm guessing it didn't go smoothly."

With a sigh, Eric finally released her and went to sit at the top of her steps. Angie followed and sat beside him. She didn't push him, instead allowing him to share however much or little he wanted to.

"I feel like there's a fight going on in my head," he finally said. "A fight between doing what I feel is the right thing and just leaving again since I'm obviously not wanted here."

A sharp stab of...something pierced her, making her want to grab on to him and not let him go. Was it fear? Was it imagined loss?

She decided to be completely open and honest.

"I can't tell you which is the right path for you, but I selfishly don't want you to go. Even if you don't live with your dad, I hope you stay in Jade Valley."

He looked over at her, lifted his hand to run his thumb softly across her cheek. How could such a simple gesture cause such a swell of emotions within her?

"I don't want to leave you either." He leaned toward her then, and she met him halfway.

After they kissed for a while, they continued sitting out under the stars as they so often did while he told her everything that had happened that day—from Camille leaving, to the work he'd undertaken, to his dad's revelation that Wes had been the one to bail him out of jail, and then their unpleasant back-and-forth until Eric had finally left.

"I hate that I walked out," he said. "I know it was probably the best thing to do right then, but I still hate it because it felt like I was running away again."

"Don't let your dad make you feel bad for leaving. You did it before to change your life for the better, which you did. And tonight you did it so that the argument didn't devolve further. Both are valid reasons to walk away. I'm a big advocate of walking away when staying is the worse option. There's no shame in it. There are times to stand your ground, and times when doing so will only add to the problem. The trick is figuring out which is which."

Eric entwined his fingers with hers and brought her hand up so he could plant a kiss on the back of it. "If you ever decide to give up police work, you'd make a great counselor."

"Are you kidding? I already am." She counseled domestic abuse victims to seek a safe place to stay and to press charges. She helped young people starting down a wrong path to change directions the way Eric had. She'd even had to convince a couple of people who felt hopeless that there was indeed hope, that they just couldn't see it right then. So many people with so many problems, and she did her best to offer solutions.

It started to sprinkle rain so they retreated from the steps.

"I should go home," Eric said.

Angie shook her head. "Not yet. I brought back cupcakes from my favorite bakery in Casper. Come in and have one. Maybe we can watch a movie."

"You've had a long day."

"But I don't work until the afternoon shift tomorrow."

It filled her with warmth that it didn't take much convincing to get him to come inside. A few minutes later, they were sitting close on the couch eating cupcakes and watching a comedy special. She'd chosen it because Eric needed to laugh.

Angie didn't realize she'd been staring at him until he looked over and caught her.

"What? Do I have frosting on my face?" He reached up to the edges of his mouth to wipe away frosting that wasn't there.

"You're so handsome when you laugh. I mean, you're mighty good-looking all the time, but when you smile…it's a whole different level."

The air around them changed as he pulled her slowly toward him and kissed her deeply. She lost track of time until the end of the comedian's routine was met with rousing applause. She giggled a little at the idea that the applause could also be for Eric's excellent kissing skills.

She curled into his side as he switched TV channels until he landed on a superhero series neither of them had seen yet. They were halfway through the first episode when she felt his arm go lax just before she noticed his breathing change. Careful not to wake him, she eased away and turned off the TV. She wished she could help him stretch out along the couch, but she didn't want to disturb his rest. Grateful the puppies were spending the night at Maya's, she walked toward her bedroom. She couldn't resist one final look back toward where Eric was sleeping.

There was no doubt in her mind anymore. She was falling for him. Probably had already fallen. She put her hand over her heart, hoping that things with his father would improve—because he deserved to have a good relationship with his only surviving parent.

And because she couldn't stand the idea of losing him.

LOUD BANGING JERKED Eric from sleep. For several seconds he was confused about where he was, but then it all came flooding back. Judging by the watery light filtering in through the windows, he'd spent the night at Angie's.

Just as her name formed in his mind, she appeared in the living room, racing for the front door wearing a pair of shorts that showed off her long legs and an old concert T-shirt. When she opened the door, a woman shorter than her pushed her way inside followed by a man so tall and broad that he seemed to consume half of the space in the living room just by stepping across the threshold.

"Mom, Dad, what are you doing here?"

"What is *he* doing here?" her mother said, pointing an accusatory finger at Eric.

Before Angie could answer, however, her mother had grabbed hold of Angie's ear, evidently painfully if Angie's yelp was any indication. Eric leapt to his feet, not willing to let anyone, not even her mother, hurt the woman he cared about. But before he could say anything or move to intervene, Angie freed herself.

"If you want to talk about something, I'll

talk, but I'm not letting you treat me like a child anymore."

"Why is there a man here this early? And why do you both look disheveled?" her mother asked. "Is this the one I heard about?"

"No, Mom, I bring home a different man every night."

"There's no need for that tone," her father said. "And Ji-An, give Angie time to explain."

Her mother crossed her arms, looking as if no explanation was going to prove satisfactory.

Eric stepped forward. "Hello. My name is Eric Novak. I assure you nothing inappropriate happened here last night."

"You don't have to explain," Angie said beside him. "We're both adults."

"And they're your parents and are obviously concerned about you." He turned his attention back to the older couple. "We were watching TV and I was more tired than I realized and fell asleep. I only woke up when I heard the knocking just now."

"You mean banging," Angie said.

"Angie had gone to sleep in her bedroom. I should have gone home when I started feeling tired, but…" He looked over at Angie. "I like your daughter a lot and find it difficult to leave."

"Well, I admire your honesty," her father said.

"How do you know he's being honest?" her mother asked.

"Are you going to call our daughter a liar?"

Her mother pressed her lips together, evidently not pleased with the current situation but not willing to go that far.

Angie's dad extended his hand. "Vernon Fox, and my wife, Ji-An Lee."

So that meant that Angie had taken her mother's surname.

Eric accepted the other man's hand but noticed that the handshake was a bit stronger than it needed to be, communicating a not so subtle message that if Eric had done anything to hurt his daughter he would grind him into dust. And judging by the man's size, he could do it.

"Let's go for a walk." It wasn't a request.

"Dad—"

"It's okay." Eric wanted to give her hand a reassuring squeeze, but he didn't dare touch her. With the way her mother was looking at him, she might actually chop off his offending hand.

The morning was damp from the overnight rain, thankfully not enough to cause further flooding. The sun was trying to break through the cloud cover but hadn't quite succeeded. Eric walked with Angie's father until they reached the fence at the far edge of her property.

"If you've been spending a lot of time with my daughter, you'll know that she's very straightforward and no-nonsense. She gets that from me. So I'm just going to ask you straight out. Do you pose a danger to her?"

It was not the question that Eric had expected and it threw him for a bit of a loop, but thankfully he recovered before too much time had elapsed.

"I do not, and if anyone else does I will defend her with my life."

Her dad nodded. "Good answer."

"It's the truth, sir. I suspect the reason you and her mother are here so concerned this morning is that you've heard about my past. I made some poor decisions when I was young, a lot of them, but that's in the past. I'm not that person anymore. Leaving behind bad influences and then my time in the army changed me."

"Military service will do that for a man."

"And women."

Mr. Fox nodded again. "Indeed."

"I'll answer any questions you have."

"I have no desire to delve into your privacy. You've answered the main question I had." Mr. Fox looked back toward the house. "Now Angie's mother is a different story. She will dig until she knows everything, including your blood type."

"Then I will answer her questions."

Angie's dad smiled a little, which softened his imposing presence a bit. "You like Angie that much, huh?"

"Yes, sir. I like her a lot."

After saying they'd best not go back to the house until they were given the all-clear, they spent a good while talking about their respective years in the service. When Eric shared that he'd been stationed in South Korea as well, they discovered they'd visited a lot of the same places.

"I'm going to warn you that Ji-An's way of testing you will be fiery. If she decides to give you a chance, she's going to try to make you miserable by feeding you one spicy dish after another. And if you complain, you won't get that approval."

Eric smiled. "Lucky for me that I like spicy food."

The front door opened and Angie's mom came outside. She pointed at Eric.

"You, go home. Come back in two hours." And then she went back inside.

Angie's dad chuckled and gripped Eric's shoulder. "Looks like you've passed the first hurdle. Prepare your stomach lining for the second one."

Not wanting to go back home, he instead took a drive toward the mountains to the west. He hadn't been up that way in years, but he drove until he reached the scenic overlook of the valley that had graced many a calendar, photograph and painting. He got out of his truck and walked over to the rock wall at the end, sat and swung his legs over to hang from the other side. The air was cooler at the higher elevation. It felt good after his day of working out under the sun. He closed his eyes and listened to the wind rustling the leaves of the tall aspens nearby.

It was the kind of peaceful that people the

world over needed more of, but he was lucky enough to have it a short drive away.

The peace was interrupted, however, when his phone rang. Thinking it might be Angie, he quickly pulled the phone from his pocket but saw it was his friend Tony.

"Hey, man. What's up?" Eric said when he accepted the call.

"Please tell me you're tired of Wyoming and are ready to come back to Texas," Tony said.

"Let me guess. You landed a big job and need help."

"I did. I could really use you."

"I'm going to have to pass, my friend."

Tony sighed. "I was afraid you'd say that. So you patched things up with your dad?"

"I wouldn't go that far." If anything, they were further apart now than when he'd returned to Jade Valley and the ranch. He gave Tony a quick rundown of everything that had happened since he'd left San Antonio. When he was done, Tony whistled.

"That's a tough spot, man." Tony had experienced a rough childhood because his mom was an alcoholic, but he was close to his own dad and thus understood Eric's need to do the right thing with regard to his father and his compromised health. But he also was Eric's friend and wanted the best for him. "Just know that the offer to come back stands. If you show up at my door, I will put you to work the next day. That day even."

"Thanks. I appreciate it."

He'd deliberately not gone into detail about Angie or his relationship with her. One, he didn't feel like getting teased about it. But, more importantly, he had no idea what the future might hold for them, what exactly he wanted, what Angie wanted.

After hanging up with Tony, Eric stared out at the valley as he tried to think of ways to get on Angie's mom's good side. But after several minutes, he decided that all he could do was be himself. Either she would accept him or not. Just as he wouldn't hide who he'd been in the past, he wouldn't pretend he was anyone other than who he was now. Angie seemed to like that version of him, so that would have to be enough for everyone else.

He hoped it was enough for her mother.

ANGIE REACHED FOR her mother's hand, to try to halt the flow of gochujang into the buldak her mother was making. The fire chicken was the hottest dish her mother cooked.

"Are you trying to test him or send him to the emergency room? And why is the consumption of volcanic food the hurdle he has to cross?"

"If he can't handle a bit of spice, then how would he handle life's adversities?"

Angie stared at her mother, wondering how in the world she thought those two things were connected.

"Not everyone has a stomach lining of steel like Dad does."

"I wouldn't count the boy out," her dad said from where he sat in the living room, scrolling through Maya's latest posts covering news of Jade Valley and beyond. "I should advertise on Maya's site."

"I'm sure she would appreciate it," Angie said.

Her dad's profession of carving miniatures of everything from trout jumping from a stream to busts of Sacagawea and Chief Washakie was some of the finest artwork she'd ever seen. The small size and intricacy of his work contrasted so much with his physical size that it often surprised people.

At two hours on the dot from when her mother had ordered Eric to leave, he knocked on the front door. Angie loved the fact that her mother could neither criticize him for being too early nor too late. She hurried to open the door before either of her parents could, then gave him an apologetic smile.

"I apologize in advance to the lining of your mouth, your esophagus and your stomach. Mom is going to try to light them on fire."

Eric smiled and reached out to give her hand a quick squeeze before releasing her.

Her mother looked smug when she placed the *buldak* on the table along with several typical side dishes.

"*Gamsahamnida*," Eric said with a slight bow of his head.

Though it was obvious he was speaking with an American accent, Angie had to admit his Korean wasn't bad. She looked over in time to see the shock on her mother's face. Angie had to press her lips firmly together to keep from laughing.

"Did you teach him that to try to impress me?" her mother asked her father.

"I did not."

"I was stationed in Korea for two years," Eric offered.

"Why did no one tell me this?" The absolute offense in her mother's voice was also amusing.

"You didn't ask, dear," Angie's dad replied.

Her mother got yet another surprise when Eric not only ate the fire chicken without complaint, but he also accepted and consumed a second large helping.

"This is delicious. It brings back good memories," Eric said.

Angie sensed her mother softening toward him ever so slightly. And every time he answered a question to her satisfaction, against her will she softened a tad more. By the time the meal was over and Eric hadn't withered under the assault of either the *buldak* or the barrage of questions, the animosity had turned to what seemed like a grudging respect.

"What do you think of Angie working as a police officer?" her mother asked out of the blue.

Angie started to interrupt to tell Eric he was about to get trapped by a trick question—

"I think she's excellent at her job, and the people of this county are lucky to have someone fair and impartial as their head of law enforcement. The world would be better off if more were like her."

Surely her mother hadn't expected Eric to say something misogynistic, such as Angie shouldn't be working in a "man's field." After all, her mom was all for women being strong and standing up for themselves, but for some reason she had this one sticking point regarding Angie's job.

"I understand you probably would rather her have a safer occupation, but is any career really without danger anymore? I do worry about her, but I like the idea that she's out there making sure that everyone else doing their jobs is safe."

Angie stared at Eric, her heart and brain sending identical messages on an express train back and forth. She was pretty sure she loved him. Not that she had a lot of experience with falling in love, but what else could the overwhelming wave of affection be? She wanted to grab him, drag him outside and kiss him until they were both forced to come up for air—and not just because of physical attraction reasons, though that was undeniably an element. What captured her heart in that moment was the conviction she heard in Eric's voice when he didn't even hesitate to answer her mom's question.

Instead of giving her feelings free rein, however, she smiled at him and hoped he could read her heart in that smile.

"What if your past endangers her job?"

This time, Eric didn't immediately answer. He either didn't have an answer for that or, worse, he did and he didn't want Angie to hear it.

"I would never do anything to endanger Angie, her family or her job."

It was the kind of answer that covered a lot of area without important specificity. Eric wouldn't meet her eyes, though he caught and held her mother's for a long moment that gave Angie a sinking feeling in her stomach. And she knew if she questioned him about it after her parents left, he would likely brush off her concern, maybe say that she was reading too much into the exchange. Instead, she would have to ensure that he was never put in the position of making that kind of choice.

ERIC SHOOK VERNON'S hand again as Angie's parents prepared to leave.

"You did good," Vernon said with a conspiratorial grin. "I suggest some ice cream if your stomach is screaming."

Eric laughed a little at that. After Angie's parents drove away, he went back inside where Angie was and she extended a pint of mint chocolate-chip ice cream toward him.

"Hope you like this flavor."

"I don't think there's a flavor I don't like."

They sank onto the couch, each eating their ice cream, staring ahead at the black screen of the TV.

"Well, I guess the fact that you came back earlier is a good sign," Angie said.

"I did get a call from my friend Tony in Texas inviting me back to work for him again. Thought about it."

Angie turned toward him, her expression telling him she didn't like that idea. His heart filled with happiness at the sight of that look.

"I thought about how I didn't want to go back." He smiled. "I'm happy here. And by here I mean on this couch with you. Less so down there." He pointed in the general direction of his dad's house.

"I'm glad you're staying, even though things are difficult with your dad. You're welcome to this couch for as long as you want it."

"I think if I took you up on that, it would erase any progress I made with your mother tonight."

"I still can't believe you ate that much *bul-dak*."

"A man will do a lot for the woman he likes."

Angie leaned over and gave him a quick, minty kiss. Despite the earlier unpleasantness with his dad, life was pretty good right now.

"I do have one question," he said.

"I think with as many questions as you answered tonight, you've earned the right to ask more than one."

"You took your mom's last name?"

"Ah, that. Mom and Dad made a deal when she got pregnant. If it was a boy, the surname would be Fox. If it was a girl, Lee. But either would have both names, just in a different order." She pointed at herself. "Thus, Angie Fox Lee."

Eric smiled at an image that popped into his head.

"What?"

"I just pictured you with nine fox tails."

Angie huffed out a single laugh. "You better hope I'm not a *gumiho*."

She might not be a creature of Korean folklore that feasted on the hearts and livers of men, but there was no doubt she'd captured his heart.

CHAPTER ELEVEN

ERIC FELT EYES on him, more than the ones that had been looking his way since he'd arrived in the middle of town along with Dean Wheeler and Gavin Olsen to build the stages for the Fourth of July festivities. He scanned the area around the square but didn't see anything different than he'd seen all morning. But he knew something was, in fact, different. The skills he'd honed as a soldier told him that in no uncertain terms.

"So, I heard you met Angie's parents," Gavin said, drawing Eric's attention.

"Yeah. And lived to tell the tale."

Gavin and Dean laughed.

"I met her mom once while we were over visiting Maya's parents," Gavin said. "She legit scared me. I wanted to hug Maya's mom for being so awesome."

"I hear she's driving Maya up the wall, though," Dean said.

"Yeah, but it's done out of love."

Dean laughed. "Have you said that in front of Maya?"

"I have."

"Well, she must love you if you're still here."

"So, what do you think?" Dean asked Eric. "Did you pass the mom test?"

"Well, as you said, I'm still in one piece, so I guess that's a yes." At least partially. He still wasn't sure Angie's mom was thrilled with whom she was dating, but she'd at least been cordial toward the end of that night at Angie's house a week ago.

In fact, in the days since then, his concern had shifted to the opinions of others. That question Angie's mom had asked him, about what he would do if his relationship with Angie threatened her career, still lingered in his mind. Angie loved her job, and he would not be the reason she lost it. But he was going to do whatever he could to make sure he never had to face that kind of decision. He was going to do good, fit in, be friendly even with those who still looked at him with suspicion, find a way to salvage at least a somewhat decent relationship with his father. Out of all of those things, the last one was probably going to be the hardest—harder than a twenty-mile mountain hike in the rain carrying forty pounds of gear.

The day grew hotter as they worked to build the main stage where a variety of musical acts were set to entertain the crowds that were expected over the holiday weekend. They would also be building a smaller one in an area a block over that had been set aside for kids' activities. He'd heard Gavin and Dean talking about taking their kids so they could play games, pet animals in the petting zoo and take pictures at several themed photo stations that Sunny, Maya and some other women were currently busy setting up. Angie wasn't among them because she was working. He'd seen her race out of town a couple of hours before, her siren wailing and lights flashing. Despite what he'd told her mother about supporting her career, he didn't think he'd ever not get anxious when she put on the uniform.

He finished hammering in a nail and reached for the towel in his pocket to wipe the sweat from his forehead. He glanced toward Main Street again and saw Angie walking toward him holding a drink carrier with four cups. When she smiled, his heart added an extra beat.

"Perfect timing," Dean said as he stepped forward and grabbed two of the drinks then handed one to Gavin.

Indeed it was, and not just because of the drinks she was bearing.

"Hey," Eric said when she came close.

"Hey, yourself." She looked at the stage in progress. "Looks like you all are moving right along."

"For a makeshift crew, we're decent," Gavin said.

Dean pointed at Eric. "He's putting the two of us to shame. He's twice as fast."

Eric shook his head. "That's an exaggeration."

"No, that construction experience is showing," Gavin insisted.

"Well, here, Mr. Hard Worker, have some fresh lemonade." Angie pulled one of the two cups out of the cardboard holder and handed it to him, then took the final one for herself.

"Busy day?" Eric took a drink of his lemonade to keep from pulling Angie into his arms and kissing her right there in the middle of town. "I saw you race out of town earlier."

"A little boy was missing, but thankfully we found him with nothing more than a couple of scraped knees. My stomach always sinks when we get calls about kids."

He suddenly wondered if she might want some of her own someday. He could imagine that she wouldn't, being so dedicated to her job, but he didn't know that for sure. Even though they were spending a lot of time together, getting closer every day, they hadn't talked about that or even their relationship long-term.

But if he was being honest, he couldn't imagine being with anyone else. This was not what he'd expected when he returned to Jade Valley, but it was a nice surprise.

"So, any progress with your dad?"

"We've moved from arguing to periodic grunts mixed with silence."

"Well, any day I don't have to come out and separate you two is a good day. I heard he wasn't thrilled with the fine and community service the judge handed down yesterday."

"Let's just say I suddenly had something to do at the very back of the ranch after he came home. He's lucky he got off so lightly."

To his surprise, Angie reached out and

squeezed his free hand. Unable to help himself, he turned his hand over to take hers. Something about the moment made his heart feel full of light and warmth that had nothing to do with the midday temperature.

He still worried about what people would think of the two of them together, not for his own sake but for Angie's. She was well-liked and respected by most of the area residents, and he didn't want to jeopardize that. But maybe he was worrying too much. He'd already started to make some tentative friendships, and Trudy always had a smile for him when he came into the café. The fact that Alma hadn't kicked him out of her place probably had more to do with who he'd been with, but at least there hadn't been an issue there either. She'd even responded with an obligatory hello when he'd spoken to her in the grocery aisle the day before. Maybe people were beginning to thaw ever so slightly toward him, giving him a chance to prove that he was different now from what they remembered.

Beyond Angie, he saw Tyler and Wes walking slowly down the sidewalk that ran along Main Street. That's who was watching him earlier. He knew it like he did his birth date and Social Security number.

"Have you made any progress on the burglaries that have happened?" he asked Angie without taking his eyes off his former friends.

Angie followed his line of sight. "No, unfortunately. If they did it, they're better at hiding it than I would have given them credit for. I've talked to everyone who might have seen anything, and I have no valid reason to search their homes."

"They've probably already gotten rid of everything anyway." He hated the idea that they had likely gotten away with yet more crimes.

"I've put in calls to pawn shops and everyone at the office has been checking online sales sites. Nothing has popped."

"Those two sure can't seem to be apart, can they?" Dean asked.

"Tyler needs an underling, and Wes needs someone to tell him what to do," Eric said. "Match made in...well, not sure where." He shook his head. "I'm more embarrassed of my past self every day."

"We all make mistakes," Gavin said. "Some people just don't learn from them while others do."

It felt good to have even one person in Jade Valley believe in him, but as others were added to that number he began to feel more like he had while serving in the army. During those years, he'd been able to leave who he'd been before far, far away. He'd made friends who'd never seen him in the back of a police car, served with fellow soldiers who depended on him the way he depended on them. They all would have given their lives to protect each other.

As he drove back home late in the afternoon, he realized he'd enjoyed working with Dean and Gavin because it had given him that sense of camaraderie again. When he parked in front of his dad's house, he didn't get out of the truck. He realized he couldn't keep going like he'd been. If he was going to stay here and work alongside his dad, he didn't want to always be expecting the next blowup or an out-of-the-blue tirade. Even if they had to wade through the most epic fight to date, he was going to get some answers. Only then could he decide his way forward, whether he would stay on this ranch or find his own place and his own way to make a living. He'd still be nearby if his father became too ill to care for himself, but not in his immediate line of fire.

As prepared as he was ever going to be, he made his way into the house. He found his dad in the kitchen making a cold-cut sandwich. Eric tried to focus on the fact that his dad didn't make some snarky remark about him doing volunteer work instead of working on the ranch—like he had when he'd first found out Eric would be helping out with the stage building.

"Dad, do you think we can have a conversation without fighting?"

"Depends."

Eric sighed and waded in despite the noncommittal answer. "I have questions I need answered."

"You can ask."

Eric heard the implied "but I don't have to answer." He'd thought about starting with some easier questions and working his way up, but he suddenly knew he just needed to ask the biggest ones right off the bat.

"Why didn't you tell me Mom was sick? Why didn't I know until after she was gone?" He barely got the second question out past the uncomfortable knot that formed in his throat.

His dad didn't have one of his snappish comebacks. In fact, he didn't say anything at all.

"Are you just going to ignore my question? You owe me an answer."

"She didn't want you to know."

That was not something Eric had considered. He'd assumed the blame lay solely with his father.

"What? Why?"

His dad looked at him as if Eric was being remarkably slow to understand.

"She didn't want you to worry, didn't want your mind to be on her when you were off toting a gun around God only knows where."

Eric felt as if he might be sick.

"I had a right to know. Even if you promised her, I had a right to know. And you didn't even tell me when she died." His voice was getting louder. "I didn't get…" He swallowed hard, trying not to let the anger consume him, anger at not only one of his parents this time.

"She's the one who kept your contact information." It was the same excuse his dad had used before.

Eric let out a curse. "You could have contacted the army. You could have asked the funeral director to help you. Angie could have helped you!"

"What good would it have done? She was gone already!"

Eric was prevented from responding by his dad's lungs deciding the yelling was too much. He was overtaken by a coughing fit. Even as mad as he was at his dad, he hated to hear the wheezing and crackling of the man's lungs. But there was little he could do to help except stay quiet and let his dad gradually bring the cough under control. When he finally did, it struck Eric how totally spent his dad looked. No matter the circumstances or topic of conversation, he didn't want to put him through that again.

"Dad, I don't want to fight. Aren't you tired of us being at each other's throats? I don't even remember when that started or why. I know I've not been perfect, far from it, but I deserved the chance to say goodbye to her if nothing else." He blinked away tears, ones he hadn't allowed to flow since right after he got the message that his mom was gone.

His dad was silent so long that Eric didn't think he was going to respond.

"I didn't know what to do." For the first time

that Eric could remember, his dad sounded small and vulnerable. "Your mother took care of everything but the work with the cattle."

Eric kept himself from mentioning that she'd had to because things would have fallen apart otherwise. Was that why she'd gotten sick? Had a life of too much work and too little happiness made her susceptible when cancer came knocking?

"Did you ever love Mom?"

Again, his dad hesitated to answer, and it made Eric want to punch a wall. But then his dad nodded slowly.

"At first. Then we grew apart."

"Your anger and bad decisions drove you apart."

To Eric's surprise, his dad nodded again.

"You're right."

Eric gripped the edge of the table until it dug into his fingers and palms. "Were you always so angry and..." Did he dare say the rest out loud?

"Lazy? Irresponsible?"

"Yeah."

His dad shook his head. "No."

"Then why have you been like that my whole life?"

"Because I didn't want this life, okay? But I got stuck with it anyway."

Eric felt as if he'd been punched in the stomach.

"I didn't want to be a rancher. I wanted to leave this valley and go do…something, anything else. But my dad got ill and I had to take over the running of the ranch or see my parents lose everything."

It was as if a fog that had always obscured part of who his dad was started to lift. In the space of a breath, so much became clear. Eric saw the parallels between himself and his father—both growing up on this ranch as only sons, both allowing themselves to follow a path paved with bad decisions and anger, both being tied to this ranch because of ailing fathers.

"I'm sorry." Eric didn't know he was going to say the words until they tumbled out. He wasn't even sure precisely why he was apologizing. Was it because his dad had felt trapped? Or the fact that Eric had been able to do the thing that his father had never had the opportunity to do? Was that why his father's animosity toward him had grown? Eric had been able to leave Jade Valley for several years before having to return. His dad had never been able to leave.

It didn't excuse how he'd behaved, but at least it was some insight. Eric couldn't help but wonder if his own path would have been different if his dad hadn't been so resentful of his plight in life that he'd taken it out on his family.

"Do you want to leave now?" he asked his dad.

"It's too late." There was a sorrow and resignation in his dad's voice that made him seem like an entirely different person than the one Eric had always known.

"It doesn't have to be." What was he saying? Was he offering to take his dad to start a new life somewhere else? A picture of Angie smiling as she brought him that lemonade sprang to mind, and he instantly wanted to take back his words.

"I've already done too much damage to myself. And it's not like I've got a lot of money socked away to go traipsing all over."

Eric refrained from mentioning that those facts were also his father's fault because it was obvious he knew that already.

This time his dad was the one who got up

from the table and walked away, leaving his food behind. Eric let him go because he didn't know what else to say. He felt as if he would need to sit at the table for a year to fully process everything he'd just learned. How his parents had gotten together in the first place and exactly how his dad had felt about his mother when the end came for her—those things he still didn't know. But he wasn't sure he could take in any more information right now. And he didn't know whether his dad would—or even could—give it.

At some point he realized his appetite had abandoned him. He wrapped up the sandwiches and put them in the refrigerator, then walked out the front door. And he kept walking, right down the driveway, up the road, all the way to Angie's front door. But when he knocked, she didn't answer. Thinking she could be in the shower or might even be sleeping after a full day of dealing with the many annoying or serious fires a sheriff had to put out in a day, he turned to leave. Maybe he'd just walk until his legs couldn't carry him anymore. How far could he get before that happened?

He'd reached the bottom of the porch steps when the front door opened.

"Hey, where are you going?" Angie asked.

Eric didn't turn around. He suddenly didn't have the energy.

"Eric," Angie said as she hurried down the steps and put herself in front of him. "What's wrong?"

Maybe he should be embarrassed by the tear that broke free. After all, he'd survived boot camp, grueling missions, extreme temperatures in inhospitable places, but right now there was a rawness deep within him that he would have never imagined. He had no idea what to do with it, how to even begin to heal it.

Angie pulled him into her arms and held him. Her unconditional love—and that's what it felt like even though neither of them had said those words—knocked the final piece of the dam loose. In the next moment he was full-on crying while Angie held him tight. It was as if every feeling of sadness, anger, resentment and loss he'd ever held bottled up inside during his more than thirty years of life rushed out of him riding his tears. He lost any sense of time or any part of the world beyond the woman in his arms.

Eventually, however, the rush of swirling emotions started to wane enough that his tears dried and the world around them came back into focus. He didn't think he'd ever felt so utterly spent, and that was saying a lot considering the missions and training he'd undertaken while serving. As perceptive as ever, Angie seemed to sense his exhaustion and guided him to sit on the steps then sat beside him. She entwined her fingers with his.

"Do you want to talk about it?"

Where did he even start?

He swiped at the tear tracks on his cheeks, surprised he wasn't embarrassed by them. He found himself wondering if his dad had ever shed tears, maybe while riding alone in the pastures of a ranch he'd never wanted to run.

Somehow his brain found a point in which to launch into the story, and over the next several minutes Eric shared with Angie the entirety of the tense conversation he'd had with his dad and the unexpected revelations.

"It's my fault I didn't know about Mom," he finally said.

"No, it's not."

"She was afraid her diagnosis would distract me, endanger me." He inhaled a shaky breath, realizing he was angry with his mom too. "I loved her. I miss her. But I also want to scream at her. She robbed me of the choice to try to see her, even if there was nothing I could do to save her."

"I hope this doesn't anger you, but I'm going to be honest here. I see both sides. You are entitled to your anger and your grief, but I can also understand where your mother was coming from. Think about if you had a child, and that child was perhaps in a dangerous situation where a moment's distraction could cost their life. Would you want to be the reason they were distracted?"

Eric sighed as he looked out across the landscape, the edges of which were beginning to fade into the approaching evening. He wanted to sit with his anger a while longer, but Angie was right. In his mother's place, he may have very well done the same thing.

"Have you eaten?"

The question made him smile ever so slightly. Though Angie had never set foot in the country of her mother's birth, it was such a Korean question to ask. He'd heard it countless times while stationed there, a question rooted in the post–Korean War food shortages and Koreans' way of asking after someone's well-being. She had probably heard her mother ask that question thousands of times.

"No, not since lunch."

"Come with me." Angie stood, not relinquishing his hand as she led him inside, not until she opened the puppy pen and let the exuberant pups free. "I think some puppy love is just what you need until I can make some food."

"You don't have to fix—"

"Shh! My house, my rules."

He smiled, more fully this time. As he sank to the floor and played with the puppies and watched Angie move about her small, not-totally-renovated kitchen, he nearly told her that he loved her. Sometime between when he'd walked up her driveway earlier and right this moment, that truth had cemented itself in his mind and his heart. Maybe there wasn't a perfect time to tell her, but on the heels of his tearful revelations about his family wasn't it. But soon. He'd tell her soon because he didn't think he could hide it from her when she was so observant. And he wanted to be the one to tell her, not have her guess.

Little Frigg licked him on the chin, eliciting a laugh from him that had seemed very far away only a few minutes ago.

"I think that one loves you the most," Angie said.

"Well, I love her too," he said, rubbing noses with the adorable pup.

"Good thing she's one of the two I'm keeping."

He looked up, surprised by how much he was dreading seeing any of the pups go.

"Don't worry," she said. "The other two are going to Maya's. She and Gavin decided that they wanted their new pup to have a playmate, and Blossom—that's Maya's cat—had no interest in filling the role."

"I can't imagine why. These little guys are so calm."

Angie's smile lit up his heart like the fireworks that would be shot off over the upcoming weekend. And he realized that more than the country's independence, the holiday was coming at a time when he felt a new sense of freedom—a freedom from all the pent-up feelings that he hadn't even really been aware he was carrying around like an invisible, fully loaded rucksack. The freedom to tell the woman he loved how he felt.

"What's that smile about?" Angie asked.

He shook his head. "Nothing."

No, it was everything.

ANGIE LAUGHED AT the way Camille waved like a queen while sitting on the makeshift throne at one of the photo stations. A party supply golden crown sat atop her freshly coiffed white hair. She looked to be having every bit as much fun as the children running around in all directions. After she'd dropped off her lemon loaf at the bakery contest booth, she'd allowed Eric to escort her through all the various vendor booths set up along Main Street. Though Angie was working, making sure all remained safe in the crowd, she'd watched Eric and Camille make their way from a booth selling homemade jams to Gavin's small tent showcasing his paintings. She'd popped over to say hello when they reached her dad's booth. Camille had taken a fancy to a carving of a bald eagle in flight, and Eric had bought it for her.

Angie wondered if Camille was filling the

void left by his mother or perhaps a grand-mother. Even if it was neither, a casual observer could tell that these two were now important to each other, a bit like family.

"You look like you're still having fun," Angie said as she approached them.

"Best day I've had in years," Camille said.

It was hard to believe this was the same grumpy woman who'd been sitting on the side of the road that day, Eric beside her for the first time. They both had a new light in them. They both smiled more often. That made Angie really happy for both of them.

"She has made me take her picture at every photo spot," Eric said.

"I'm old. I have to have all the fun I can while I can." Camille grabbed Angie's hand, then Eric's. "Speaking of fun, come with me."

She practically dragged them to the end of Juniper Street, which had been blocked off for the kiddie booths and photo stations. She stopped in front of the photo spot that looked like it had come right out of a Valentine's Day high school dance. Red, pink and white balloons, some shaped like hearts, floated next to fluffy white teddy bears, empty candy boxes and a white wooden bench.

"Sit so I can take your picture," Camille said.

"I'm not exactly dressed for fun photos," Angie said.

"You could be wearing a feed sack and this boy would still love you."

Angie froze and she sensed Eric doing the same beside her. Had he said something to Camille and she'd let it slip? Or was she just pushing her matchmaking agenda? Deciding not to comment, she pretended that she hadn't noticed the word *love* and instead sat down in what could only be deemed a love-themed photo spot.

"Come on," Camille said. "You look like two strangers forced to take your driver's license photos together at the DMV."

Eric wrapped his arm around Angie's back and pulled her close. It was the most physical affection he'd shown her in public, another sign that he was relaxing and fitting into Jade Valley as the new person he was, not the angry, troublemaking boy he'd been. There was still a long way to go until he was fully accepted, if full acceptance was even possible, but at least it was a lot better than when he'd first arrived. He'd gotten gratitude for helping out with the stages and compliments on how he was looking after Camille.

There were still those, however, who looked at him as if he was wearing a facade, that he hadn't changed at all and was just playing everyone. No doubt people like Dan Lintz, and probably Wes and Tyler, were feeding that fire. She hoped Eric didn't give those people any space in his mind.

"Now kiss," Camille said as she held up her phone.

"Camille," Eric said in a voice of warning. "Angie's on duty. She has to be professional."

Had anyone ever understood her so well?

"I love you." The words flew out, but she was glad they did. They were the truest ones she'd ever spoken.

Eric jerked his head around to stare at her just as Angie heard the click of the camera on the phone.

"Sorry. Bad timing, huh?" Angie asked.

"No," Eric said, obviously startled. "I... I just wanted to say it first."

"Then why didn't you?"

"I was looking for the perfect time?"

Angie laughed a little and rolled her eyes. "The perfect time is when you realize it."

"Then I would have told you when I was sitting in the middle of your floor playing with the puppies and you were making me a grilled ham and cheese."

Angie couldn't help it. Despite the fact she was in uniform, she leaned over and planted a quick peck on his lips.

"If I weren't on duty with half the county milling about, that kiss would be a bit hotter. Alas, as you said, I'm a professional."

Eric smiled, and there was a touch of a wicked gleam in his eyes.

"I guess I have to begin counting down the minutes until you're not on duty anymore," he said. Angie smiled and started to stand, but Eric stopped her. "I love you too. I just needed to say the words."

When Eric looked over, Camille was gone. He stood as Angie weaved her way back through the crowd. He scanned the faces nearby then a bit farther away. Finally, he spotted Camille talking to some other ladies down by the bakery contest tent. He had to laugh. The old woman had to be feeling pretty smug about her matchmaking abilities.

But he'd give her all the credit if necessary because Angie had told him she loved him.

He wished he could rewind time so he could hear her say it again. If only there hadn't been so many people around, many of them little kids, he would have shown her exactly how much he loved her.

Though he had dreaded returning to Jade Valley with every mile he'd driven away from San Antonio, he now felt as if it had been the best decision he'd ever made.

CHAPTER TWELVE

"LET'S GO TALK at the office," Angie said to an agitated Dan Lintz, wanting to get him away from the crowd before too many people heard him making accusations.

"I don't want to go to the office." Dan stabbed a finger in the direction of the Novak ranch. "I want you to go out there right now and do your job, what the taxpayers of this county pay you to do. Or we will find someone who will."

"I don't take kindly to threats."

"Well, I don't like having things stolen from me and then showing up on your boyfriend's ranch." He said it loud enough that several heads turned their way. "Are you protecting him?"

"You need to talk to her with more respect." The steely command in Eric's voice was 50 percent soldier and 50 percent angry boyfriend.

"You don't get to tell me how to talk, you

thief. I knew you were guilty. You were always no good, just like those friends of yours. All of you should have been run out of town years ago. Your no-account father too." Dan returned his gaze to Angie. "Looks like you're no better than Genovese."

Eric took a step toward Dan, but Angie quickly stepped between them.

"Both of you step back. Now." She used her stern voice, the one that left no room for argument or doubt that she was serious. "How did you come to this conclusion that your property is where you say it is?"

Dan pulled out his phone and thrust it at her. "Someone sent me proof."

Angie took the phone from him and scrolled through the photos in the text message. Some matched the descriptions of the items taken from Meecham's. Her heart sank when other pictures showed the entrance to the Novaks' barn. She could even see Oscar in the dimly lit interior. A shot of fear went through her at the thought that she could have been wrong, blinded by her feelings for Eric. But then her facts-only mindset kicked in as she noted that none of the pictures of the stolen items also showed anything identifying their location as the barn on Allen and Eric's ranch. They could be completely unrelated.

Please don't let those items be there.

But duty required that she start the process to check. She noticed all the locals currently staring at her and Eric. Even ones who'd been warming up to Eric now appeared as if they were questioning that decision. If she didn't treat this situation the same as she would with any other accused, it would erode public trust in her and her department. And she'd spent too much time and effort rebuilding that following the wrongdoing of the previous sheriff to allow that to happen.

"It will require a search warrant."

"Not if he gives you permission," Dan said.

"Eric doesn't own the property."

"Then his dad better give permission, unless they have something to hide."

Angie couldn't say she'd ever particularly liked Dan, but she'd never known him to be quite so hateful.

"Search all you want," Eric said.

Angie looked at him. "Are you sure about that?"

Was she?

"I don't care if this guy wants to sift through hay and horse dung."

She gave a single nod. "Fine. If your dad also gives permission, I will go and check the validity of the claim."

"Not without me, you're not," Dan said. "I don't trust that you won't cover up for your boyfriend." The way he said *boyfriend* had a nasty edge to it, and she could sense Eric tensing behind her. Thankfully, he kept himself in check, though she had no doubt it took effort. "And I'm not taking my eyes off you," Dan said over Angie's shoulder to Eric. "I don't want you texting your dad to move the stuff out."

"It's a really ugly look, accusing people of things they didn't do," Eric said, his voice seemingly flat and emotionless. But Angie heard the carefully concealed anger vibrating within him.

"Let's go and take this away from the people just here to have a good time today," Angie said.

Angie looked over at Mike, who she needed to hand off the festival patrol to because, one, the crowd required at least one uniformed officer visible and, two, she saw the way he was looking at Eric, as if he might tear him apart if he'd fooled and hurt her.

"What the—?"

Angie turned at the sound of Dan's exclamation to see that Camille had just hit him on the back with her substantial purse.

"Camille!" Angie knew the older woman could be cantankerous when it suited her, but she'd never seen her assault someone.

"Why did you hit me?" Dan asked.

"Because you deserved it. What a rude mouth you've got. I knew your parents. They didn't teach you that, so I don't know where it came from. Wherever it was, it needs to go back. And I know the Meechams are hands-off the business these days, but you better believe I'm going to be calling them and telling them what a nasty piece of work they've got running their store."

Angie took Camille's arm and forced a bit of distance between her and Dan, enough that she couldn't swing and hit him again.

"Camille, you can't go around hitting people you don't agree with."

"If that hurt him, then he needs to toughen up."

"Camille." Angie's voice was filled with warning. "You owe Dan an apology."

"I most certainly do not. Why should I apologize to someone who is accusing people of crimes without evidence?"

"I have evidence!"

Camille made a *pfft* sound.

"Here, look for yourself," Dan said, shoving the phone at her.

Camille acted as if she'd never seen a smartphone before when Angie knew for a fact she played word games on the one that was no doubt in her weapon of choice. Something was going on. Was she hoping to give Dan a different target for his anger in order to protect Eric? While sweet in a way, nothing was going to protect Eric other than proving the accusation wrong.

"How do I see all these?" Camille asked Angie, indicating the photos on the phone. When their gazes met, there was a twinkle of satisfaction in Camille's.

Angie humored the other woman, though, and showed her the photos.

"Well that doesn't prove anything," Camille said, echoing Angie's earlier thought. "You could have taken these yourself," she said to Dan.

"Why would I steal my own stuff?"

"Insurance money."

When Dan looked like he was going to explode, Angie held up a hand to stop him.

"I will check to see if there is any merit to

the claim. Dan, do you wish to press charges against Camille for assault?"

"Assault!" Camille's surprise sounded not entirely feigned.

"I'm not going to throw an old woman in jail."

"But a good, innocent man is okay?" Camille asked, poking the proverbial angry bear with a pointy stick.

"Camille, that's enough," Angie said, growing more frustrated.

Throughout the entire exchange, Eric had remained so quiet it would have been easy to forget he was there if not for his imposing physical presence. He could squish Dan like a bug if he so chose, but he hadn't moved. When she looked at him, it wasn't even obvious he was breathing. The fact that she couldn't read his expression bothered her. Was he simply holding his anger in check so he didn't make the situation worse? At the thought that Dan could be telling the truth and Eric knew it—no, she couldn't believe that. Absolutely nothing during her time of knowing him pointed toward him still being a thief, toward him lying to her. But there was a first time for everything, and it wasn't impossible she was wrong.

Even though she didn't believe he was guilty, she had no choice but to prove his innocence. With a sick feeling in her stomach, she forced herself to look away from the handsome face of the man she had confessed her love to not even an hour before. If she could prove he wasn't guilty, she still hated that the day they'd both told each other how they felt was going to be marred by the public accusation Dan had hurled in the middle of the Fourth of July crowd. She didn't miss the fact that Dan was evidently hoping to take away a man's freedom on a holiday celebrating freedom.

"Mike, you and Kevin take care of things here. Call Jace or Andrea if you need to." He nodded, though she suspected he'd rather go with her and be the one to click the cuffs into place on Eric if he was guilty.

Angie turned her attention to Camille. "Do not hit anyone else."

"No one else here deserves it," Camille said under her breath as she crossed her arms.

With a sigh, Angie led Dan and Eric to her department vehicle. As she drove toward the ranch, neither of the men spoke. The hot dog she'd had a few minutes before Dan found her started churning in her stomach, but she didn't have time to be sick.

When they arrived at the ranch, she was surprised to see Allen out mowing the small front lawn. She hadn't asked Eric why his dad hadn't come with him to the festivities in town, but maybe he was being grumpy again. Or it could simply be that he knew most people didn't like him much. It was honestly sad to think about how he'd managed to ostracize himself. After Eric had told her about Allen's past, she'd felt some compassion for the man and hoped he could find a way to redeem himself the way Eric had been doing.

But now all of Eric's work was in danger because of Dan's loud mouth.

Please let Eric be innocent.

When Allen saw her park and the three of them get out, he let the mower die and then, in the next moment, started coughing. She couldn't help but wince at the sound of his lungs. He managed to bring the coughing under control but was out of breath. She wanted to tell him to go inside where it was cooler and get something to drink, to rest, but she doubted he'd appreciate her comments.

"What's going on here?" Allen asked.

"We've come to get my stuff," Dan said.

"Let me handle this," Angie said, growing more exasperated with Dan by the moment. She was beginning to sympathize with Camille and her purse swinging.

Shaking her head at the unprofessional thought, she explained the situation to Allen.

"Maybe if you had a proper security camera, you'd know who took your stuff," he said to Dan.

"Let's just move this along," Angie said, growing more nervous by the fact that Eric still wasn't saying anything. Was he upset that she was here? Did he take it as her not believing him? But he knew how dedicated she was to her job. A wave of nausea hit her as she considered that maybe he was just preparing for his crime to be revealed, and then she felt even sicker for having that thought even though it was her job to consider all possibilities. No, he would have insisted on the warrant if he was guilty. It would have given him time to move the stolen items. "Do we have your permission to search the barn?"

Allen coughed again, then motioned toward the barn. "Knock yourself out. Look wherever you want. You ain't going to find anything that I don't own."

Her stomach twisted more at Eric's continued silence. She possessed a good sense about people, but again she wondered if her romantic feelings had somehow clouded her judgment. No, she didn't believe that. Even so, the hot dog threatened to make an unwanted reappearance as she walked into the shaded interior of the barn.

Dan immediately started looking in stalls. When she moved to stop him, to tell him he was not the investigating authority here, Eric reached out and lightly touched her on the arm.

"Let him do whatever he wants."

There was an "I expected this" resignation in Eric's voice that broke her heart. Not only had the progress he'd made fitting in eroded among the citizens of Jade Valley. It was every bit as depleted on his end, maybe even more so. She imagined she could hear his thoughts, things like *Why did I even bother?* or *Nothing is ever going to change.*

Had he been able to sense her momentary doubts as well? She hated the idea that he had, especially since he was not acting like someone who was guilty of wrongdoing.

Oscar sidestepped in his stall when Dan loudly closed the next stall door over.

"Don't be so rough," she said. "Just because

you're justifiably upset because of the theft doesn't give you the right to treat other people's property with anything less than respect."

Dan didn't reply but he at least stopped slamming things. After checking all the stalls and the tack room, he climbed the ladder to the loft. Angie followed and simply stood back and watched as he looked around and between all the hay bales and various old ranching detritus. Obviously agitated, he stalked to the edge of the loft and looked down at Eric.

"Where is it? What did you do with it?"

"I don't have it, never did," Eric said, his voice calm and emotionless. At least that's how it would seem to most everyone, but Angie knew better. Though she'd never seen him the quiet kind of furious, that's exactly what he was. She knew it in her bones. Her instincts were telling her that he felt that way because he'd been wrongly accused yet again, but despite that she had to keep approaching the situation like a professional by setting aside her personal feelings.

"I don't believe you," Dan said, his anger not abating.

"I really don't care what you believe. You could look in the house, under the house, in our vehicles, even in our stock tanks. You're not finding something I didn't steal. Maybe you should ask yourself why someone is going to the trouble to make you think I did."

An excellent question, and one to which Angie fully intended to find an answer as soon as she could.

"He's bluffing," Dan said, pointing at Eric. "Search the house."

"Dan, you may be a taxpayer, but you're going to want to dial back the demanding tone you're using with me as well as the accusations and threats." It was the closest she'd come to really telling off a resident in a long time.

"Just do it," Eric said. "He's not going to leave it alone until he's satisfied."

"I'll be satisfied when I get every bit of my property back and every single person who was involved is in jail."

Angie refrained from pointing out that the stolen property didn't actually belong to him. Just because he'd been put in charge when Mr. and Mrs. Meecham retired to Arizona didn't make him the owner.

As they moved from room to room in the house a few minutes later, Angie hated every minute of the invasion. And that's what it was, an invasion of privacy based on weak "evidence."

When Dan made like he was going to start opening dresser drawers in Eric's bedroom, Angie put an end to it.

"That's enough. Do you really think something the size of a saddle or a generator is going to be in a sock drawer?"

"The tools could be."

Eric suddenly stalked into the room. Angie moved to stop him, thinking he was about to punch Dan. Instead, he started pulling out drawers, turning them upside down so that a parade of T-shirts, socks and underwear fell into a pile on the floor.

"Eric, stop," she said.

"No. We're going to show him every nook and cranny." He grabbed a photo album. "Would you like to look inside my dead mother's photo albums? Maybe the laws of physics have changed and I hid everything within the pages."

Angie's heart ached as she reached for him and gripped his forearm. At first she didn't think he would move, but he finally made a sound of disgust and stalked from the room.

She spun on Dan. "When I find out who really did this, I will ensure that they are punished and the store receives either the property back or adequate compensation. And then you will apologize to Eric and Allen for the incredibly disrespectful way you have behaved today." Not allowing him time to retort, she pointed toward the bedroom door. "Walk out of this house, do not say a word to either of them and wait for me outside."

He must have seen how close she was to losing the cool she always tried to maintain because he complied. She took a moment to inhale then slowly exhale a calming breath that actually did little to calm her. She'd seen so much worse in her time as sheriff, but the sight of Eric's clothing in a pile on the floor made her want to cry. It felt wrong to stare at it, so she turned and made her way into the living room where Eric was standing.

"I'm sorry."

"I gave you permission." He sounded so distant that she wanted to pull him into her arms. But the rigidity of his stance told her he might not welcome it. Best to come back when she wasn't wearing her uniform.

"I'm still sorry. I'll find out who did this." Yes, her words implied she believed him even though her job required she go where the truth lay. She wanted to tell him that she would clear his name no matter what it took because she was certain now that Eric had nothing to do with the break-in at Meecham's, but she held those words in check. They were true, however, even if she didn't say them. She just had to find the actual culprit—or culprits—to prove it.

Though she wanted to touch him, she didn't. Instead she told him she'd call him later then headed out the door, trying not to think about how quiet he was, how he wouldn't look her in the eye.

ERIC REINED OSCAR to a stop at the highest point on the ranch and let the sun beat down on him, punishing him for believing that he could have a normal, happy life in Jade Valley. Fate was cruel to have given him glimpses of that kind of life, getting his hopes up, only to slap him upside the head with the reality he'd temporarily forgotten—that he would always be seen as a thief and good for nothing here.

It had been two days since Dan Lintz had, with one loud accusation in the middle of Main Street, erased any chance Eric had of making a good, respectable life here. And since that moment, Eric knew that he couldn't take Angie down with him. He'd heard with his own ears the threat to her job, to her good name, and he was the cause.

Why had he told her he loved her?

He did, of course. But sometimes loving someone evidently meant pushing them away, which he'd already begun to do despite his promise to her that he wouldn't do that. It had been somewhat easier than he'd expected since she hadn't come by. Between her normal work, her assertion that she was working hard to find the real culprit and him making sure he was "busy" whenever she said she could meet him, they hadn't seen each other since she'd left with Dan in tow. If he kept it up for a bit longer, maybe she'd just get the message and cease communication on her own—because if he had to stand in front of Angie, he didn't know if he was strong enough to break things off with her.

Of course, there was a voice inside his head telling him that she was the one hoping that this time apart would grow until it was just natural not to see each other anymore. On the day when Dan had made his public accusation, there had been a couple of moments when he'd seen doubt in Angie's eyes—a suspicion that Dan was telling the truth and she'd been a fool.

He gave voice to his anger, but there wasn't even a breeze to carry the hot, heavy words away. Instead, the anger settled on him, seeping back into the place deep within him where it had originated.

Scanning the nearly cloudless sky and the miles and miles of familiar hills and pasture flanked by two mountain ranges, he hated the idea of leaving it. Texas, while it had its pretty spots, couldn't hold a candle to Wyoming's natural beauty, at least in his eyes. But was this land worth staying in a place where everyone would always look at him like he was a criminal? Where the woman he loved was nearby but untouchable because one or both of them had pushed the other away?

But if she really did believe him innocent, he knew what she'd say if she heard his thoughts—that he was being stupid and unnecessarily self-sacrificing. But that question her mother had asked about what he would do if he put Angie's job in jeopardy kept echoing in his head. And he'd heard the threat to her job straight from Dan Lintz's mouth in the middle of Main Street, where lots of other Jade Valley voters could hear it too. Even if Angie wanted to stay together, would she eventually resent him if she lost the faith of the local residents and thus her job? He didn't want to put her in the position of having to choose.

Tony had said his offer of employment in San Antonio would always be there for Eric if he chose to come back. Was that what he should do? Go back to Texas and take his dad with him, listing the ranch for sale before they headed out of town? After all, his dad had never really wanted the ranch, had instead wanted to go somewhere else. Maybe he finally could. And they had good medical facilities in San Antonio where he could get treatment and see specialists without having to drive long distances—if he wasn't too stubborn to do so.

Eric took off his hat and ran his fingers back through his hair. Was he really thinking about moving with his father somewhere they'd be in even closer proximity without acreage where they could escape each other when necessary?

His phone rang, which seemed out of place in this spot out of view of any other human or even a man-made structure. He pulled it out of his pocket and saw it was Camille. Hoping she was okay, he quickly answered.

"Get your butt back to this house before my

excellent cooking gets cold," she said before he could even say hello.

"What?"

"I said come back to your house. I brought food."

Despite his low mood, he laughed a little. "Yes, ma'am."

If nothing else, he owed her a hug for being his unconventional knight in shining armor—or grandma with a big honking purse. As he turned Oscar in the direction of home, the idea of also leaving Camille alone if he left Jade Valley sat heavy on his heart.

When he came within view of the house, however, Camille's car was not the only one he saw parked along the driveway. He reined Oscar to a stop and stared at Angie getting out of her personal vehicle. He knew the moment she spotted him in the distance because she stopped walking and shaded her eyes from the sun. He supposed if she wasn't in uniform, she wasn't there to arrest him.

Though he knew he should keep away, for both of their sakes, he urged Oscar to move forward. He told himself that he needed to see her one last time. If he stayed in Jade Valley, he'd do his best to avoid her. And if he left… well, he desperately and selfishly wanted at least a few more minutes of memories to take with him.

Still, he took his time unsaddling and tending to Oscar's needs, second-guessing all of his decisions regarding Angie and his mind swirling with what and how much to say to her. Wondering how he could push her away without hurting her, if that was even possible. Going from hearing her say she loved him to where they were now in only a matter of days felt like the euphoria of reaching the peak of Everest followed by immediately falling off the mountain.

"Are you avoiding me?"

He closed his eyes for a moment, trying to ignore how just the simple sound of her voice affected him. Part of him wished he'd stayed out in the farthest pasture.

"I've been busy. I'm sure you have been too." He hadn't meant the hint of hurt to reveal itself in his voice, but it was impossible to retract it now.

Angie entered the barn and walked right up to him so he couldn't avoid seeing her. "I'm pretty sure I know what you're doing, and I want you to stop."

He sighed, not daring to pretend ignorance. Did she really believe in his innocence? While her actions pointed toward the answer being yes, he knew what he'd seen in her expression when Dan had shown her those photos of this very barn. Still, his heart pushed him to believe what he wanted most to be true. Either way, he needed to protect her.

"You heard what Dan said about you right out there where half the county could hear him, casting doubt about your ability, endangering your job. Those types of whispers spread quickly. They're infectious. You know that."

"You don't need to worry about that. I'm a grown woman and perfectly capable of taking care of myself. I've been at the mercy of others, and I don't intend to ever be again."

He hated that he'd made her remember that night when Genovese had put his hands on her.

"I know you're strong and capable, but—"

"No buts," She placed her palm firmly against his chest. "Part of my job is standing up for those who are wrongfully accused, making sure that they are not railroaded by mobs acting on feelings instead of evidence."

"Do you really believe in my innocence?" He needed to know for sure, whether he was leaving or not.

"I do." She didn't hesitate for even a moment. Still…

"I saw doubt in your eyes that day."

This time she didn't immediately respond, and that hesitance hurt more than it should. She had so many reasons to doubt him.

"I admit, I questioned whether my feelings for you could have possibly blinded me. But once I mentally took a step back and looked at the evidence alone, I realized that there was nothing concrete. Even the circumstantial evidence was weak at best. I asked myself how I would treat you if we weren't in a relationship, and the answer is that I wouldn't do anything different. If I'd never met you before, I would look at the so-called evidence and come to the same conclusion. So I'm going to find out who is really behind the thefts and set things right."

He marveled at the woman in front of him, loved her even more and experienced an even more powerful need to protect her and all she'd worked to achieve.

"I admire your idealism—I really do. But I've been thinking about this ever since your mom asked what I'd do if my reputation endangered your job."

"My mom would be thrilled if I lost this

job so she could pressure me to take up one she felt was more appropriate. So I don't intend to lose it. But if people insist that I badger and arrest people without evidence, then I will walk and not look back."

"Angie—"

"Dan is an angry blowhard. People know this, now more than ever. Give them time to remember that and the fact that I've never given them a reason to doubt me."

"Because I wasn't here. You weren't... hanging out with me." He truly didn't mean to sound self-pitying, was simply stating the obvious.

"Hanging out? Is that what they call dating now?" She removed her hand from his chest and instead gripped his hand. "You have to give me time. I've made some progress, but I need to make more."

"Was it Wes and Tyler?"

"I don't know yet, but I think whoever it was may have been here the night I came over to take care of Oscar. It's possible they were scouting so they'd know where to put the stuff if they got the opportunity to hide it here. But they never did for some reason. Maybe they were also here another time when they took the pictures of the outside of the barn that were texted to Dan, but it's possible they had to leave because you or your dad returned." She shook her head, looking confused. "Though why they would send Dan those photos when there was nothing here, I don't know. It doesn't make sense."

"Let me guess. The phone the photos were sent from is untraceable."

She nodded. "Prepaid burner phone. We're doing what we can to try to figure out where it came from and who bought it, but it's a long shot at best."

Eric sighed and looked up toward the roof. "Of course it is."

Angie squeezed his hand, but he kept his gaze away from hers. The more he looked at her, the more difficult it would be to say goodbye. Because no matter how much he wanted to stay, any faith he'd had that things would work out had been severely shaken. In this valley, things just didn't go his way—at least not for long.

"Did you mean what you said to me in that photo spot?" Angie asked.

No matter how much easier it might make pushing her away, he couldn't lie to her. Wouldn't.

"Yes."

"Then promise me right now, again, that you won't pull away, that you won't push me away, that you won't try to be some sort of romantic martyr. It won't help the situation. It'll only hurt us both and let whoever did this win, whether that's Wes, Tyler or someone else trying to set you up so you'll leave." She squeezed his hand harder. "Don't let them."

The intensity with which she said those final three words unexpectedly kindled a fire in him, one that made him want to do the opposite of sacrificing his new happiness. A fire that would lead to him finding out who had made the false accusation against him and to being able to hopefully build a future with Angie if she still wanted him when all this was over.

"Okay."

Evidently he couldn't say no to her either, not for long anyway. He told himself that if it became necessary, he could always change his mind later. It would be harder, but he'd leave if it became obvious there was no other choice to protect Angie and her job.

But for now, he couldn't keep his hands off her any longer. He pulled her close and kissed her deeply, hoping he wasn't making the biggest mistake of his life.

CHAPTER THIRTEEN

ERIC PUT OFF going to town as long as he could, but the food supply was pretty low and it wasn't as if Jade Valley had grocery delivery. He wasn't sure anyone would deliver to him and his dad anyway. As he made his way quickly through the store aisles, tossing more of everything that he'd typically buy into the cart despite his dwindling funds, he kept his gaze from meeting anyone else's. He had a feeling many people's feelings about him hadn't changed despite the fact that the accusation against him had proven false. He was certain at least some would believe he'd moved the stolen goods elsewhere or already sold them, but nothing he could do or say would change those opinions.

When the cashier rang up his purchases and he handed over the cash to pay for it, the teenage girl picked up one of those markers used to check for counterfeit bills.

"I'm sorry," she said. And she truly did sound sorry, as if she wouldn't check if she hadn't been told to by her boss.

"It's okay," he said, surprised by how much the small act of semikindness meant.

He was on his way across the parking lot to his truck when someone stepped into the path of his shopping cart. When he looked up he saw it was Wes, and he was wearing a confused expression.

"How did your girlfriend manage to keep you out of jail? I heard you're the one who broke into Meecham's."

Eric simply stared at Wes, resisting the powerful urge to run over him with the cart. But the last thing he needed was to give Wes a reason to accuse him of assault.

"I guess the sheriff isn't as squeaky clean as she likes everyone to think," Wes said.

"The next words out of your mouth better not be anything about her." Eric had to keep his cool, but Wes was making it difficult.

Wes's expression shifted from confusion to a smirk. "Did I hit a sore spot?"

"Wes!"

They both looked toward the sound of Tyler's angry voice, and Wes's smirk dropped off his face. He glanced back at Eric and shook his head, seemingly in disbelief, before he headed toward where Tyler was sitting in his idling truck. Tyler gave Eric a look that would have caused a chill to run down the back of many people. But Eric had dealt with bigger bullies than him. If Tyler was put in some of the situations he'd been in, he'd probably wet himself. That mental image made Eric chuckle. Tyler must have seen and not liked that reaction because Wes barely had the passenger side door closed before Tyler peeled out of the parking lot.

"I don't think you're their favorite person anymore."

Eric looked behind him to find Trudy Pierce, who appeared to have bought every loaf of Texas toast the store had stocked. When she saw him staring at all the bread, she laughed.

"My bread delivery got delayed because of an accident. Evidently there's bread all over the I-25." She nodded in the direction Tyler had left. "I'm glad you don't have anything to do with those two anymore."

"How do you know I don't?" He didn't mean for his question to have quite the defensive edge to it that it did, but Trudy didn't seem to notice.

"I've been feeding this town for more than three decades. I'm pretty good at reading people."

One of those annoying knots formed in his throat again.

"Thanks for believing in me." Simple moments of support like what Trudy offered added weight to the side of the scale urging him to stay in Jade Valley, counterbalancing the worries that he was just endangering Angie's career and reputation, possibly even her safety, by staying. If he hadn't promised her he wouldn't leave, he might already be on the road to Texas.

"I know it's tough, fighting to remake your reputation. But don't give up. For yourself and for Angie. That girl is obviously head over heels for you because I've never seen her work this hard on a case, and that's saying something because she's the best law enforcement officer we've had in this town for as far back as I can remember."

"I wish there was something I could do to help her."

"You might not be able to help with the investigation, but I'm sure you can find other ways to support her." Trudy's wink caused Eric to actually blush.

She laughed, patted him on the arm and headed off across the parking lot with her bags of bread.

On his way home, Trudy's words kept echoing in his mind, so much so that after he got home and put away the groceries he headed over to Angie's house. She'd given him a key so he could take care of the puppies while she was working long hours.

After setting up the portable puppy fencing outside in the shade, he brought the puppies outside so they could run around and play.

"I think you all are doubling in size every time I see you," he said as he placed them inside the fenced area.

Free of their pen inside, they immediately started running and rolling around with each other, getting excited when they spotted a little yellow butterfly flying nearby. Eric crouched and petted them all, rubbed some chubby little bellies, allowing their pure, uncomplicated joy to shove aside the frustration he'd experienced when he'd had the run-in with Wes and received the death stare from

Tyler. He honestly didn't understand why they couldn't just leave him alone. Whatever grudge they had against him for leaving, for not picking up where he left off with them, whatever slights they might feel—it was all just so dumb.

But then they weren't the brightest bulbs either. Of course, neither was he. But he liked to think he'd matured and learned a lot during his time away. No, he knew he had. He was satisfied with the person he'd become. If only everyone else could really see and believe that the new Eric Novak was the real one.

With the puppies enjoying fresh air and playtime, he got to work. Angie had bought lumber to replace the weathered floor of her front porch but hadn't had time to undertake the task. This was totally in his wheelhouse, so he started ripping up old, springy boards that had probably been in need of replacing when he was a kid and cutting new ones to fit.

The sound of a vehicle approaching drew his attention. To say he was surprised to see his dad pulling into Angie's driveway would be an understatement.

"Something wrong?" Eric asked when his dad exited his truck.

His dad waved him off and walked toward the pups, then stood and watched them for several seconds. Little Frigg noticed him and put her paws up on the fence. To Eric's further surprise, his dad bent over to pick her up and cuddled her to his chest. When Frigg licked his dad's chin, Eric heard something he'd not heard in...he couldn't remember how long. Laughter.

He and his dad hadn't fought lately, but they'd not suddenly become a warm and open father-son duo. He'd considered peacefully coexisting the best he could hope for, but hearing his dad laugh made him wonder if more was possible.

"I see she has charmed you as well."

"She's a cute little thing." His dad reached up and let his hand hover above Frigg's head as if he was afraid of hurting her or possibly wasn't sure how one went about petting a puppy.

Something about the scene in front of him hurt Eric's heart. He'd been angry at his dad for so long, and admittedly his dad hadn't helped any in alleviating that anger, but now he wondered if his dad had been wrapped in so many layers of resentment and frustration that he'd forgotten how to be happy.

"Do you want to leave here?" Eric asked.

"I didn't come to fight."

"No, Dad. Here as in the ranch, Jade Valley." He'd promised Angie he wouldn't leave her because of some misguided idea of trying to protect her from wagging tongues, but what if his dad was still miserable? Despite everything, he couldn't say his dad deserved to live the rest of his life as unhappy as he'd evidently been during most of his adulthood.

His dad shook his head. "This is home. I wouldn't know what to do out there now." He made a gesture that seemed to indicate the world outside the valley.

"You said you hated ranching."

"I resented having no choice when I was young." He looked toward their land in the distance. "I think…" He paused for so long that it seemed as if he wouldn't finish his thought. "It's not terrible. I convinced myself it was years ago because it wasn't what I chose."

Fate had instead chosen it for him.

"But if you don't want to do it, I'll sell off the herd and all the land but what the house is on." The way Camille had after her husband's passing.

Eric suddenly wondered if all the times his father had been silent recently hadn't been because he was upset or just trying to avoid arguing. Maybe he'd been trying to make sense of all the thoughts and feelings that he was voicing now.

"I assume you're going to stay," his dad said, nodding toward the house but obviously meaning Angie.

"I want to, if I can." He'd not said it out loud to anyone, not even himself, before that moment. Rebuilding his reputation yet again wasn't going to be easy, especially if Angie couldn't find out for certain who had broken into Meecham's, but he was willing to try if he felt it wouldn't do her harm. Even if he had to make people see him for who he really was one person at a time, being with Angie was worth it. Standing up for himself was worth it.

"Good." His dad ran his hand over Frigg's head and back slowly, treating her as if she was as fragile as dandelion puffs. "You have to be happy before you can make her happy. Don't fail at that like I did."

The pain of not only his mother's death but also the hard life she'd lived threatened to bring Eric's long-held anger back.

"I did your mother wrong, and I'm sorry for that."

Eric knew how difficult it was for his father to say those words. He'd never been one for admitting when he was wrong or apologizing. That he was doing both in one sentence was nothing short of remarkable.

"I wish you'd said that to her."

"I should have when she was still here, but..." He cleared his throat. "I went to the cemetery and told her today."

If his father had taken one of the boards and hit him with it, Eric couldn't have been more stunned.

"I'm not telling you that for forgiveness. I just wanted you to know. I don't deserve to feel better about it, but I hope she does."

Eric honestly felt as if he was looking at a different man than he'd known his entire life. He couldn't say all the old anger and hurt had gone away. It might never all totally disappear. But this was a start.

"Now, you want some help or not?" his dad asked, obviously trying to get past the uncomfortable sharing-feelings moment by adopting some of his usual gruff exterior.

"Sure."

Eric was amazed by how well they actually worked together, but then they'd never actually given each other a real chance before. If his relationship with his dad could begin to change like this, then anything was possible.

The two of them were sitting on the front steps, drinking bottles of water and watching the puppies run free in the yard, when Angie arrived home. When she got out of her truck, she looked tired.

"This is a nice surprise." She was evidently talking about their presence because when she noticed the newly completed porch floor, she stopped in her tracks. "Oh my, you two have been busy. You didn't have to do that."

"I wanted to. And I think Dad helped so he could play with the puppies."

Allen huffed like that was the dumbest thing he'd ever heard and stood. "Time for me to leave."

Eric bit his lip to keep from laughing. He couldn't remember a time before today when his dad had done anything that made him want to laugh. Maybe there were some hazy memories when he was little, but too much had happened since then to block them. But there was no changing the past, so it seemed a healthier choice to focus on the present and the future. And based on this day alone, he had hope that things between them going forward would be much better than they'd been in the past.

"Allen," Angie said, drawing his dad's attention. "Thank you."

His dad nodded, uttered an *um* to indicate he'd heard and resumed his trek to his aging truck. The door squeaked loudly when he opened it.

"Oil those hinges!" Angie called out.

"Quit being so bossy!"

Angie just laughed in response, which made Eric do the same. As his dad headed back down the road toward the ranch, Angie came to sit in the spot he'd vacated beside Eric.

"Seems there has been some progress," she said as she pointed toward his dad's retreating truck.

"Yeah. I would have never bet any money on him changing, but he is—at least to some extent."

"I'm glad." She reached behind her and patted the new porch. "This is also pretty awesome."

He reached over and took her other hand, entwined his fingers with hers.

"You've been working so hard, trying to solve this case in addition to your other work," he said. "I wanted to do something to thank you."

"I haven't solved it yet."

"I have confidence you will. You're very good at your job." He leaned over and kissed her. "I've often heard how good men look in uniform, but you don't look half bad yourself."

"I guess we can add flattery to your list of talents," she said, smiling at him in a way that made him feel hotter than he should even after working all day.

Eric reached up and tucked some of the hair that had escaped her ponytail back behind her ear. "I would ask you out to dinner, but I don't think now would be the best time for us to be seen together."

"I want to argue with that, but I can't. But not for the reason you think. I'm confident in my decision of who to be with," she said.

"However, I don't want to draw extra attention to you until I can prove who did perpetrate the thefts. I have leftover rotisserie chicken and potato salad, though."

"Perfect."

As they stood, Angie's phone rang. She quickly checked the caller ID and gave Eric a "wait a moment" sign.

"You're kidding," she said after listening to whoever was on the other end of the call, sounding both surprised and excited. "I'll be there as soon as I can."

Eric's heart thumped a little harder. Was it possible there had been a break in the theft case? Did he dare get his hopes up?

"I'm sorry," she said as she looked up at him after ending the call. "I've got to go."

"What is it?"

"Hopefully the proof we need, but I don't want to say too much until I'm sure." She stood on her toes and kissed him on the cheek before jogging toward her vehicle.

"Be careful," he called to her.

"Always am. Love you!"

He smiled at how easily she seemed to toss the endearment toward him. Unwilling to let Angie go without showing her how much he loved her in return, he ran to catch up and spun his girlfriend into his arms. After pulling her close, he kissed her as if she was leaving for the other side of the world.

"Wow," she said when he finally lifted his mouth from hers.

"I love you too," he said softly.

Moments later, he watched the woman he'd given his whole heart to disappear into the coming night, once again asking whoever was listening to keep her safe.

ANGIE PULLED UP to the large log home at the edge of the county. Located on a bend in the river with the towering mountains as a backdrop, she was certain the property and home cost more than she'd make in her lifetime. The owner, a handsome gray-haired man she'd met some months ago, lived in California, some sort of company CEO if she remembered correctly.

"Mr. Childress, good to see you again," she said as she drew close to where the man was standing with Jace, the deputy who'd called her. "Though not under these circumstances."

"Sheriff Lee," Samuel Childress said.

Jace held up an evidence bag that held a

disposable phone. "I checked it already, and it's the same one."

Finally, the break she'd been combing not only the county but also a significant portion of the state to find.

Jace and Mr. Childress filled her in on what had transpired, which was remarkably bad timing for the man sitting in the back of Jace's patrol vehicle but lucky for everyone else. Well, maybe not everyone. Only time would tell on that. Mr. Childress, thankfully, had only scared the soul out of the man he'd found carrying a box full of expensive items out of his house instead of shooting him with the gun he'd had strapped to his hip.

Angie left Jace to finish up with Mr. Childress as she walked over to the patrol car and opened the back door.

"Well, well, Wes, we meet again." She held up the evidence bag with the phone. "You know what this is?"

"I know my rights."

As many times as he'd been read his Miranda rights, he probably did.

"Was Tyler here too?"

Wes remained silent.

"You can stay quiet all you want," she said.

"But think about what Tyler would do in your situation. If he could save himself even one night in jail, he'd toss you under the bus."

Wes looked up at her, and she could tell he wanted to tell her she was wrong. But he couldn't without opening his mouth, which he'd apparently decided he wasn't going to do anymore.

"Suit yourself. Let me know if you remember how to talk." She wanted to say something like, "You better like jail because you're going to be staying there for a good, long while," but she didn't. She kept her professional composure and simply shut the door, hoping that time, solitude and incarceration would bring out his chatty side. As it was, she had a key piece of evidence tying him to the accusation against Eric. That plus what Eric had told her about meeting Wes in the grocery store parking lot and Wes being surprised that Eric wasn't in jail were enough to start building a case even without the stolen merchandise. She did need something more solid, but she was way ahead of where she was only an hour ago.

When she arrived home the second time, Eric wasn't there. He'd brought the puppies in, fed them and given them water. He'd also left a package of her favorite oatmeal cookies on her kitchen table with a note to call or text him when she got home. After she warmed up some chicken then took it and the entire container of potato salad to the couch, she texted him.

Back home safely.

Can I call or are you going to sleep?

Call.

The phone rang immediately and she answered just as quickly. She didn't even wait until he asked what she knew was uppermost in his mind.

"Wes was arrested midtheft, and he dropped the phone that was used to text Dan those photos."

"What about Tyler?"

"He wasn't there and Wes isn't talking. At least not yet. We'll see if a few days behind bars change his mind."

The one thing still troubling her was why Wes would send those photos implicating Eric when the stolen items weren't actually there. She couldn't imagine him making that kind of move without Tyler's guidance or approval because Wes was a lackey, not a leader. But while neither of them was the brightest of humans, she didn't think either of them was dumb enough to make an accusation when it would be so easy to prove it wrong. Something wasn't adding up. Did they just want to make people suspect Eric to get back at him? Sometimes that's all it took to ruin someone's life, and she could see them being that kind of vindictive, especially Tyler. Even if that was the case, it meant they had at some point had access to the items that had been stolen from Meecham's.

But where had Tyler been tonight? If he'd been there and abandoned Wes, and Wes still didn't give him up, then Wes was a bigger sucker than everyone already considered him to be.

"You're wondering where the stuff taken from Meecham's is, aren't you?"

"Yeah. And why, if Wes and Tyler are the ones who stole the stuff from Meecham's, they would go through the trouble of setting you up without actually putting the items in your barn."

"Maybe they wanted to punish me but also wanted the money they could get out of the merchandise."

Angie nodded, even though she couldn't quite figure out the missing pieces of the puzzle. She had to find those pieces to make sure she could totally clear Eric.

"Possibly." But she wasn't so sure. She depended most often on tangible evidence, but sometimes she had to pay attention to her gut instinct because it was insisting she do so.

And right now it was jumping up and down, waving its arms and screaming.

ANGIE WALKED OUT of the sheriff's department with a pounding headache. Between a particularly volatile domestic call early in the day, Wes's continued silence and Dan continuing to stir up some of the locals with talk that she wasn't fit for her job, it hadn't been one of her favorite days of work. She walked straight to Trudy's and bought the biggest fully caffeinated soda she could.

"One of those days, huh?"

She looked over as she paid for the drink to see Stevie standing there.

"You could say that."

"Well, maybe this will help. Tyler was down at The Bar drinking earlier and he seemed very irritated with Wes. There were several unflattering comments about his lack of intelligence."

Angie could imagine the colorful language Tyler had likely used. "Did he happen to blurt out an admission that he and Wes have been the ones thieving all over the county?"

"Sorry, no. But would he be that upset just over Wes getting himself tossed in jail? It didn't seem like it was simply because he was down an underling."

If only Tyler would admit all if she questioned him, but he was indeed smarter than Wes. While Wes knew enough to keep his mouth shut, Tyler would go a step further and point the blame elsewhere. That persistent gut instinct was telling her that was exactly what he'd done to get back at Eric for not simply slipping back under his thumb when he returned to Jade Valley.

The truth was Angie had a difficult time imagining Eric ever under Tyler's influence.

While Tyler was a few steps smarter than Wes, Eric put them both to shame. But somehow he'd fallen into that subservient position when he'd been a kid looking for a place to belong and someone to praise him.

"Thanks for telling me," she told Stevie. "If you hear anything else—"

"I'll let you know immediately. Tyler is one customer I'd be happy to do without."

Angie headed out of the café while trying to think of a way to get either Wes or Tyler to slip up and confess their crimes. Her phone rang as soon as she stepped onto the sidewalk. Seeing it was Camille and thankful for a distraction, she answered.

"I need you to come over to my house," Camille said.

"What's up? Do you need something?"

"Yes, for you to come over."

Camille knew that Angie and Eric were together, so surely it wasn't more matchmaking. Since Camille's place wasn't too far off her path home anyway, she said she'd be there in a few minutes. What she didn't expect to find was Allen's truck sitting in Camille's driveway. Wondering if Eric had borrowed it for some reason, she got out and headed toward the house. When Camille let her inside, however, it was Allen sitting in a chair, not Eric.

"Okay," she said slowly. "My 'something's up' sense is tingling right now."

Camille motioned for her to follow her into the extra bedroom. As soon as Camille flicked on the light, Angie stopped in her tracks at what she saw. Then she spun to look back at Allen.

"He didn't steal it," Camille said. "And I sure didn't."

"So do you care to enlighten me how this bedroom is filled with stolen property?"

"When Dan was making that scene on the Fourth of July, I had a sinking feeling someone had set Eric up. So I called Allen, and thank God he answered the phone. I told him what was going on and to get that stuff out of the barn as fast as possible, to bring it here, because who is going to think a woman my age is a thief?"

Angie turned back toward Allen, hands on her hips. "Is this true?"

He nodded. "I had barely gotten back when you all showed up at the house. I fired up the mower to have an excuse for why I was so out of breath. I thought I was going to die getting all that stuff out of the loft, to the truck and over here. I haven't moved that fast in years, and my lungs just about gave out."

"Well, whose fault is that?" Camille asked.

"I'm aware," Allen said, obviously irritated at being scolded.

Angie paced while running her hand back over her hair. "Why didn't you two tell me this sooner?"

"We knew how it would look if you found out these things had been right where Dan said they were," Camille said.

"You needed to find the real thief first," Allen added. "And Maya reported that you did."

Angie closed her eyes and took a slow breath, trying to calm herself. Never in a million years would she have imagined this scenario.

"I do not have an ironclad case against Wes, and so far I have nothing against Tyler."

"Dust for fingerprints," Camille said. "Isn't that the smoking gun you're looking for?"

"There are probably dozens of fingerprints on that stuff. They were sitting in a store. Not to mention your prints."

"We didn't touch it with our bare hands,"

Camille said. "We're not dumb. I've seen enough cop shows to know not to do that."

"Plus, there's stuff that didn't come from Meecham's," Allen added.

Angie went back into the bedroom to verify that statement. Sure enough, she saw items reported missing from Pippa Anderson's place along with some things she couldn't immediately identify from police reports. If Wes and Tyler had stolen all this, why in the world hadn't they offloaded it yet? Had they been waiting until news of the thefts faded to make it easier to sell?

She pulled out her phone and called the office, dreading the fact that it was Mike on duty. He was a good deputy, but he held no love for anyone with the last name Novak. Hopefully, the fact that this had been Camille's brainchild would mitigate the situation.

"You really don't know what off duty means, do you?" he said by way of answer.

"I need you to bring a fingerprint kit out to Camille's place, and keep it quiet." She wasn't trying to hide anything, but she also didn't want anyone else showing up nor rumors spreading.

"Did something happen to Camille?"

"No, she's fine." At least she was at the moment, if Angie didn't decide to wring her neck for putting her in this position. But she also understood what she and Allen had done. This was just going to be complicated if she couldn't get a rock-solid case against at least Wes. She was afraid it was too much to hope that Tyler would have messed up as well.

When Mike arrived and she filled him in on why he was there, he shot Allen a hard look.

"If you're passing out those looks, she deserves one too," Angie said, pointing at Camille. "But let's focus on the positive, okay? We're recovering stolen property, and hopefully it will lead us to who actually stole it."

Mike looked very much as if he wanted to say something else, probably that he believed one of the culprits was sitting in the living room. But to his credit, Mike nodded and got to work. They took their time, and when they finally completed the task and got everything loaded in their vehicles her stomach was growling. And hers wasn't the only one. As if she'd heard the sounds of hunger too, Camille came out of the kitchen with two thick sandwiches and plastic glasses of tea. She didn't even look contrite. Camille was a woman who did what she wanted, when she wanted, why she wanted. If Angie was being honest, Camille was a good person to have in your corner. She'd protected Eric as if he'd been her own child or grandchild. Angie had to admire that, even if it was legally iffy at best.

"I can't decide if when you arrive at the Pearly Gates, if Saint Peter is going to have a stern word with you or just chuckle and wave you in," Angie said.

"My money's on the latter. Everyone could use a good laugh."

She wasn't wrong.

When Angie met Mike outside, his posture was still stiff.

"I know you don't like Allen or Eric," she said without preamble, "but personal feelings have no place in enforcing the law. Evidence does, and I intend to get that evidence tonight." She shared with him an idea that had been percolating in her mind as they'd dusted every item for fingerprints.

Mike's sour mood gradually changed, and he surprised her by smiling. "I like it."

She inhaled the sandwich and tea on the drive back to the department. When they arrived, she and Mike both put on fresh sets of sterile gloves and started toting the evidence in. Thankful the jail cells were within view of the deputies' desks, she and Mike brought the first load of stolen goods in and started placing them within easy view of where Wes was sitting.

"Good thing you've gotten used to being behind bars," Mike said to him. "You and Tyler are going away for a while now that we have the stuff you stole back and your fingerprints. I can't believe you two were so stupid. I mean, you yes. You're not that bright. But wow, Tyler messed up big-time."

"Cut it out," Angie said, just as they'd planned. She looked toward Wes, sighed and shook her head. "It may have gone easier for you if you'd confessed what the two of you did."

She started to turn around to go fetch another load.

"Wait!"

Angie forced the smile off her face before she turned around.

"Can I still talk? Will it help me?" he asked, suddenly sounding desperate.

"A judge may look more favorably on your charges if you cooperate." She couldn't and wouldn't promise him anything because that was beyond her control. But if she could get him to confess and rat out Tyler while they waited on the results of the fingerprints, it was worth a bit of acting on her part.

By the time they finished with Wes's videotaped confession and statements regarding all the thefts, how Tyler had picked the targets and never listened to Wes's ideas, and how Wes had decided to act on his own at the Childress place in order to prove to Tyler his ideas were good too, Angie was beyond tired. Mike offered to log all the property into evidence, but she shook her head and helped him complete that task as well.

When everything was done, she was exhausted but still had one more thing to do.

"Are you going to be okay to drive home?" Mike asked.

"I'm fine. Thanks for your help."

"Are you kidding? That was really satisfying." He hesitated for a moment, seemed to be trying to find words that were difficult to say. "I'm sorry about how I've treated Eric. I owe him an apology."

"Yes, you do. But you're not the only one. Speaking of satisfying, I'm going to take great pleasure in hearing Dan apologize."

"I wouldn't hold my breath if I were you."

"You might be surprised."

She rolled the windows down in her truck as she drove out of town again, letting the wind help keep her awake. Despite her fatigue, she drove past her house then made the right turn into the Novak ranch. Allen's truck was back in its spot, and the lights were on in the house. She wondered if Allen had told Eric what he'd done and, if so, what his reaction had been. Would he be thankful? Angry? Some confusing mixture of the two as she'd been? She was about to find out.

When Eric opened the front door for her, he asked, "Are you here to arrest Dad?"

One look at his face, how he couldn't quite meet her gaze, told her how the conversation had gone. He was pulling away again, probably partly out of guilt about his dad's actions and partly because of that persistent need to protect her and her job.

"If I were going to arrest him, I would have

done it earlier." She wanted to touch Eric but refrained. "But, good news, one Tyler Langston will be behind bars soon, thanks to a fine bit of acting on my and Mike's parts, if I do say so myself."

Eric did meet her gaze then, and she saw both hope and concern in those amber eyes.

"Come in before you let in every bug in Wyoming," Allen called out from his favorite chair.

"Sorry," Eric said, moving back so Angie could step inside.

"Did Wes rat out Tyler?" Allen asked.

"He did indeed."

Allen snorted. "I knew he'd cave eventually."

"Really?" Eric asked her, as if he was afraid to believe that he'd also not been implicated as well.

She smiled and reached out to gently squeeze his forearm. "Really. I made it abundantly clear to Wes that he was best served by telling the entire truth, leaving absolutely nothing out, and that he'd better not lie about one bit of it. Not only are we now solving the thefts we knew about, but also three others we didn't. I'm not a judge or jury, but my educated guess is that you're not going to have to worry about Wes or Tyler for quite some time."

Eric pulled her into his arms and hugged her as if she'd just saved his life. Maybe in some respects it seemed that way.

"Thank you."

"I just did my job."

"No, you went above and beyond."

"Well, I'm not the only one. You had a couple of guardian angels." Sometimes cranky guardian angels, but guardians nonetheless.

"I already thanked them, right after I yelled at them."

Angie leaned around Eric to speak to Allen. "Never knew you had a bit of superhero in you."

"Don't encourage him," Eric said.

Allen made a dismissive wave at them. "Can't you two go be lovey-dovey somewhere else and let me watch TV in peace?"

Eric took her hand and led her outside, back to that bench where they'd shared their first kiss. She laid her head on his shoulder, and he wrapped an arm around her and pulled her close.

"I should let you go home and sleep, but

I'm feeling selfish right now and don't want to let you go," he said.

"I don't want to leave either. It feels as if a giant weight has been lifted, doesn't it?"

"Yeah. I'm almost afraid to believe it."

She lifted her head and looked at him. "It's solid."

Eric cupped her cheek. "Thank you."

"You already said that."

"It's worth repeating." He stared at her, something in his eyes communicating that he was debating saying something further.

"What is it?"

"When I came back here, I had more than a few doubts. I think when I left Texas, I at least halfway thought I'd be back before long. To be honest, I've pulled out my travel bag and started filling it more than once since being back. But despite everything that's happened, coming back here was every bit as good a decision as the one I made to leave here. When I left, it allowed me to break a destructive pattern and remake myself." He ran his thumb across her cheek, causing an intoxicating shiver to run through her. "But coming back gave me so much I never expected. An actual relationship with my dad, a grandmother figure…and a woman I love more than I ever imagined possible."

"I'm happy for you," she said. "But I'm also happy for me. For a long time after that night I was pulled over, I didn't want to even be around men. It took me two years to go on a date. But like you, I didn't want to continue down that path. I wanted to take control, not let others dictate how I thought about myself, how others viewed me or how I saw the world."

"And you succeeded."

"I did. And you're succeeding too. You're not all the way there yet, but it's happening. And it's not just because of me or your dad or Camille." She lifted her hand and placed it against his chest above his heart. "Most of it is because of you, the person you are now. The man I love."

Eric lowered his mouth to hers for a kiss that said more than words ever could.

CHAPTER FOURTEEN

ERIC STOOD OUTSIDE the wrought iron gate that served as the entrance to the cemetery. He'd been thinking about coming here for days, knew it was something he needed to do before he moved on with the next phase of his life. His relationship with his dad was remarkably decent now. Some days he was still stunned by what his dad had done to protect him. He wouldn't have thought it was physically possible for him to undertake the moving of all that stolen property out of the barn loft let alone do it at the pace he had. And yet he had.

With things between him and his dad going okay, it was time to make peace with his mom. He'd come here to do the thing he'd not been able to do before—say goodbye. Even though she wasn't really here, this was the closest he could get.

He reached out and opened the gate, stepped inside the cemetery, then closed the gate behind him. Though he'd not been here in many years, he still remembered where his grandparents were buried. His mom had been laid to rest next to her mother and father.

He'd prepared himself for a lot of different reactions when he finally saw her name on a tombstone, but calm acceptance wasn't one of them. And yet that's how he felt as he let his gaze run over her name, her birth and death dates and the flowers carved into the stone. It was the sight of his father's name next to hers and the blank spot waiting for his death date that was more startling. It felt almost like tempting fate to put one's name on such a grave marker while still alive though he knew people did it all the time.

He leaned over and placed the bouquet of multicolored daisies next to his mother's side of the stone.

"Hi, Mom. It's been a long time. Sorry I didn't come sooner, but I had to work out some things on my own first." He paused and took a deep breath. "I needed to not be so angry at you for not telling me you were sick. But Angie—that's my girlfriend—helped me to see things from your point of view. I still wish I had known, that I would have had the chance to come see you before it was too late, but I'm not mad at you anymore."

A slight breeze wafted across the cemetery, stirring the leaves in the nearby trees. He knew it wasn't anything so otherworldly as a caress from his mother, but for some reason it still eased some of the tension in his shoulders.

He'd planned for this to be a brief visit, but he found himself lowering himself to the ground and sitting cross-legged beside his mother's grave. And words just started tumbling out. He told her about his years away, the places he'd seen, the friends he'd made, why he'd left in the first place and why he knew it was the right decision. Then he shared everything that had happened between him and his dad since his return, the difficulties of changing people's opinions of him, his unexpected friendship with Camille, how he'd considered leaving more than once and the improvements he'd made around the ranch.

"I think you'd really like the kitchen. Angie didn't know yellow is your favorite color, but that's the color she helped me pick out for the walls. She's awesome like that." He proceeded to tell his mom about Angie and the puppies, about the trial-by-*buldak* her mother had put him through. He looked toward his mom's name on the piece of hard granite. "I love her, and I hope someday she'll be your daughter-in-law. I'd ask her today but maybe it's too soon. I'm not so good with choosing the right timing on things like that."

By the time the flow of stories stopped, he'd been sitting there in the cemetery for almost an hour and a half. He was surprised Angie hadn't called him yet to ask where he was. He needed to hurry or they'd be late for Maya and Gavin's wedding.

Once he was standing he looked at his mom's name again.

"I miss you, Mom. I hope wherever you are, you're happy now. Don't worry about us. We're doing fine."

With those words still hanging in the air, he turned and walked away—leaving the sorrows of the past in the past and heading straight toward a happier future.

"Wow." Eric stared at Angie in her pink-and-white dress, like some wearable combination of a cloud and a field of pink wildflowers, her long black hair free of its customary ponytail, and almost forgot how to breathe. "You look beautiful."

"I clean up okay, right?" Angie's smile added to her beauty. "And I have to say, you look not half bad yourself." She stepped forward and adjusted his light blue tie then ran her palms lightly across the lapels of his new dark suit. "I may have to protect you from all the singles today, what with romance in the air."

"I won't even see them." How could he when he had this stunning woman beside him?

"You're getting better and better at the smooth talking. I like it." She gave him a quick peck on the cheek. "But we need to go. We're running late."

He hadn't been to a wedding since his second year in the army when one of his buddies had tied the knot in a no-frills service before they headed to Afghanistan. Hopefully, Maya and Gavin's marriage lasted longer than that one had because Mark had been served divorce papers just shy of his first anniversary. From what he'd seen of Maya and Gavin though, they appeared to be in it for life. As he glanced over at Angie while they walked hand in hand to his truck, he wondered what it would be like to be married to her. He liked the idea of waking up with her in his arms every morning instead of rolling over to send her a good-morning text.

But it was too soon for that kind of step. He was happy just having her in his life. Since Tyler had been arrested a month ago and Maya had revealed the truth in great detail through her reporting, life had gradually changed for the better. Not only had he and his dad settled into a peaceful coexistence, Eric had remarkably convinced his dad to make some positive changes for his health. Whenever Eric went to town now, he no longer felt suspicious stares. Occasionally, he'd notice someone avoiding him, but on the whole his relationship with the locals was a great deal better. He'd even been hired on to work part-time with a local builder, which along with running the ranch with his dad kept him busy—but not too busy to spend time with Angie when she wasn't on duty. They worked side by side on renovating her house, and he had to admit it was going to be really nice when she was done. She'd even gotten him to watch home improvement shows with her.

Other days they'd escape for a hike in the mountains, a float down the river, even a day trip to Jackson. It honestly didn't matter if they were laying tile in a bathroom or eating in a nice restaurant, the most important part was being with her. His dad and Camille teased him about how head over heels he was, and he didn't even care because it was the truth. Tony had teased him too when he'd told him about Angie, but then had said he understood because not only was Angie pretty, she'd also helped to give him the life he'd never had but always wanted.

"What are you thinking about?" Angie asked from the passenger seat.

"How lucky I am," he said without hesitation and reached across to take her hand.

"So am I." She pointed at the steering wheel. "Ten and two."

Eric laughed. "Even looking like a fairy princess, always the consummate law enforcement officer."

When they arrived at the ranch Sunny and Dean ran with Sunny's dad, it looked as if half of Jade Valley was attending the wedding.

"It's always good to come bearing well-wishes and gifts for the woman who decides how to write the local news," Angie said as Eric parked.

Eric wondered if he and Angie got married someday, would they have a similar turnout because it was wise to stay on the good side of the sheriff?

As they walked hand in hand toward the gazebo by the river that was decorated in flowers and that fluffy see-through fabric, his stomach tensed. Even after getting to know more area residents, working with or for some of them, even after Dan Lintz begrudgingly apologized to him right before Dan got fired, Eric still couldn't totally banish the idea that it could all come crashing down.

Angie squeezed his hand. "Stop worrying. It's in the past now."

"Are you sure you're not a mind reader?"

"Positive. I just know you."

She did indeed, better than anyone—even his own parents—ever had.

When he spotted Camille, who had saved two seats for them, he couldn't help a chuckle.

"Did you somehow find the biggest hat in Wyoming?" he asked her.

"I'm going to take every chance I get to

wear a fancy hat. You two better hurry up and get hitched before I kick the bucket."

Eric nearly choked, and it must have showed because he heard a few good-natured laughs from people seated nearby.

Angie leaned close and whispered, "Sit down before you pass out."

He glanced at her and saw a mischievous grin tugging at the edges of her mouth.

They'd been in their seats only a couple of minutes when the wedding party arrived via SUVs and started making their way toward the riverside gazebo. Laughter ran through the crowd as Gavin's son walked down the aisle between the seats with little pups on leashes. Each one was wearing a big bow, and a lot of phone cameras started snapping shots.

"Aww, they look so cute," Angie said.

All through the wedding ceremony, Eric kept picturing a different couple at the front— Angie in a white dress, him placing a ring on her finger, both of them promising to love and cherish each other for the rest of their lives.

Now might not be the right time to propose to Angie, but he knew in that moment that someday he would. And hopefully her answer would be yes.

ANGIE SAT BACK and enjoyed watching Eric talking with Dean, Sunny's dad and a couple of other guys. When he laughed at something that was said, it filled her heart with happiness. And, wow, did he look great in that suit. He was handsome all the time, but the first glimpse of him in a sharp, three-piece suit had taken her breath away.

"You look like a woman in love."

Angie managed to pull her gaze away from Eric to see Sunny had slipped onto the chair next to her, a glass of wine in her hand.

"That's because I am."

Sunny smiled. "I'm happy for you, for both of you. I admit I never would have imagined this when I knew Eric back in high school, but I'm glad he found a new path and it led to you."

"Me too." Angie looked around. "Who's on kid duty?"

"Maya's mom and aunties are having a ball playing with the twins, Max and the puppies. Too bad the other two pups aren't here too."

"Allen tried to act like he was doing me a huge favor in puppy sitting today, but I've got his number. They've totally won him over."

Sunny shook her head. "Another change it's

hard to believe. But you have that effect on people, same as Maya."

"I wouldn't say Maya and I have the same type of personality."

"Well, no. She's of the fun, ray of sunshine variety, but you believe in people so much that it enables them to believe in themselves."

Angie couldn't have asked for a better compliment.

"Okay, it's time for the bouquet tossing," Sunny said, then looked over toward where Eric was still talking with her husband. "Should I tell Maya to aim it at you?"

"Let fate decide where it goes. I'm not knocking people out of the way to catch a superstition."

"But just think how happy your mother will be," Sunny teased.

"Aren't you needed somewhere else?"

Sunny laughed as she stood then walked away to attend to her matron of honor duties.

The fact was, Angie's mom probably would be happy if she got married, and she'd warmed considerably toward Eric. No doubt she would have picked someone different for her only daughter, but that ship had sailed.

"Come on, let's go," Camille said as she almost literally dragged Angie from her chair to join the group of unmarried women hoping to catch a flying bouquet of roses.

Angie laughed. "Are you trying for the bouquet?"

"I'm old, not dead."

"All the single men better watch out," one of Maya's cousins said, causing more laughter to move through the crowd.

Maya, who looked beautiful in her simple but stylish wedding gown, stepped forward. Angie thought she caught a wink directed at someone before Maya turned her back and tossed the bouquet. Right then, someone shoved Angie. Not used to wearing heels, she stumbled a bit and reached out to catch herself.

She caught the bouquet instead.

Stunned, it took her a moment to notice the laughter and applause. She turned to see who'd pushed her. Camille looked very pleased with herself.

Instead of reacting how a lot of people probably expected her to, she decided in the spur of the moment to have fun with the situation. So she searched the crowd until she found Eric and spun the little bouquet in the air.

"So, what do you say?"

More laughter erupted at her good-natured teasing.

"I say yes."

Angie froze and forgot to breathe. She barely heard the chorus of surprised exclamations from those around them over her accelerating pulse banging against her eardrums. Eric wasn't teasing. She could tell by the way he was looking at her, as if he possessed all the love in the world and he was offering it to her.

"Good."

Eric slowly started moving toward her, the crowd parting before him until there was a clear path. Her heart beat harder with each step he took, making it difficult but not impossible to hear the rising excitement and calls of support from the crowd. When Eric was no more than a step away, he stopped.

"Did you just ask me to marry you?"

"I think I did," she said.

"Do you want to back out?"

"No."

He smiled and laughed a little. "You keep saying and doing things before I can."

"You shouldn't dilly-dally."

"Okay, I won't." He grabbed her then, bent

her back over his arm and kissed her like his life depended on making her world spin.

He evidently was going to live a very long life.

EPILOGUE

ANGIE COVERED HER mouth to hide her laughter.

"This is better than any TV show ever," Eric said.

It was indeed. Watching her mother explain all the Korean street food to Allen and answering his countless questions was one of the best parts of the trip yet, and that was saying a lot because her first trip to Korea had been amazing so far. Sure, it was unusual to bring all the in-laws on one's honeymoon, but it also seemed right. Her mother was getting to see her home country again. Her dad and Eric were reliving memories of their service years on the Korean Peninsula. And Allen had finally gotten that trip far away from Jade Valley.

Preparing for the trip had been quite the undertaking—her scheduling time off from work, Eric getting Dean to watch after Oscar and the herd, Maya agreeing to puppysit, and getting Allen both a passport and clearance from his doctor for the overseas adventure. They made sure he wore the good face masks on the bad air quality days in Seoul, but he hadn't complained once. She'd teased him, saying she wondered if he'd gotten switched out with someone else going through customs.

After examining all the food stalls' options at least half a dozen times, Allen finally chose *jjinppang*, a warm steamed dumpling filled with red bean paste.

"I knew he'd go for the plainest option," Eric said.

She playfully swatted her husband's arm. "Let him gradually warm up to the more adventurous dishes."

Angie bit into her really unhealthy but delicious Korean hot dog, a deep-fried concoction on a stick that would feel at home at many state fairs. Unsurprisingly, her dad and Eric went for the spicy *tteokbokki* stir-fried rice cakes, while her mom indulged in *eomuk*, fish cakes she didn't have to make herself.

"What's next?" Eric asked.

They'd already toured Gyeongbokgung Palace, at both her mother's and Sunny's urging, as well as the art galleries and tea houses of Insadong. Eric wanted to revisit some of the history museums but those would be better for a different day.

Angie pointed toward the cable cars carrying people up Mount Namsan toward the N Seoul Tower. The mountain was ablaze with fall color, and she wanted to see the view from the top with her own eyes.

When they left the cable car station at the top, they took their time going from one vantage point to another so that they didn't overtax Allen's lungs. Angie didn't mind the slow pace because it gave her time to really soak up the experience and the views. Her parents wandered off, hand in hand.

"I think they're reliving their dating years," she said to Eric.

"This is the happiest I've ever seen your mom."

"I don't think she allows herself to miss Korea too much because she didn't think she'd ever come back after her parents passed. But I heard them talking about going hiking more when we get back home." She glanced over to where Allen was looking out over the expanse of Seoul and the Han River.

"Amazing, isn't it?" she said.

Allen nodded without taking his eyes away from the view.

"Hard to believe that there are more than fifteen times as many people living in Seoul than there are in all of Wyoming."

Allen looked behind him at the walkways and trees, at the families laughing and enjoying snacks and coffee.

"I understand why they would come to a place like this, to get out of the hubbub down there."

Angie agreed. She loved the energy of Seoul, the deep history that was interwoven with her family's, but Wyoming was home. She would enjoy her time here fully, then go back and enjoy the life she was building with Eric. Slip back into her uniform and protect the people of Jade Valley.

"You two go explore," Allen said as he sat on a bench that afforded an unobstructed view far into the distance. "This is your honeymoon. Go hold hands, kiss or something."

Angie couldn't help herself. She leaned over and planted a peck on Allen's cheek. He grumbled and swatted at her like a fly. With a laugh, she took Eric's hand and led him farther into the park. When she spotted the beginning of the love locks, she felt like a giddy teenager with her boyfriend.

"Let's get one," she said.

"Why not?"

They chose a pink heart-shaped lock and took turns writing something on the sides. When they were finished, she handed the lock back to Eric. She watched as he read "To the man who captured my heart." He brought her hand to his lips and kissed it.

She accepted the lock so she could read his message. The first thing she noticed was the little heart he'd drawn in the corner.

"*Gwiyeobda*," she said softly. Cute.

Then she saw what he'd written, and her heart squeezed with emotion.

"To the woman who gave me hope. *Saranghae.*"

She wasn't someone who cried often, but tears threatened when she looked up at him.

"I love you too. More than I can ever adequately express."

He pulled her close and planted a sweet kiss on her forehead. Then he took her hand and guided her to the side of the viewing platform. They found an empty spot in among the thousands of locks and snapped it into place.

She smiled at this little symbol of their love. When they were back on the other side of the world ranching, policing, and loving each other, this lock with their names would still be here proclaiming their love as it looked out over the city where her parents had fallen in love.

Thank goodness her dad liked spicy food. Thank goodness Eric did too.

* * * * *

Get 4 FREE REWARDS!

We'll send you 2 FREE Books plus 2 FREE Mystery Gifts.

FREE
Value Over
$20

Both the **Love Inspired®** and **Love Inspired® Suspense** series feature compelling novels filled with inspirational romance, faith, forgiveness and hope.

YES! Please send me 2 FREE novels from the Love Inspired or Love Inspired Suspense series and my 2 FREE gifts (gifts are worth about $10 retail). After receiving them, if I don't wish to receive any more books, I can return the shipping statement marked "cancel." If I don't cancel, I will receive 6 brand-new Love Inspired Larger-Print books or Love Inspired Suspense Larger-Print books every month and be billed just $6.49 each in the U.S. or $6.74 each in Canada. That is a savings of at least 16% off the cover price. It's quite a bargain! Shipping and handling is just 50¢ per book in the U.S. and $1.25 per book in Canada.* I understand that accepting the 2 free books and gifts places me under no obligation to buy anything. I can always return a shipment and cancel at any time by calling the number below. The free books and gifts are mine to keep no matter what I decide.

Choose one: ☐ **Love Inspired**
Larger-Print
(122/322 IDN GRHK)

☐ **Love Inspired Suspense**
Larger-Print
(107/307 IDN GRHK)

Name (please print)

Address   Apt. #

City   State/Province   Zip/Postal Code

Email: Please check this box ☐ if you would like to receive newsletters and promotional emails from Harlequin Enterprises ULC and its affiliates. You can unsubscribe anytime.

Mail to the **Harlequin Reader Service:**
IN U.S.A.: P.O. Box 1341, Buffalo, NY 14240-8531
IN CANADA: P.O. Box 603, Fort Erie, Ontario L2A 5X3

Want to try 2 free books from another series! Call 1-800-873-8635 or visit www.ReaderService.com.

*Terms and prices subject to change without notice. Prices do not include sales taxes, which will be charged (if applicable) based on your state or country of residence. Canadian residents will be charged applicable taxes. Offer not valid in Quebec. This offer is limited to one order per household. Books received may not be as shown. Not valid for current subscribers to the Love Inspired or Love Inspired Suspense series. All orders subject to approval. Credit or debit balances in a customer's account(s) may be offset by any other outstanding balance owed by or to the customer. Please allow 4 to 6 weeks for delivery. Offer available while quantities last.

Your Privacy—Your information is being collected by Harlequin Enterprises ULC, operating as Harlequin Reader Service. For a complete summary of the information we collect, how we use this information and to whom it is disclosed, please visit our privacy notice located at corporate.harlequin.com/privacy-notice. From time to time we may also exchange your personal information with reputable third parties. If you wish to opt out of this sharing of your personal information, please visit readerservice.com/consumerschoice or call 1-800-873-8635. **Notice to California Residents**—Under California law, you have specific rights to control and access your data. For more information on these rights and how to exercise them, visit corporate.harlequin.com/california-privacy.

LIRLIS22R3

Get 4 FREE REWARDS!

We'll send you 2 FREE Books plus 2 FREE Mystery Gifts.

FREE Value Over **$20**

Both the **Harlequin® Special Edition** and **Harlequin® Heartwarming™** series feature compelling novels filled with stories of love and strength where the bonds of friendship, family and community unite.

YES! Please send me 2 FREE novels from the Harlequin Special Edition or Harlequin Heartwarming series and my 2 FREE gifts (gifts are worth about $10 retail). After receiving them, if I don't wish to receive any more books, I can return the shipping statement marked "cancel." If I don't cancel, I will receive 6 brand-new Harlequin Special Edition books every month and be billed just $5.49 each in the U.S. or $6.24 each in Canada, a savings of at least 12% off the cover price, or 4 brand-new Harlequin Heartwarming Larger-Print books every month and be billed just $6.24 each in the U.S. or $6.74 each in Canada, a savings of at least 19% off the cover price. It's quite a bargain! Shipping and handling is just 50¢ per book in the U.S. and $1.25 per book in Canada.* I understand that accepting the 2 free books and gifts places me under no obligation to buy anything. I can always return a shipment and cancel at any time by calling the number below. The free books and gifts are mine to keep no matter what I decide.

Choose one: ☐ **Harlequin Special Edition**
(235/335 HDN GRJV)
☐ **Harlequin Heartwarming Larger-Print**
(161/361 HDN GRJV)

Name (please print)

Address   Apt. #

City   State/Province   Zip/Postal Code

Email: Please check this box ☐ if you would like to receive newsletters and promotional emails from Harlequin Enterprises ULC and its affiliates. You can unsubscribe anytime.

Mail to the **Harlequin Reader Service:**
IN U.S.A.: P.O. Box 1341, Buffalo, NY 14240-8531
IN CANADA: P.O. Box 603, Fort Erie, Ontario L2A 5X3

Want to try 2 free books from another series! Call 1-800-873-8635 or visit www.ReaderService.com.

---

*Terms and prices subject to change without notice. Prices do not include sales taxes, which will be charged (if applicable) based on your state or country of residence. Canadian residents will be charged applicable taxes. Offer not valid in Quebec. This offer is limited to one order per household. Books received may not be as shown. Not valid for current subscribers to the Harlequin Special Edition or Harlequin Heartwarming series. All orders subject to approval. Credit or debit balances in a customer's account(s) may be offset by any other outstanding balance owed by or to the customer. Please allow 4 to 6 weeks for delivery. Offer available while quantities last.

Your Privacy—Your information is being collected by Harlequin Enterprises ULC, operating as Harlequin Reader Service. For a complete summary of the information we collect, how we use this information and to whom it is disclosed, please visit our privacy notice located at corporate.harlequin.com/privacy-notice. From time to time we may also exchange your personal information with reputable third parties. If you wish to opt out of this sharing of your personal information, please visit readerservice.com/consumerschoice or call 1-800-873-8635. **Notice to California Residents**—Under California law, you have specific rights to control and access your data. For more information on these rights and how to exercise them, visit corporate.harlequin.com/california-privacy.

HSEHW22R3

THE NORA ROBERTS COLLECTION

40% OFF!

Get to the heart of happily-ever-after in these Nora Roberts classics! Immerse yourself in the beauty of love by picking up this incredible collection written by, legendary author, Nora Roberts!

YES! Please send me the **Nora Roberts Collection**. Each book in this collection is 40% off the retail price! There are a total of 4 shipments in this collection. The shipments are yours for the low, members-only discount price of $23.96 U.S./$31.16 CDN. each, plus $1.99 U.S./$4.99 CDN. for shipping and handling. If I do not cancel, I will continue to receive four books a month for three more months. I'll pay just $23.96 U.S./$31.16 CDN., plus $1.99 U.S./$4.99 CDN. for shipping and handling per shipment.* I can always return a shipment and cancel at any time.

☐ 274 2595   ☐ 474 2595

Name (please print)

Address   Apt. #

City   State/Province   Zip/Postal Code

Mail to the Harlequin Reader Service:
IN U.S.A.: P.O. Box 1341, Buffalo, NY 14240-8531
IN CANADA: P.O. Box 603, Fort Erie, Ontario L2A 5X3

*Terms and prices subject to change without notice. Prices do not include sales taxes which will be charged (if applicable) based on your state or country of residence. Canadian residents will be charged applicable taxes. Offer not valid in Quebec. All orders subject to approval. Credit or debit balances in a customer's account(s) may be offset by any other outstanding balance owed by or to the customer. Please allow 3 to 4 weeks for delivery. Offer available while quantities last. © 2022 Harlequin Enterprises ULC. ® and ™ are trademarks owned by Harlequin Enterprises ULC.

Your Privacy—Your information is being collected by Harlequin Enterprises ULC, operating as Harlequin Reader Service. To see how we collect and use this information visit https://corporate.harlequin.com/privacy-notice. From time to time we may also exchange your personal information with reputable third parties. If you wish to opt out of this sharing of your personal information, please visit www.readerservice.com/consumerchoice or call 1-800-873-8635. Notice to California Residents—Under California law, you have specific rights to control and access your data. For more information visit https://corporate.harlequin.com/california-privacy.

NORA2022

Get 4 FREE REWARDS!

We'll send you 2 FREE Books plus 2 FREE Mystery Gifts.

FREE Value Over **$20**

Both the **Romance** and **Suspense** collections feature compelling novels written by many of today's bestselling authors.

YES! Please send me 2 FREE novels from the Essential Romance or Essential Suspense Collection and my 2 FREE gifts (gifts are worth about $10 retail). After receiving them, if I don't wish to receive any more books, I can return the shipping statement marked "cancel." If I don't cancel, I will receive 4 brand-new novels every month and be billed just $7.49 each in the U.S. or $7.74 each in Canada. That's a savings of at least 17% off the cover price. It's quite a bargain! Shipping and handling is just 50¢ per book in the U.S. and $1.25 per book in Canada.* I understand that accepting the 2 free books and gifts places me under no obligation to buy anything. I can always return a shipment and cancel at any time by calling the number below. The free books and gifts are mine to keep no matter what I decide.

Choose one: ☐ **Essential Romance** ☐ **Essential Suspense**
                        (194/394 MDN GRHV)   (191/391 MDN GRHV)

Name (please print)

Address   Apt. #

City   State/Province   Zip/Postal Code

Email: Please check this box ☐ if you would like to receive newsletters and promotional emails from Harlequin Enterprises ULC and its affiliates. You can unsubscribe anytime.

Mail to the Harlequin Reader Service:
IN U.S.A.: P.O. Box 1341, Buffalo, NY 14240-8531
IN CANADA: P.O. Box 603, Fort Erie, Ontario L2A 5X3

Want to try 2 free books from another series! Call 1-800-873-8635 or visit www.ReaderService.com.

---

*Terms and prices subject to change without notice. Prices do not include sales taxes, which will be charged (if applicable) based on your state or country of residence. Canadian residents will be charged applicable taxes. Offer not valid in Quebec. This offer is limited to one order per household. Books received may not be as shown. Not valid for current subscribers to the Essential Romance or Essential Suspense Collection. All orders subject to approval. Credit or debit balances in a customer's account(s) may be offset by any other outstanding balance owed by or to the customer. Please allow 4 to 6 weeks for delivery. Offer available while quantities last.

Your Privacy—Your information is being collected by Harlequin Enterprises ULC, operating as Harlequin Reader Service. For a complete summary of the information we collect, how we use this information and to whom it is disclosed, please visit our privacy notice located at corporate.harlequin.com/privacy-notice. From time to time we may also exchange your personal information with reputable third parties. If you wish to opt out of this sharing of your personal information, please visit readerservice.com/consumerschoice or call 1-800-873-8635. **Notice to California Residents**—Under California law, you have specific rights to control and access your data. For more information on these rights and how to exercise them, visit corporate.harlequin.com/california-privacy.

STRS22R3

⟨H⟩ HARLEQUIN
HEARTWARMING

#463 HER AMISH COUNTRY VALENTINE
The Butternut Amish B&B • by Patricia Johns

Advertising exec Jill Wickey knows all about appearance versus reality. So why does she keep wishing that spending time with carpenter Thom Miller—her fake date for a wedding in Amish country—could be the start of something real?

#464 A COWBOY WORTH WAITING FOR
The Cowboy Academy • by Melinda Curtis

Ronnie Pickett is creating a matchmaking service for rodeo folks—but to be successful, she needs a high-profile competitor as a client. Former champ Wade Keller is perfect...but could he be perfect for her?

#465 A COUNTRY PROPOSAL
Cupid's Crossing • by Kim Findlay

Jordan's farm is the only security he's ever had. So when big-city chef—and first love—Delaney returns home with suggestions for revamping it, Jordan isn't happy. But Delaney has a few good ideas...about the two of them!

#466 A BABY ON HIS DOORSTEP
Kansas Cowboys • by Leigh Riker

Veterinarian Max Crane didn't expect to find a baby on his porch—or for former librarian Rachel Whittaker to accept the job caring for his daughter. Now, most unexpectedly of all, they are starting to feel like a family...

YOU CAN FIND MORE INFORMATION ON UPCOMING HARLEQUIN TITLES, FREE EXCERPTS AND MORE AT HARLEQUIN.COM.

HWCNM0223

HARLEQUIN
PLUS

Try the best multimedia subscription service for romance readers like you!

Read, Watch and Play.

Experience the easiest way to get the romance content you crave.

Start your **FREE TRIAL** at
www.harlequinplus.com/freetrial.

HARPLUS0123